SNOW HUNTED

S.N. MOOR

NOTE

This is a Kindle Vella series Episodes 1-41. This is an ongoing series with no planned end.

Season 2 will be called Huntress Snow – where the Hunted become the Huntress and will start at Episode 42 in Vella.

WARNING:

This is an adult book, not a child's fairytale. It is an adult paranormal romance fantasy reimagining of Snow White. It is a why choose with enemies to lovers, forced proximity, some kinky fuckery, one bed, and other yummy tropes. There are werewolves, shifters, mages, sirens, hseins, and witches and some more I am sure. ;)

HEY DAD

IF YOU'VE MADE IT this far past the Note and the Warning then I implore you to stop reading now. I super love your support, but this isn't the book for you. You've read Snow White before and this is just like the many many others out there so no need to read... all done. The End! Actually, seriously it's not, which is why you have a page dedicated to you in this book. You can just text me and be like OMG girllll that was totes your best book ever! The twists and turns... wowzers! Can't wait for your next one (which you also won't read) and obviously you will scribe above text in your words, or just copy and paste.

Love you! Now go read a book about the Appalachain Mountains or something!

Thanks to all you smutty fuckers out there who opened my eyes to the world of word porn. Go charge your toys, clean your hands or don't (dirrrty girdies!), light some candles, run a bubble bath, get some pop rocks... wait what? Sit back, lay down, slouch, whatever floats your boat and enjoy the book!

CONTENTS

PROLOGUE

EVERYONE KNOWS THE STORY of my mother, the beautiful Queen, who on a day much like today sat by her window looking out, admiring the beautiful falling snow while she sewed. Startled by a blackbird, she pricked her finger with her needle, causing blood to pool. Laughing graciously at her mishap, she stroked the bird's head, wishing she could finally bore the King a child.

What the Queen didn't know is the blackbird was in fact an evil witch and when she made her wish and rubbed the bird, the witch cast a spell on the Queen, binding it to her life.

Some months later, I was born and my mother was dead. My father loved me dearly and tried to raise me as best he could, but knew I needed a mother, so he went looking for one. After searching for over a year, he found a beautiful woman who would make a suitable wife. Fair and youthful skin with dark hair- she reminded him of his Queen.

I don't remember the day she came to live with us, or much about my mother, or what my dad was like before she came.

I only remember the after.

She was a darkness, rooting herself in the castle, casting her evil shadow over everything.

My father was too heartbroken and weak minded to stop her and I never understood why....

CHAPTER ONE

SNOW - MIDNIGHT RUN

"SHOOT! TAKE THE SHOT, Snow!" the huntsman urged.

I chuckled and released the arrow out of the bow, striking the rabbit square in its eye. It fell to the ground immediately. "I told you I knew what I was doing. You've taught me well." I smiled at the huntsman, shifting my weight into him.

He shot me a weary side glance but didn't speak as he made his way over to the rabbit. I stood up and wiped the dirt from my dress, following behind him. "How did I do?" I grabbed his arm to peek over.

He gently pulled his arm out of my grasp and looked at me again. He wasn't a man of many words and liked to keep things strictly professional between us. I had a natural curiosity about the man and found him quite attractive and sometimes I would have dreams about him... inappropriate dreams.

He was a full head taller than me, clean-shaven face, brown eyes, wide shoulders, and very muscular. Aside from my father, the King, he was the only man I knew and one of the few people I ever talked to. I used the term 'know' loosely since he wouldn't even tell me his name. I would call him Hunter if I needed to get his attention because Huntsman seemed too long and too formal.

I watched him as he pulled the arrow out of the rabbit's eye. The muscles in his arms flexed, and it made my stomach feel things... like butterflies dancing.

"It was a clean kill."

"I had an excellent teacher." I smiled.

"Snow." He lightly reprimanded.

"What?"

"You're flirting with me. We've talked about this."

I laughed, spinning in a circle. "I'm turning eighteen tomorrow and will be a woman."

"Snow." He said, pulling out a knife and laying the rabbit on the ground.

"What? All I'm saying is that I will be a woman and I have no prospects. I'm not allowed to attend parties and aside from the cook who leaves me food, you're the only other person I know. I'm going to die alone in that castle."

"You won't." He took the skinned rabbit and ran a stick through it from head to tail.

"You don't know that. For my birthday," I paused, waiting for him to stand back up, "Can you give me a kiss? That way, if I die alone, at least I would have kissed a man before... you know."

"No," he said matter-of-factly.

I shook my head. "Ass."

"Language."

"Give me a fucking break. I hear you cuss all the time."

"You're a lady."

I rolled my eyes. "Who you've taken under your wing and taught how to hunt? Doesn't seem very lady like to me. And again, I go back to, it doesn't matter. No one knows I exist."

He ignored the latter part of my argument. "You looked lonely and seemed to have a natural skill for shooting."

I studied him, quietly.

He continued. "I would watch you shoot apples out of the tree."

"You watched me?" I asked, almost too excitedly.

He cocked his head to the side.

"You creeper." I teased.

"It wasn't like that, Snow."

"Why do you say my name like that? Like it's a bad thing. Like I'm a bad person?" I walked over to him and placed my hand on his arm.

"Snow." He warned, but didn't pull away.

"What?" I stared him in his eyes and could see a look of panic. "Do I make you nervous?"

"No."

I pressed my body up against his and it felt like my heart was going to pound out of my chest. "I don't?" I said the words quietly. I raised up and his beautiful face looked down at me and in that moment I knew what he didn't want me to know.

He found me attractive.

He wanted me to kiss him.

"Kiss me." I pleaded softly.

He didn't say anything as the entire world around us froze.

"Hunter." I encouraged.

A bird chirped, bringing us crashing back to reality.

He shook his head like I'd captured him in a trance and backed away from me. "Snow. I said I would not kiss you." His words were short.

"Whatever." I grabbed my bow off the ground and started walking back to the horses.

"Snow." He called after me.

"Leave me the fuck alone." I shouted, not turning around.

A few minutes later, I untied my horse from the tree and gave it a loving pat on its neck. "Let's go boy." I threw my leg over and bounced solemnly back to the castle.

"Get up, child! Get up!" I stirred from my sleep to find my father standing over me, shaking my arm.

It had been at least a month since I had seen or talked to him.

"What?" I sat on the edge of the platform bed and rubbed my eyes.

"Get up Snow. You must leave." His words were rushed and quiet.

"Leave?" I was awake now.

I watched him race around the little room and stuff as many things as he could into a bag in his hand. I didn't have much. The evil bitch of a Queen made sure of that when she banished me to this Goddess-forsaken room.

Room?

More like a closet. Big enough to hold a mattress on a wooden table, a small sink and a bucket for my other needs. I had a small dresser that held a few changes of clothes and a secret compartment that held my mother's necklace- the only thing I had left from her. One of the staff had found it and swiped it away for me when I was little.

"Why in the hell do I have to leave?" I stood up and grabbed his arm. "Dad. I'm talking to you."

"Snow, we don't have time." He lightly reprimanded.

I shook my head in disbelief. "I have nowhere to go."

"You must go."

"Where?" I yelled.

He slapped his hand over my mouth and looked around, panicked. I pushed him off, but didn't speak.

"I've called a friend to help guide you out of the castle grounds."

I snatched the bag from him and dumped all the contents on the bed. None of them meant anything to me. I refilled the bag with two outfits, my toothbrush and brush. I popped the secret bottom out of the drawer and pulled out my mother's necklace and quickly slipped it on, tucking it under my gown and jacket.

I caught my father looking at the necklace longingly.

"Don't. You don't get to miss her. You let that bitch lock me away in this fucking closet and didn't do a goddam thing to stop her. She is evil- a disease taking over everything."

"You're right Snow. But I'm trying to save you now. You turn eighteen at midnight and you can't be on property when you do. She'll..." His words trailed off.

"What? What will she do?" What more could she do? She left me completely isolated in this room. I barely saw my father and had no one else, except my horse and the few birds or mice that came to visit occasionally.

He shook his head. "It doesn't matter. You need to go!"

I heard a dog howl outside.

"It's time. Let's go." My father nearly pushed me out of the room, looking both ways before he shoved me into the spiral stairwell. "Let's go Snow, let's go."

"I'm going as fast as I can." I seethed in frustration.

I stepped outside and felt a bag thrown over my head.

"No!" my father shouted.

Obviously, this wasn't part of the plan.

I swung my arms around, catching a man in the face because I heard him let out a grunt and my fist stung like it had touched fire.

"Stop her!" I heard a woman's voice command off in the distance.

It *was her*.

The evil bitch and cause for all this misery.

I suddenly remembered my necklace and reached up to grab it, yanking it off, the metal burning against my skin as the clasp broke.

"Please don't hurt her." My father pleaded.

I quickly pulled the chain into my hand, balling my fist around it. I only hoped the distraction of my father and the Queen was enough to pull their attention away from me.

"What do we have here?" The Queen queried, walking up. I could hear the gravel parting under her feet the closer she got.

"Please don't do this." My father pleaded.

"Don't do what?" She snapped before quickly regaining her composure.

"She's not a harm to you."

"You know nothing, you idiot. My mirror told me what's going to happen."

"Your mirror is lying. I won't hurt you." I added.

"My- My mirror does not lie! Take the bag off her head." She thundered.

I shook the hair out of my face and looked around and realized I had punched my father in the jaw. Part of me figured he deserved it, but the other part felt guilty. I loved him, even though he never protected me from her. "Queen." I said with as much disgust as I could manage.

"Snow." Her one word equally dripped with hatred. Then she looked at my father. "What were you doing?"

He was still rubbing his jaw, but he put his hand down before he spoke. "I can't let you do this. I can't let you kill her."

She gasped, clutching her chest. "I'm not going to kill her."

I looked between the two of them.

My father seemed confused. The clarity I saw in his eyes was fading fast, second by second. "I... I heard it. I heard you. Your mirror said Snow was a thousand times fairer than you. You yelled out..."

She walked over to him and extended her hand, gently rubbing it across his face. The cut on his cheek healed, and he stood up taller, like he was in a trance. "What you heard, my King, was the frustrations of an old woman." She laughed. "Nothing more. I," she paused, "would never harm a hair on our precious daughter's head."

"You wouldn't?" He dribbled out.

"Darling. No." She shot her wicked gaze at me.

The semantics of her words- she wouldn't hurt me, but that didn't mean she wouldn't have someone else do it for her. Did my father actually believe this garbage?

"You go back up to your room and we can talk about this in the morning."

My father nodded and started walking back to the main part of the castle, like the mindless drone he'd become.

The Queen glared at the man behind me and spoke in hushed tones. "See to it that he goes straight to his chamber and try not to mess this up!"

"Yes, my, my Queen. Right away."

"Now what to do with you?" she asked, circling me.

I turned my head following her and saw my bow and quiver was propped on the wall near the door, just out of arms reach. "I could leave." She stopped in front of me, so I pretended like I was scared, taking a step back closing the distance to the door.

She bobbled her head from side to side. "See, that doesn't work for me." She took another step closer to me, sticking her nose in the air. "You smell... so sweet... So youthful." She looked at the sky. "It's almost midnight." She clasped her hands together.

I realized I was running out of time and had to move quickly. I reached down and looped my arm through my quiver and grabbed my bow, swinging it at her and striking her across the face. I heard her yell out in pain, but I ran as fast as I could, not turning back. A flame shot past my head and landed in the field in front of me. I dodged to the right and saw another ball of flame land just to my left.

I grabbed an arrow and placed it in the bow, drawing the string before I looked over my shoulder. I waited for a beat and then turned, found her and released the arrow at the same time a ball of fire was coming straight at me. I dodged as the arrow was shooting out, so I knew my aim was off, but I heard her scream out and fall to the ground.

I knew I didn't kill her, so I kept running.

I ran as far and as fast as my legs would carry me.

CHAPTER TWO

DARK QUEEN - HEALER AND THE HEAD

"MY QUEEN, MY QUEEN, are you ok?" One of the house staff ran outside.

A flash of anger crossed my face, but I reeled it in and opted for the poor, distressed Queen. "Please... help me..." I pleaded, reaching up from the ground.

"My Queen. What happened?" They asked, rushing over. It was a frumpy little woman in a bland brown dress with a bonnet tied around her head, holding a candle. I didn't know their names. They weren't important enough to me.

"My goodness, thank you. I think you saved my life. Snow..." I paused, shaking my head. "I thought..." I wiped the invisible tear from my eye. "She tried to kill me."

"Snow?" she said in utter disbelief. Of course, who would ever think that wretched girl would do something so heinous?

"It shocked me too." I feigned. "Until this." I pointed at the arrow the dreadful bitch had managed to shoot into my side. I was just about to pull it out when the housemaid called out.

"Oh, my!" Her hand shot to her mouth.

"Please help me." I reached up for her again.

"Right away my Queen."

"I wonder..."

I could tell the simple-minded woman was still trying to figure out how something like this could happen, so I began crafting my story. "I heard arguing which stirred me from my beauty sleep, so I rushed to see what was going on, fearing that something bad was happening to the poor girl." I sighed, shaking my head, "I found her out here arguing with her father. The King! Can you believe it?" I paused for a moment, standing, then continued. "I don't know what they were arguing about, but then she punched him!"

"What?" She recoiled in shock.

"Yes. Punched him on the cheek." I pointed to mine. "When I got to them, he had a slight cut."

The woman was shaking her head. "Her mother was cursed, and I feared she was cursed as well. Banished away to this tower was the best thing for her." She nodded her head agreeing with herself.

I had to prevent myself from rolling my eyes. "But she didn't think so." I stated as somberly as I could.

"Those young children don't always know what's best for them." She swiped at the air.

"No, they certainly do not." I was in a lot of pain, and this woman was grating on my last nerve. "Anyway, when I approached, she swung her bow at me, cut me here across the cheek and took off running." I pointed to the field that was on fire. "She threatened to burn this place down, and when I told her I wouldn't let her, she shot her arrow at me."

"My Queen, I will call the healer right away."

"Please take me to my room before you do."

I rolled my eyes. I could have had this arrow out of me by now and healed myself if it wasn't for this frumpy, meddling, hag.

We got back to the main house a few minutes later, and she helped me to my bedroom door. "I got it from here." I nearly snapped out. Fortunately, she seemed to think my short temper was a result of the pain I was in and less about her.

"My Queen, you've been shot. Please let me help you to your bedchamber."

"No." I barked, startling the poor woman. "I mean to say," I steadied my voice. "You have already done so much for me. I can make it these last few steps while you call the healer."

"Right ma'am." She looked around and in a hushed tone said, "I will let the staff know Snow is not allowed on property."

"Thank you. Please call the healer right away and get me the name of the town's best huntsman."

"Right away my Queen."

Once the door was shut, I broke the arrow and pulled it through, tossing it to the ground. I slipped out of my clothes and walked over to my kit of potions, which hid in my closet, and pulled out a handful of ingredients and began concocting them into a salve. I rubbed it over the wound and watched it heal quickly. "That's better." I muttered to myself, popping the cork back into the bottle of toad's tongue.

I looked out of the window at the smoldering flames in the field and slammed my fists onto the table, knocking several jars in my kit over. Tonight had not gone as planned. I should be feasting on her heart and liver right now, not mending my own wounds.

I put my kit in order and tucked it back into the closet.

How did the King learn of my plans to kill his beloved daughter? How did he get close enough to her?

I glanced around the room, wondering if anything looked out of place. I shook my head. He was not that clever.

I walked over to my mirror on the wall.

Mirror, mirror on the wall,
tell me... how did the King

learn of my plans tonight?
My Queen, he came to check
on you for dinner and heard
you in here screaming.
Why didn't you say something?
My Queen, you did not ask.

I screamed out in frustration, pounding my fists against the wall on either side of the mirror. Stupid mirror!

There was a cautious knock at the door.

The healer. I rolled my eyes, irritated that I had to keep up this facade.

I opened the door, staying behind it to shield myself, allowing the man to enter.

"I was told you..." He stopped talking when he saw me standing in front of him, completely nude.

I closed the door and gently grabbed the bag from his hand. He was a handsome enough fellow.

"I wanted to see you."

"M... M... Me?" He stuttered.

I led him over to the bed and pushed him down.

"H... H... how do you know about... me?" His eyes were wide with shock, but the growing bulge in his pants told me he was excited to see me.

"You?" I slid the jacket off his shoulders and placed my knee between his legs, letting it rub the inside of his thigh. I leaned over and whispered in his ear as I was undoing his tie. "The healer."

"I... I..."

"Shh." I placed my finger over his lips and pulled his tie off with my other hand.

He shook his head. "I don't think..."

"Don't think." I grabbed his hands. "I need healing." I pouted, placing his hands on my swollen breasts, and squeezed his fingers around them. I gasped out in pleasure as his nails bit at the skin, letting my knee rub against him.

"I... I..."

I ripped off his shirt and traced my fingers across his chest, letting my nails dig in, leaving traces of red lines. I pushed him back on the bed and pulled his pants down, freeing his hard cock, pausing to appreciate his size. This will do.

"I... I have a wife."

I smiled at the poor bastard.

"I have a husband." I retorted.

I crawled over top of him, letting my pussy brush against the tip of his dick and hung my breasts over his face, letting them swing on either side of his lips. I lowered my hips onto him slowly, letting just his tip go in and then raised back up. "Do you like that?"

"I... I..."

I rolled my eyes, lowering myself again, just so the tip went in and then pulled back up and then shimmied down, grabbing his cock in my hand. I slowly pumped it up and down and put my lips on his slit, which was already oozing with delight, swirling my tongue around.

"If you want me to stop, just tell me." I lowered my mouth on his shaft, taking him as deep as I could go.

"I..."

I slowly pulled out and then took him in my mouth again, squeezing around the base. I pulled his dick and moved on top of him, placing my pussy just on the tip. "Do you want me to stop?"

He shook his head.

"I need to hear you say the words."

"Don't stop." He stuttered out before wincing like I'd struck him.

"You don't care about your wife?"

His eyes grew enormous, but I sank my hips down a little lower.

He shook his head.

"I need to hear you say it."

"I... I don't care about my wife."

"Good boy."

I sank down fully, taking him in and letting him fill me fully. I sat up on my legs and pulled up slowly and then sank back down quickly, letting him shove into me. I sat back on my heels and began to grind and move my hips as his hands went up to grab my breasts. I had him. He was hungry and he yearned for me, for nobody but me.

I moved faster, bouncing up and down, until I could tell he was close. "Come for me. Spill your seed inside me." That's all it was to me- his seed.

"I..."

"Do it now." I lowered my voice, commanding him to come. I continued to circle my hips around and around and felt him stiffen, feeling the warmth inside me oozing back out.

I climbed off of him and laid on the bed beside him, trying to preserve as much of him inside of me as possible. When he didn't move, I glimpsed at him and saw a doe eyed look on his face.

"Come on." I pushed his arm.

He looked shocked.

"Let's go. You aren't staying here all night. I'm healed, thank you. You can go." I waved my hands in the air, dismissing him.

"I didn't do anything."

"You did plenty. Thank you."

He looked around, confused, as he was pulling his pants up.

"Your shirt is over there." I pointed to the cloth on the floor.

He lifted his shirt and examined it. "You ripped it off me."

"No, I didn't. You took it off along with your tie and put them over there."

He touched the buttons. "I saw them pop off."

"Did you?" I stood from the bed and grabbed his shirt. "All the buttons look like they're attached."

He slipped his shirt on and tied his tie.

"Thank you for your help tonight. I really appreciate it." I ushered him to the door. I leaned near his ear. "And if you say one fucking word about this to anyone, I will murder you and your wife, but not before I tell her you're an adulterous whore."

He shook his head quickly, nearly stumbling out of the door.

I saw the frumpy lady from earlier walking back down the hall with a pitcher of water, staring after the man, confused. I waved at her quickly, then shut the door.

CHAPTER THREE

SNOW - HOUSE IN THE WOODS

I DON'T KNOW HOW far I had run or for how long, but my feet and my legs screamed out in pain. I could feel open cuts and scrapes on the bottoms of each of my feet, but I didn't let that stop me for too long. I had to keep moving.

I paused by the base of a large tree and looked at the sun, set high in the sky and guessed it was sometime in the early afternoon. The air was warm, but starting to get that muggy afternoon weight and the insects were starting to come out to prepare for their evening serenade.

I had only stopped a few times to get a sip of water from the creeks before moving through them and hoped doing so would lose the trackers that evil bitch would surely send after me.

I continued to walk, slowing my pace considerably as nearly every part of me ached. I looked around for any sign of life, but there was nothing in this forest- just trees and bushes, bushes and trees, there weren't even clear paths marked.

I stopped by a berry bush and plucked off a handful of vibrant red fruit and sat on the ground, looking around as I popped them into my mouth one at a time, savoring their sweetness. My stomach growled in delight. Too bad it was the main course for today's meal, I thought sorrowfully.

I looked around trying to piece together any clues as to where I was, but I was lost and alone. Being stuck in the castle for my entire life and not being allowed to visit neighboring villages was really hurting me right now.

I took the bag off my shoulder and rifled through it, finding my mom's necklace at the bottom. I pulled it out, examining the chain, and saw the loop at the top had only been pulled apart just a bit. I searched on the ground and found two small, thin rocks and placed them on either side of the loop and pushed the pieces back together, closing it. I clasped the necklace and slipped it back on, watching as it dangled on my chest.

"Mother. I don't know if you can hear me, but if you can... can you please help me find a way out of these woods? I have grown up alone and unloved, even hated for no reason and now I have been forced from the only home I've ever known- away from papa and away from your memory. Although I don't remember you, I miss you. The way the King misses you tells me you were a kind and loving woman."

I heard twigs breaking behind me and stopped talking, slowly reaching my hand into my quiver to extract an arrow. I threaded it slowly into the bow, careful not to move too fast. I continued to listen, confused how the Queen had someone this close to me already. I had been careful, crossing in several creeks and took as many precautions as I could. My heart was nearly pounding out of my chest.

After what felt like an eternity, I heard some more twigs breaking. I sank further onto the ground and slowly rolled over so I was lying on my stomach and peeked around the base of the tree. My heart nearly leapt out of my chest with what I saw. Standing just a few feet away was my caramel brown horse staring at me- waiting for me. I dropped my bow and let my body flop on the ground as relief surged through me, relaxing my taut muscles.

I jumped up and ran over to him. "What are you doing here, boy?"

He neighed and put his head down. I patted him gently on the shoulder and went back to the tree to grab my stuff and climbed onto his back.

I looked at my necklace and couldn't help but wonder if my mother had sent him. I shook my head in disbelief. Surely not, but also how likely was it that my horse followed me for who knows how long?

We rode slowly through the woods as I had to duck under low-hanging branches and dodge overgrown bushes that littered the path, but it didn't matter. My feet were getting a much needed rest.

"I don't know where we need to go, boy." I leaned over to pat him and was hit with a wave of exhaustion. "We need to find something soon though, because it's getting dark." I looked up at the falling sun.

Minutes turned to hours when a cottage appeared, built into the base of a large tree. It was the first sign of civilization I had seen since I ran away from the castle and thought for a minute I was hallucinating. After blinking hard a few times I realized it was real and it was getting closer. "A house. You did it, boy!" I patted him on the shoulder.

The horse trotted quickly to the house and I jumped off and ran up to the door, knocking on it, but no one answered. I moved behind the small row of bushes and peeked through the window to find an empty house, but saw a pot of stew steaming over a slow burning fire. My mouth began to immediately salivate. It had been almost a full day since I'd eaten anything aside from the random berries I found on the trail.

I went back to the door and jiggled the handle, and it opened. I felt guilty for letting myself in, but also had to hope these people were nice and wouldn't mind helping someone in need.

Inside was a quaint little space, but also roomy at the same time. To the right was a long dining room table, perfectly sat for seven- seven plates, seven cups, seven sets of silverware. To the left were several couches and recliners and on the far side of the room was a kitchen with a large island table top. Tucked in between the living room and kitchen were a set of hand carved wooden stairs leading up.

I looked through their cabinets and saw there were no extra bowls, just the seven on the table. Perhaps I could use one and pour myself a bowl of stew and clean it before they got back, and they wouldn't be the wiser. I rushed quickly to the table and grabbed a bowl and a spoon and made my way back to the pot on the fire and carefully ladled out a spoonful. I wanted more, but also didn't want to be too greedy.

I hovered over the kitchen counter and slowly brought the spoon to my lips, blowing on it to cool it off. The mixture of smells was causing my stomach to grumble in anticipation. I tipped the stew into my mouth, ignoring the slight burn on my tongue and swallowed it. It was the best food I had ever tasted and nearly melted into the ground in happy satisfaction. The meat was cooked perfectly, falling apart in my mouth and the carrots and potatoes were fresh. After eating, I quickly washed and dried the bowl, sitting it on the table exactly where it was before, careful to line up the spoon perfectly alongside it like the others.

I walked around and realized there were no pictures of anyone, no names, nothing.

I walked up a set of stairs and found two rooms on the first platform. I had to imagine that is what was on the rest of the platforms the higher I went, but I couldn't go any further. My legs and my bones ached and with a full belly, I was doing everything I could to stay awake, so I decided to take a quick nap. I walked into the first bedroom on the left and climbed into the bed and realized immediately, it was huge, fit for a king, and soft too.

I sank right in and fell asleep.

"My dearest child, Snow." The words echoed throughout the room in a singsong voice.

I looked around the elegant room but didn't see anyone. "Hello?"

"Over here, darling." A woman stood up from the high-back hunter green chair that was facing the window.

"Mama?" The woman was dressed in a long, flowing navy blue satin gown with a gold ribbon tied around her waist.

She tilted her head to the side and smiled lovingly. "Yes, dear."

"How? I don't understand." I stood frozen in my spot, trying to wrap my head around what I was seeing... what I was hearing.

"No need to worry about that now." She walked over to me, floating gracefully, and reached down to touch the necklace. "I'm glad you have this. It was a special gift to me on my wedding day."

"It was?" I looked down at it.

She dropped the necklace and rubbed her hand across my cheek. "Oh, my darling, you are more beautiful than I could have ever imagined."

My heart fluttered with contentment. She looked like me- soft skin, long dark hair, enormous emerald green eyes. "Thank you, mama."

She turned and walked back to the chair by the window.

"What is it mama? Why did you come to see me?"

She sighed heavily.

"It's your father."

"My father?" I panicked. I had left him alone with that vile woman. Who knows what kind of torture she is inflicting on him as punishment for me. "Is he..."

"He's alive... for now, but I don't know for how much longer."

"I left him there with that wretched woman. She is dreadful. Horrible. I don't know why he married her."

"She's a witch, Snow, and practices in the dark arts." She sighed.

"A witch?"

"You have to find a way to defeat the dark Queen."

"How? How do I do that?"

She shook her head and I could tell she was fading away. "There are things you need to know that I cannot tell you, but once you know, you'll understand everything."

She was like a fine mist, floating away in a breeze.

"No. Don't go! Don't leave me!"

CHAPTER FOUR

GAGE - HARD DAYS WORK

A SCREAM ECHOED THROUGHOUT the hills that sounded like a cross between a shrilling wingawhomp and a child.

"What was that?" Jace asked with a look of concern spread across his face.

"I don't give a shit, Jace." I said matter-of-factly. I wasn't in the mood for questions with no answer.

"Someone's in a good mood." Enzo chimed, bouncing in from who knows where. He propped his elbow on my shoulder, but I shrugged it off.

"I'm in a fine mood. I just literally could give two shits about what that noise was."

"But what if someone's hurt?" Enzo asked, clasping his hands to his lips in a panic, mocking Jace.

"Stop." Jace moaned. "Just because I have a natural concern for others doesn't mean I can't kick your ass."

I chuckled because Jace was right. Even though he was the gentler one of the group, he was still an intimidating size for most people. He stood tall, at over six foot three with a muscular build- nothing on me, and not as wide as Enzo, but strong none the less. Enzo bounced around in front of Jace and then took off.

"Where are you going?" Calix asked.

"I'm going to find some rabbit for your stew tonight, brother!" Enzo bellowed, somewhere off in the distance.

"It's dark out. You won't be able to see anything!" Jace yelled after him.

"You care too much." I said, pushing a twig out of my way.

"Ouch Gage!" Gideon said as the twig swung back and smacked him in the face. "You could've warned me."

"Watch out Gideon." I said deadpan.

"Very funny. What's got you in such a sour mood?"

"He's always in a bad mood." Enzo said, bouncing back in.

"I hoped you had gotten lost." I said, pushing another branch out of the way.

"Damn it Gage." Gideon moaned again.

"Maybe don't walk behind me." I rolled my eyes.

Gideon grumbled about something and moved to the front of the line by Calix and Jace.

"You don't mean that. You would miss me." Enzo chimed.

"Would I?"

"Yes." Enzo said, trying to rub my nose, but I batted his hand away before he ran off again.

"Boundless energy, that one." Barrett said, walking up beside me.

I looked over at him. Barrett was probably the only one who got me. If there was a leader in our group, it was him. He was no non-sense like me, which was nice in a house of buffoons like Enzo and caretakers like Jace.

"You did good work today."

"I always do good work Barrett... it's why you keep me around."

"Well, that and your charm." He chuckled.

Another scream sounded, echoing in the trees around us.

"What is that?" Jace asked from up ahead.

"Go find out and take Enzo with you." I suggested.

Enzo jumped backwards, so he was now walking beside me. "Gage, you big softy."

"Seriously, shut the fuck up!"

"You know it's true."

I looked at Barrett. "I haven't made you choose between us yet, but I will one day and that day is getting closer and closer."

"Pish posh Gagey Poo." Enzo continued.

"Barrett." I warned.

"Enzo, leave Gage alone. He had a rough day." Barrett commanded.

I saw Enzo stick his tongue out before running ahead again.

"It sounds like it's coming from our house." Calix observed.

"You're just hoping to catch whatever it is so we can cook it up and eat it." Enzo teased.

"Gross." Calix said.

"Well, we'll be there soon." Dresden said, walking up.

"Where have you been?" Barrett asked, looking over his shoulder.

"I found some nice wood back there. Thought I would bring it home and see what I can make out of it this weekend."

"Do you ever rest?" I asked.

"Wood working is restful to me. It allows me to get my thoughts out."

"Whatever."

"Is that a horse?" Enzo asked.

"No." Barrett said, dismissing him, then paused. "Wait... I think that is. Why is a horse wondering around this area?"

Of course, Jace walked over to it and put his hand on his neck. "Here boy."

"What if it's a girl?" I remarked without emotion.

Enzo bent down. "Definitely not a girl. His schlong is almost as big as Gagey Poo's."

I didn't dignify his comment with an answer.

"Let's get back to the house. We need to shower and eat and if it's still out tomorrow, we will figure out what to do with it." Barrett advised.

The house was just as we left it, with the flickering fire casting shadows in the living room, but something felt different even though I couldn't put my finger on it.

We all took our shoes off and sat them in the grassy bed by the front door, stacking them neatly in a row.

Calix walked over to check the stew and gave it a light stir, bringing the spoon to his mouth to taste. He let out a moan of satisfaction. "Oh boys. We're eating good tonight."

"Let's jump in the showers and clean this dirt off us before we eat." Barrett suggested.

"Fine, but I get the middle one tonight!" Enzo bounded up the stairs.

"You know that's mine, Enzo." I reminded.

"Not if I get to it first."

"I will kick your ass tonight, Enzo. I'm not in the mood for your games."

"You can kick it in the middle shower."

"Boys." Barrett scolded. "Enzo. That is Gage's."

"But it's so big." He whined, looking up at the ceiling.

"Because... You know what... nevermind." I didn't have it in me to explain anything to him tonight. I knew he was trying to get under my skin and I was letting him.

We all walked up the two flights of stairs to the shower room and stripped out of our clothes, leaving them in a pile by the door. Around the edge of the large wooden room were six showers, and one in the middle. Each shower was enclosed with a chest-high wall, offering a modicum of privacy and a shower head.

Enzo had taken his usual shower stall- the left on the back wall. I walked into the middle shower and switched the water on, letting it hit me in the face. I looked down to see the water turning a nice brown color from all the dirt in my hair and on my body. It was my favorite part of taking a shower, the cleanliness of it all and watching all the dirt wash away.

We all finished around the same time and grabbed the towel on the wall just outside our shower stalls. I made my way down the flight of stairs to my room. I was looking forward to putting on a clean set of clothes, getting some stew, and then going to bed. Tomorrow was the last day of the week and I couldn't wait.

I flicked the light on, tossing my towel on the bed as I walked to my dresser, and that's when I heard it.

A gasp.

Chapter Five

SNOW - FIRST ENCOUNTERS

I FELT SOMETHING WET and heavy hit my face.

Oh no!

Someone was in the room with me.

I sat up in the bed, removing the towel from my head, and standing before me was a bare ass man sifting through his dresser. His legs were twice the size of mine and muscular like the rest of the body. His arms... his back... the way the muscles moved and flexed. He was a beautiful statue of a man.

A God.

He had to be.

I heard the uncontrolled gasp escape my lips before I could do anything. I had hoped the man hadn't heard.

But he did.

His back straightened and he slowly turned around.

I looked into his eyes and he looked into mine.

"I'm-"

"Who the FUCK are you? And why the FUCK are you in MY bed?" He yelled, enunciating each fuck.

His eyes flashed from a brilliant electric blue to as black as his hair in under a second, and the intensity of his stare caused me to retreat further up the bed, so my back was pressing against the headboard.

"I'm sorry." I couldn't help but stare at his beautiful chiseled body and his... oh my... it was so... big. I had never seen one before in person, but that must be why all the women screamed!

He covered himself up. "I don't give a shit what you are! Get out of my bed! Now!"

"What's going-" a man with purple hair skidded into the doorway. He, too, had tan skin with a chiseled body and soft blue eyes. "Holy shit! Gage has a girl in his bed!"

Gage. I made a mental note as I looked back at the handsome and dark beast of a man.

"A what?" I heard another voice, followed by another as head after head peeked in the room. The first man with purple hair had dropped to his knees, perching his chin on his fist. I presume he squatted so the others could get a view of the spectacle I was the center of.

"What's going on?" A last voice asked. He seemed as curious, but it held a note of something else. Authority, maybe?

I watched as the others moved out of his way as he walked through the crowd.

"Barrett." Gage said, pointing at me.

"Who are you?" Barrett asked.

"I'm... I'm..."

"Spit it out!" Gage demanded.

"What. Is. Your. Name." The purple hair man spoke slowly and paused after every word.

"I'm not an idiot. You all just startled me." I said, cutting my eyes at him.

"Startled you?" Gage interjected.

I snapped my head in his direction.

"What's your name?" Barrett asked again, oozing calmness in the chaos.

I crossed my arms, looking at him... at them all.

The purple-haired man smiled and then I heard him mumble "Feisty," to the light brown skin man beside him who shoved him in the arm, never taking his eyes off me.

"Your name?" Barrett asked again, his tone now betraying his irritation.

"Sn-carlet." I answered, unsure. I didn't want them to know my real name, or that I was a princess. I needed to hide from the Queen and I had no idea where I was or how far her reach was.

Gage huffed. "Your name is Snacarlet? What kind of name is that?"

"It's Scarlet. You have me flustered."

"So flustered you forgot your own name?" He asked incredulously.

"No... I just. I'm sorry. I will go." I looked around and counted seven men. Seven very muscular men all wrapped in towels who were likely bare behind it, staring at me with a mixture of expressions. Some were curious, some intrigued, and others angry.

"Damn right you will!" Gage waved his hands. "Out!"

"How old are you?" One of the ones in the back asked. He seemed nice, with blonde hair and blue eyes that were soft.

"I'm..."

"You don't know how old you are?" Gage huffed.

I snapped my eyes at him. "If you would stop interrupting me every two seconds then maybe I would be able to get a complete thought out."

"Oh, shit." The boy with the purple hair said, bouncing up and down excitedly then settled back on the ground and looked at me with a serious face, "Be careful with that one." He nodded to Gage. "He's a little rough."

I took in a deep breath.

"You're right. I'm sorry."

"So you keep saying."

I bit my tongue and looked at the man who asked. "I'm eighteen. Today's my birthday." My brow furrowed. "Was my birthday? I honestly don't know. I've been running all day, and I fell asleep, so I have no idea what time it is."

"Are you hurt?" His eyes swept over my body and landed on my feet. "Your feet."

"I looked at them, bloodied and bruised.

"Oh, for fuck's sake." Gage moaned. "My bed is a complete fucking wreck!" He jerked the cover off with one pull, and it popped out from under me like I was nothing but a feather.

"I will clean that. I promise. I didn't know."

"Get her out of my room right now!" Gage warned as the vein near his temple was pulsing.

"Let's go. Let's go." The man with purple hair said, standing up pushing the other's back. I hopped out of bed and nearly crumbled to the ground as the pain shot through my feet. I hadn't noticed before, perhaps because I was too tired or they were too numb.

The man with soft eyes and the one with purple hair rushed to my side and helped me up. "Let's get you downstairs and I will look at your feet." He smiled. "My name's Jace."

"Nice to meet you, Jace."

"I'm Enzo." The purple-haired man said.

"Nice to meet you Enzo. I love your hair."

He blushed before chuckling. "She likes my hair." He looked over his shoulder. "Did you hear that, Gage? She likes my hair and not your gigantic cock!"

"Enzo." Jace reprimanded.

"Oh. Right. Sorry."

I chuckled. "It's fine."

They helped me onto the couch while the others stayed on the stairs with their mouths dropped open.

"You stay right here." Jace said. "I'm going to go change." He looked at Enzo and added. "We are going to go change and then we'll be right back down."

"I don't think I could run away right now if I wanted to." I said the words then mentally slapped myself in the face. Why did I just admit to a house of very large, muscular strangers that I was pretty much unable to run away if I wanted? I tried to remember where I had left my bow, but was so delirious with exhaustion I didn't remember much that had happened after my horse found me.

"You don't want to leave?" Enzo asked, obviously only hearing what he wanted. He was jumping up and down so much his towel came loose, but he grabbed it at the last second.

"We'll be right back." Jace said, patting the air as he walked back up the stairs with Enzo bouncing behind him.

The others had led Enzo and Jace up the stairs, and it was now quiet. I heard some excited or not so excited whispers on the platform above, but I couldn't make out what they were saying. I looked around and everything slowly started coming back to me from earlier. The stew, the bed.

A few minutes later, the light brown man Enzo had spoken to earlier came down the stairs. He cast a sympathetic glance at me before turning his back and stirring the stew. A few seconds later, he turned around and looked at me. "My name's Calix."

I smiled. "Hi Calix. I'm-" I laughed, embarrassed. "You already know who I am."

"The mystery girl who wandered into our place of all places." Another man said. He was darker than Calix, and his eyes held a beautiful golden tone to them. "My name's Gideon."

"Gideon questions everything, so take nothing he says personal." Calix smiled.

Enzo was hopping back down the stairs and plopped on the couch right beside me, slinking his arm around my shoulders. "She's off limits, boys. Barrett's orders."

"I think he was just talking to you." Calix laughed, taking a sip of his stew.

"No." Enzo's brow furrowed, like someone had punched him in the gut.

Jace walked down next with a bag in his hand.

Enzo leaned over. "Jace gets off on this stuff."

"What stuff?"

"Helping people."

"I've saved your ass quite a few times, and it didn't seem to bother you then."

Enzo rolled his eyes, making me laugh. He definitely seemed to be the liveliest one of the bunch and if I had to guess the one who was always getting into trouble.

Jace got on his knees in front of me. "May I?" He asked, looking at my foot.

I nodded, and he gently lifted it off the ground. His hands were rough against my skin, but he was delicate with my foot, gently pressing and prodding.

"My goodness."

"Is it really bad?" I recoiled a bit.

He rifled through his bag and pulled out a jar of liquid and some gauze. "Well, it's not good."

He began dabbing the wet pad on my foot, causing me to flinch in pain.

"Calix, do you have anything that can help her? This is probably going to hurt quite a bit." He said looking at me, then looked over his shoulder, "There are cuts all over her foot, with wooden shards, rocks and who knows what else."

Calix answered, "Yes." He reached under the cupboard and pulled out a bottle of brown liquid and grabbed a cup off the table. "Here, drink this. It may not taste very good, but it should help numb the pain."

I grabbed the cup and tossed the entire drink back and felt the slow burn move down my throat into my chest.

"Can I marry her?" Enzo asked, clasping his hands together.

I laughed and gazed at his boyish good looks and grabbed his hand as Jace continued dabbing and plucking, dabbing and plucking.

I let out a muted scream as I felt something large being pulled from my foot.

"Holy shit balls. That's huge." Enzo said, looking at a rather large splinter.

Although, I don't even know if you could call it that since it was so big; it was like the size of a small twig.

Jace pressed the cloth to my foot and I felt the burn only for a second.

"Here, have some more." Calix offered me another glass of the brown liquid.

I smiled at him as I knocked it back. This time it didn't burn so bad.

"She's drinking my ale too!" Gage said, pounding down the stairs in a pair of dark pants that hugged the muscles in his thighs and a white shirt that fit tightly around his biceps. If I wasn't so startled by him, I would probably be drooling.

"I'm sorry."

"You don't need to apologize to him." Enzo said, squeezing my hand.

I looked between him and Gage, but didn't speak.

"One foot down, one more to go." Jace said as he finished wrapping the bandage around my toes. He lifted my other foot and sighed. "Well, this one isn't as bad as the other."

"That's dandy." I said, laughing, and then paused. Why did I say dandy?

"Great, now you've gotten her drunk." Gage moaned from the table.

Gideon was sitting beside him, staring at me, but not speaking.

"I'm not drunk." I defended. "I just feel... happy."

"You're drunk." Gage fired back.

I snarled my lip at him. "Perhaps you could use some of your ale to put you in a better mood."

A red-headed man with a beard had come down and sat at the table, followed by Barrett.

"How's she doing?" He asked.

Jace looked up at him after he finished wrapping my foot. "I'd recommend she stay here for a day or two. She tore up her feet pretty bad, and I'm scared they may get infected."

Barrett looked at the pile on the floor. "You pulled all of that out of her feet?"

I leaned forward and nearly toppled out of the seat, but fortunately Enzo caught me.

"And she's had a bit of Gage's ale, too. So…" He shrugged, bobbling his head from side to side.

"I see." He looked around at everyone watching him, like they were waiting for his decision, so I looked at him too, although I was having a hard time focusing. "She can stay through the weekend and we will reassess."

"We don't even know what she was running from. Must have been bad if she did that." Gage said, pointing at the ground. Even though his tone was filled with malice, there was an underlying note of something else in his gaze.

"That's a good point." Barrett looked at me. "What were you running from?"

I looked around the room and knew if I told them the truth, they would surely send me on my way, so I settled for a half truth. "My stepmother tried to kill me… so I shot her with an arrow and then ran away."

"Shit." Gage said.

"Shit." Enzo said.

Same word, but completely different meanings. Gage understood the potential severity and Enzo seemed impressed, while everyone else just looked around in silence.

Enzo looked at Barrett. "Please, can we keep her? We need to protect her. Please?"

"She's not a fucking pet Enzo."

"I know that, Gage. I'm just saying. She's obviously scared for her life and," he paused, looking at me, "it's her birthday." He clasped his hands together and held them under his chin.

Gage rolled his eyes.

Barrett nodded. "What kind of hosts would we be if we kicked a woman out on her birthday after enduring such an agonizing journey?"

"Yes!" Enzo cheered.

"Here, drink this." Jace offered. "It will help with any infection."

"Thank you. Thank you all so much." I let out a sigh of relief. "You won't even know I'm here."

"That's impossible." Gage muttered under his breath.

I looked at him, but continued. "I can cook and clean... and I can hunt."

"We don't need a cook. We have Calix." Gage clapped back.

"Ignore him. He's always like this. It isn't you." Enzo defended.

"Would you care for some food?" Calix offered.

I didn't feel like I should tell them I already ate some, especially since I used the bowl sitting in front of Gage. "Yes please. I'm starving."

"There's only seven bowls." Gage reminded.

"I have one in my shop," the man with the red hair said, jumping up from the table.

"That's Dresden. He's our wood worker. He's created most of what you see here." Jace said.

"Wow. He's amazing."

"Thank you," he said, walking back in and setting a chair and a bowl at the opposite end of the table across from Gage.

"Let me help you." Jace and Enzo offered, lifting me from my arms and carrying me across the floor.

Calix poured everyone some stew in a bowl while Gideon hopped up to pour everyone a drink. From what I could surmise, it seemed everyone had a job. Calix was the cook, Jace, the healer, Dresden, the woodworker and builder, Barrett, the leader... but I still wasn't sure about the others, even though I'm sure they somehow contributed.

"Thank you again. I really appreciate it."

"You're welcome." Barrett nodded.

Everyone ate their dinner in silence and I couldn't help but wonder if it was because of me or if this was how it always was. I had to assume I was the cause for the tension in the air.

I tried not to look at Gage, but there was something about his rough features that drew me in like a moth to a flame. He had a thin cut beard that was as dark as his hair, and his eyes, the way they sparkled...

As I was finishing my bowl of stew, I was hit with the sad realization this was the first time I had ever had dinner with another person for as long as I could remember. Here I was surrounded by a complete set of strangers and yet there was nowhere else I wanted to be.

Calix sat a muffin in front of me with a candle in it. "It's nothing much, but you should make a wish."

"A what?"

The already silent air became even more silent- like everyone had stopped breathing.

"You blow your candle out and make a wish for your birthday." Enzo said slowly, tilting his head in confusion.

"Oh. I've never... I've never done that before."

Enzo laughed, then stopped. "Oh, you're not kidding."

My lips flattened into a hardline. "Would you believe me if I told you this was also the first time, that I can remember anyway, where I had a meal with someone else?"

Gage's eyes landed on me, but he didn't speak. I felt like he was trying to stare into the depths of my soul, there was something there. A familiarity?

"My stepmother banished me away in the... house. She gave me a closet to sleep in, where she had a ser-... person, bring me food on a tray."

"You were a prisoner?" Jace whispered.

"Well. I could go outside, but at night I had to be in and I wasn't really allowed to see anyone or be seen."

The room was so silent you could hear a needle drop.

I looked around and then my eyes landed on the melting candle so I gave it a blow. "I wish that-"

"NO! Stop!" they all yelled... well, all except Gage.

"You don't tell us or it won't come true." Enzo said.

"You believe that?"

"Of course we do."

"Not all of us." Gideon chimed in.

"Well, of us, except for Gideon, who has to study everything and maybe Gage... who, well, is just an ass."

"Oh, ok."

"Close your eyes and make a wish." Enzo encouraged with a smile spread across his face, leaning forward ever so slightly in his seat.

I closed my eyes and thought long and hard. I had never had a chance to make a wish for anything before and I felt it needed to be good, but there were so many things to wish for. So I worked through each one and settled on it and then opened my eyes.

"Thank God. She's alive." Gage mocked, no doubt commenting on how long it took me to come up with a wish.

"It was her first time. Give her a break." Jace defended.

Gage rolled his eyes. "I'm going to bed."

"We need to figure out where Scarlet is sleeping tonight." Jace said.

"I can sleep down here. I don't want to burden anyone."

"Perfect. Problem solved. Goodnight."

"Just wait." Enzo said, grabbing a bottle at the center of the table and spinning it. "Open end is the winner."

I watched as it spun and spun and slowed to a stop, pointing at Gage.

"No fucking way. Try again."

"It's really ok. I can sleep down here."

"Nonsense. You can have my room." Enzo offered.

"You're at the very top. You want her to walk up five flights of stairs?" Jace inquired.

"Good point." Enzo puckered his lips out.

Jace looked at me. "You can have my room. It's on the first level, right across from Gage."

I stared at Gage, but didn't say anything.

"Great. Can I go to bed now?" Gage asked, not waiting for an answer.

"Yes. Did you want to take her with you?" Jace asked.

"Not a chance in hell."

CHAPTER SIX

HUNTSMAN - A DEAL WITH THE DEVIL

"CALM DOWN, GIRL." I said to my brown-haired mutt, who was jumping up and down by the window and barking. I walked over and patted her on the head, and peeked through the dirty glass pane. "There's no one out there. Come on and get some dinner." I grabbed her collar and led her away from the window to her bowl across the room.

While she devoured her food, I sat my boots by the door and had a flashback to last night. I saw Snow rush out of the door, right into the arms of the Queen's waiting henchman. He had just arrived right before she walked outside, so there was no time for me to warn her or the King. I thought about intervening, but saw the Queen walking up and knew there was nothing I could do except make matters worse. At least if she didn't know I was a friend of the family, then I could try to still help them.

Snow ran into the woods, just down from where I was waiting on the edge of the field. She was too far for me to catch up to her, but I erased the tracks she left to help her as much as I could.

There was a knock on the door. I looked at the dog, but she still had her nose buried in her food. "Some guard dog you are," I mumbled, walking past her to the door. I opened it to find a man standing there with a royal hat on and a roll of parchment in his hand. "Can I help you?"

"Huntsman, is it?"

I had a name, but no one seemed to know or care. "Yes."

"The Queen requests your presence at the castle right away."

I looked down. "Right this second?" I was still in my sleeping clothes.

"Well, you can change, of course. I will wait."

I shut the door and walked over to my dresser. This can't be good. Had the Kind betrayed me and told her the truth about our relationship? Who knows what the Queen has done to him...

Ten minutes later, we were on horseback heading towards the castle. I was curious what condition she and the King would be in. Her, because she was shot with an arrow and the King... well... because she was shot with an arrow. The Queen would surely punish him for his daughter's actions.

I didn't know the Queen well, but from what Snow had said and what little I'd seen I knew she wasn't a good person. She was definitely a different kind of Queen than his former wife who was a light that radiated kindness and beauty, this woman just seemed dark.

We pulled up to the castle, and the little man ushered me in. I couldn't tell if he was the one from last night, but I had a feeling. He had a similar stature and general presence of an asshole.

"My Queen." He bowed. "I present to you, the Huntsman."

I took my hat off and bowed the same as him.

"Very well. You may leave us Seamus."

I stood up and looked at the man. Without his hat on, he looked like a little rat with small beady eyes and a pointed nose. He quickly glanced at me, then scurried away.

"Huntsman." The Queen uttered, looking at me from head to toe like I was a statue on display. She reached forward and grabbed my arms. "So strong."

"Thank you, Queen." I lowered my shoulder just slight enough so my quiver would fall off my shoulder so I could pull my arm from her mangy grasp to adjust it. "What can I do for you today?"

She tilted her chin up and looked across her nose at me. "Do you use that bow often?"

A flashback to Snow with the bow flashed before me. "I've been practicing with it lately. I usually prefer a blade."

She shuddered in ecstasy. "How animalistic."

Her seductive stare made me cringe on the inside. She was a beautiful woman on the outside, but I could see past the facade and saw the evil simmering within her.

"Thank you, Queen."

She tossed her head back and cackled. "A man of simple words. I appreciate that."

I nodded. "What can I do for you, Queen?"

"In my chambers." She waved me down the long, window laden hallway, which echoed with our footsteps.

I couldn't help but notice the large portraits on the wall of the late kings and queens, specifically of the current king's late wife. I was shocked to find it was still hanging up and would've imagined that it'd been one of the first paintings to be destroyed when the dark Queen took over the house. I paused only for a second to admire the late queen's beauty, on the inside and out. It even radiated from the painting on the wall.

The dark Queen pushed the door open and walked in, turning to wait for me. "I don't bite... unless you ask." Her cackle made my skin crawl.

I smiled and walked in, staying as close to the door as possible.

"There is a delicate matter that requires your personal attention and I've asked around and heard you're the best huntsman in the area. Accurate, lethal, and discreet."

I nodded, knowing exactly where this was going.

"Last night," she paused for dramatic effect and held her hand up, reaching for the handkerchief on her table, so I grabbed it for her. "The princess." She paused again, wiping the tear from her eye. "Just dreadful." She peeked at me for a brief second, then continued. "She attacked her father and I." She let out a sorrowful sob.

"Queen. Are you ok? Is the King ok?" I was more concerned about the King, but knew I had to play her stupid little game.

"Yes, yes." She patted the air.

"How can I help?"

"After the attack, she fled the scene like the coward she is."

I didn't speak, but continued to stare at her, waiting.

"Yes. Well then," she nodded. "I need you to track her down."

"Of course, Queen. Where would you like me to bring her once I locate her?"

She laughed, a wicked, pitchy laugh. "No. I don't want you to bring her anywhere. I want you to kill her and cut out her liver and heart and bring it to me as proof."

I swallowed, knowing this was the likely request. Not so much the heart and liver part, but the death of the princess. It wasn't a secret the Queen loathed the princess. When the dark Queen first moved into the castle, it didn't take long at all for the princess to vanish. "Of course Queen."

"Not even a flinch. I think this will be a very good partnership indeed." She dropped her handkerchief on the desk and reached into her drawer. "I will give you partial payment now and the rest when you bring me her liver and heart." She handed me a box. "Please put them in this." It was a silver box adorned with a raised bird on the lid.

"As you wish." I grabbed the silver box and placed it in my side duffel.

"I think this goes without saying, but for good measure... no one, and I mean no one, including the King, is to hear about this." She paused, looking over her shoulder. "His mind is in such a fragile state right now. The grief he still faces from the death of his first wife and now the betrayal of his daughter's attack last night." She shook her head.

"Understood. Please give my condolences to the King."

"Of course." She nodded and reached behind her neck to unclasp her dress.

"I'll see myself out."

She looked at me and frowned as I was leaving.

"Can you tell me where the attack happened or where you think she may have gone?"

She smiled. "Over near the animal pens. She ran out across the field into the trees."

I nodded and left, making my way towards the animal pens. I could feel her eyes on me through her bedroom window, so I walked around searching for clues about what happened, even though I knew the answer. I walked through the field and made my way to the wood line where she exited, trying to figure out a way around this.

I knew I couldn't go against the dark Queen, or it would mean my certain death, but I also knew I couldn't kill Snow. While I had tried to keep myself at a distance from her emotionally, I had grown fond of her.

CHAPTER SEVEN

SNOW - SCARLET THE DISRUPTOR

I WOKE UP TO find Enzo at the foot of my bed. Startled, I pulled the sheet around me and sat up.

"Good morning!" He jumped to his feet.

"Good... morning. Have you been watching me long?" My mind was filtering through a variety of feelings. I was nervous he had been here for who knows how long, while at the same time, flattered. Or was it moved? Happy? I wasn't sure. I'd never had someone that seemed to care about me before, so this was different, but also so nice.

His eyes squinted into small slits as he whispered. "I'd rather not answer." Then yelled, "Jace!"

Jace was walking up the stairs a few moments later. "I was wondering where you went. Have you been up here this whole time?"

Enzo cocked his head at Jace like he wanted him to stop talking.

Jace looked at me. "How are you feeling?"

"I feel good. Rested. Thank you so much for letting me sleep in your bed last night. It was the most restful night's sleep I think I've ever had." I laughed.

"Of course. Let me check your feet."

I scooted towards the edge of the bed and slung my feet off, while Enzo jumped onto the bed to sit beside me. "Here, you can grab my hand." He said with twinkling eyes.

"I think she'll be fine." Jace chuckled.

"She might or she might not." Enzo rebutted, bouncing his shoulders up and down playfully.

"Thank you Enzo." I interlaced my fingers between his and could feel the warm roughness of his palm against mine. He looked at me with puppy dog eyes, eager for affection. I felt his thumb rub the inside of my wrist briefly, which sent a shiver down my arm. I looked at him, but he was watching Jace.

"How are they looking?" I turned to Jace, embarrassed by the slightly awkward moment with Enzo.

He was unwrapping the second bandage. "They look fantastic. Better than I could have expected." He said, shocked. "Perfectly healed, in fact."

"Really?" Enzo asked, his tone somewhere between shock and sorrow. "But she probably should stay for a couple more days, just in case, right?" Enzo prodded.

Jace looked up, reading between Enzo's words, and said solemnly, "I have to tell Barrett what I see and let him decide."

"Who put him in charge?" Enzo pouted.

"We all did." He chuckled.

Enzo rolled his eyes.

"We have to go to the mines to work now, but we can talk about it tonight." Jace said.

"The mines?" I asked.

"Yes. We work at the mines on the sixth mountain."

"What do you mine for?"

"Ore and gold."

I was impressed. I had never met a miner before, or anyone really except the huntsman and the few people around the castle. "Is that why you are all so strong?" I grabbed Enzo's arms and squeezed.

He blushed. "Yes. We swing our pickaxes all day into the mountain. It makes for long days and sore bodies. But after today, we have the next two days off." He stuck out his chest.

"Calix made you a plate for breakfast if you're hungry."

"Famished."

"Do you need help down?" Enzo offered.

I smiled. "I don't think so. My feet feel fine."

"Great." Enzo said quietly.

I followed Jace and Enzo downstairs and saw the rest of the house sitting between the table and the living room. Everyone greeted me except for Gage, who was reading the paper on the couch.

"Good Morning."

"How is our mystery guest doing?" Gideon asked.

His words weren't rude, but there was an undertone in the way he said them that told me he didn't fully believe my story.

"All healed up."

"Hooray." Gage mumbled. "Now we can get back to normal."

"Good Morning Gage." I said as cheerful as possible.

He pulled the paper down briefly to look at me, but said nothing.

"We will talk about it tonight. Barrett said she could stay today." Enzo defended.

"She's a person, Enzo, not your pet."

"I know that, Gage. Read your paper. At least you're more tolerable then, because you aren't talking."

Dresden walked in carrying something behind his back with a smile on his face and I realized I never saw him sneak away. "I made this for you this morning." He handed me a chair and a bowl. The chair is less wobbly than the one you sat on last night and the bowl is more smoothed out on the inside.

"For me?"

"You've got to be kidding me." Gage sighed, shifting the paper in his hand.

"I love it. Thank you so much."

"So now you have a place to sit at the table."

"For the one more meal she's going to have here?"

"Shut up Gage!" Enzo threw a muffin at him, which seemed to really piss him off.

"This is fucking absurd. She is some random chick who broke into our house and slept in our bed and ate our food. We don't know her story or who she is or why she's on the run and we just welcome her in with open arms!" Gage stood up and threw the paper down.

"Why are you so scared of me?" I knew I probably shouldn't have said that, but he seemed really fun to poke and it seemed to make Enzo happy and I enjoyed watching his eyes twinkle.

Gage stalked over to me and ripped the chair out of my hand and threw it down. "I'm not scared of a little twat like you. I just don't like you and I don't trust you."

"Gage. She was just teasing." Calix stepped in.

I raised up on my toes and pressed my finger into his chest. "I don't give a fuck what you think. I told you what happened last night, so believe me or don't. But don't take something that Dresden created and throw it on the ground. It's disrespectful."

Gage looked at me and didn't speak for a moment, and then turned and walked out of the house, slamming the front door.

"Holy shit. Holy shit. Holy shit." Enzo dropped to his knees and began bowing towards me.

I laughed and looked at Dresden. "I'm sorry he did that with your chair. I love it." I picked it up and placed it at the end of the table while he took the other one back to his shop.

"What's going on in here?" Barrett asked, walking in.

"She's a little spitfire." Calix nodded his head towards me while chopping carrots.

Barrett looked from me to Enzo, who was still sitting on the ground.

"Gage just rushed her and got all in her face yelling and she stood up to him. Tiny little Scarlet stood up to him. Finger in the chest, I don't give a fuck what you think... don't disrespect Dresden." Enzo stood up. "Epic!" He said, twirling around.

"You have caused quite the stir in the house, Scarlet." His words held a note of disapproval. He looked at Jace. "How is the patient?"

Jace looked from me to Enzo, and then back to Barrett. "Her feet have completely healed, but there's still a chance for infection. After tonight, I will have a better idea."

I let out the breath I'd been holding. He didn't lie, but he also bought me a little more time and that's all I needed to put a plan together.

"I see." Barrett said, looking around the room. "Well, it's time for us to go to the mines." He looked at Calix. "You aren't ready?"

"Sorry, all the commotion in here distracted me."

"Don't worry about it." I chimed in. "I will handle it. Tonight, I will cook dinner. It's the least I can do."

"Do you know how to cook?" Calix asked.

"I'll figure it out. How hard can it be?"

Calix laughed. "How hard can it be? Shit."

Barrett and the others started walking outside while Calix was listing off things to do, what to cut, where to put it, and everything else.

"I got it! Go!" I laughed, ushering him out of the door. "I don't want to be more of a disrupter." I winked, causing Calix chuckled.

CHAPTER EIGHT

BARRETT - JERRYPOO ON A HUMDINGER

"GAGE SEEMS EXTRA BROODY today." I mentioned to Gideon, taking a break from swinging the pickaxe. Gage had found a corner of the mine and just started pounding away into the wall, relentlessly.

"Scarlet really gets under his skin for some reason and this morning when she didn't back down from him... I don't think he's used to having someone push back."

"Yea. I heard about that. Had Enzo riled up."

"He's like head over heels for her or something. He's always the free spirit, but he has stuck to her like jerrypoo on a humdinger."

"Oh that bad?"

Gideon nodded his head towards Enzo, who had his chin resting on the shaft of his pickaxe.

"Enzo! Get to work! This mine will not dig its self."

"Right! Right! Sorry Barrett."

"What do you think about her story?" Gideon asked.

I stared at him for a second, trying to understand the ask behind his question. "Seems like she could bring trouble."

"Maybe. You don't buy that they basically locked her away in a closet her entire life and then her stepmother tried to kill her, so she ran, do you?"

"I don't know. Something just seems odd about it. Like there's a sizeable chunk of the story she isn't telling us."

"Does it matter? Are we really considering letting her stay?"

"I don't know. Jace and Dresden seem to like her and obviously Enzo would be heartbroken."

"It's been a day. Hell. Not even."

"You know how he is, though. He's like a flitterbug, flitting from one thing to the next. This just happens to be his next." I let out a sigh. "So that leaves Calix."

"Yea, but he always plays things close to his chest. I guess it all depends on how badly she screws up his kitchen today." Gideon laughed.

"I don't know. Seven mouths is a lot to feed, one more..."

"Plus, having a girl... I mean woman, she is apparently eighteen now, in the house... that dynamic... could you imagine if anything happened with one of the guys... what that would do to the others..." Gideon started shaking his head. "I don't know if we can deal with that kind of drama."

"Well, you know the boys have been known to share, especially Jace, Enzo and Calix." I laughed. "Kidding aside, I don't want to think about the dynamic. We have a good thing going right now, and I think Gage would probably run through the fucking wall if that happened." I clarified. "The drama, not someone else sleeping with her." I chuckled.

"I don't know. He seems to have a certain fondness for her. I've never seen him like this with anyone before."

We both laughed out loud, garnering the attention from the others for a brief second.

"Sometimes it sucks being the one in charge." I took a swing at the wall.

"Why do you think I nominated you? I didn't want that kind of responsibility."

"Thanks." I said sarcastically.

"And we knew Jace was too soft and Enzo is too emotional to make the tough decisions. Gage is just angry all the time and would be horrible to have to listen to. Move here. Sit there. Eat that." Gideon teased in a deep voice. "Calix has his food and Dresden his woodworking, so that left you and me."

"It sucks being the responsible ones, huh?"

"Don't I know it, brother?"

The day came and went and while we were walking back to the house, I pulled Enzo aside to break the bad news to him in person before I told everyone else.

"Enzo."

He looked at me and his eyes immediately fell.

"What's wrong?" I asked.

"I know what you're going to say."

"You do?"

"Yea. I saw you and Gideon with your heads together most of the day."

"How observant."

"I know you think I don't pay attention, but I do." He said solemnly.

I nodded.

"Ok. Let me have it."

"We're going to have to ask Scarlet to leave?"

"Wait, what?!"

"Wait. Huh? What did you think I was going to say?"

"I wasn't pulling my weight today. I know I was slacking a little, but that's because-"

"Because you were thinking about her?"

"No."

"You weren't?"

He didn't say anything.

"That's why she has to go. She's only been at the house for a day and already you're off daydreaming and Gage is on edge way more than usual. Imagine if-" I stopped, not sure I wanted to have this conversation with him.

"What?"

"What if she stays and then becomes involved with one of the guys? How are you going to feel then?"

"I."

"It will cause tension and drama at the house and we don't need that."

"I'd be fine with it."

"You would? So the fact I saw her and Jace kissing last night when he took her to bed?"

"He WHAT?" He yelled. I saw him searching out Jace with a look of hatred on his face.

"That's my point right there. Look at you right now. And no. They didn't kiss, but this... this is what we don't need."

"I'm sorry. I may have overreacted, but that won't happen again."

I laughed. "It's cute, you think that."

He said nothing for a moment. "She's pretty, Barrett. Like really pretty. Probably the prettiest girl I've ever seen, and she doesn't know any better. She's been locked in a closet her entire life and then her stepmother tried to murder her."

"That's another thing that concerns me. We don't know anything about her. What if she's lying?"

"About being in a closet and trying to be killed? Why would she lie about that?"

"I don't know. We don't know the kind of person she is."

"She seems compassionate, sweet and perhaps a little feisty at times, only because I've never met a girl that wasn't terrified of Gage when he gets all Gagey. But I don't know... there's something about her that seems like she's a good one. You took a chance on all of us. Why can't we do the same for her?"

"I just don't think it's a good idea."

"Well, the house is still standing." Calix chimed from up ahead. "She didn't burn it down, now only to hope she followed my directions and cooked an edible dinner."

"It better be edible." Gage snapped.

"Oh Gagey poo. I see swinging your axe did little for your mood today." Enzo teased.

"Shut it Enzo."

"Maybe Gage needs a female figure around to give him the love his mother never did." Enzo retorted.

Gage stopped walking and turned to face Enzo. "You leave my fucking mother out of this." His nose was touching Enzo's and his finger was pointed right near his eye. After a beat, he turned around and continued to walk with the others.

"I think I peed myself a little." Enzo rebounded.

I shot a glance over at him, silently pleading for him to leave Gage alone. They always seemed to have this love hate battle going on, but for whatever reason, Scarlett seemed to bring out the worst in both of them.

We kicked our shoes off and walked in to find Scarlett standing in the kitchen with an apron tied around her waist, her hair piled on top of her head in a messy bun with flour spread across her hair and face.

"Oh my God! You're home!" She looked over our shoulders. "It's dark out, of course you're home." She spat off, frazzled.

"Have a good day?" Enzo asked, walking into the kitchen to look over her shoulder.

She looked at him, and I saw it there in her eyes. She was smitten with him. Great! I thought. I hate being the bad guy!

"I did. I changed all your bed linens, washed the sheets, and folded them. Washed your clothes and put them back in your drawers, cleaned the house, and harvested the vegetables in the garden. I also collected the eggs from the henhouse and went hunting to replenish your stock of fowl and rabbit."

"You did all that today?"

"And I cooked." She laughed, using her arm to brush the fallen piece of hair out of her face. "I'm just so appreciative of you letting me stay here. It was the least I could do."

"I can think of something else." Gage mumbled, walking up the stairs.

"Name it! I'll do it."

All the boys looked around at one another. "I think you did plenty today." I smiled.

"Wait." Enzo said, counting on his fingers. "That means tomorrow we can sleep in. We don't have to wash clothes, change our beds or work in the garden because she's already done it." He started hopping up and down. "You're amazing!"

She laughed a beautiful, melodic laugh. "I really am thankful." She looked directly at me as if she knew what I had to tell her.

"Ok." I looked around and saw Enzo still.

"We're going to go take a shower and talk about you staying here and while you're getting cleaned up after us, we will vote on it. Know that no matter what we decide, it's not a reflection of you. There are just certain dynamics we have to maintain."

"Understood."

She looked down and continued stirring the bowl of whatever she was mixing.

"Let's head to the showers, boys."

"Dinner will be ready when you come back down and the cake will be in the oven."

"Cake?" Calix called over his shoulder to Dresden.

"She said cake."

"She cooks, cleans and harvests the garden. I could get used to this."

"You know you would still want to cook." Dresden said.

"Of course, but to have the option would be nice."

We all got to the showers, except Gage, who was already there.

"Did you tell her the bad news?" He asked, scrubbing his arms.

"We're voting on it after showers, while she's washing up." Enzo said.

"Well, in case you don't know my vote. It's a big hell no for me."

"Noted." I said.

"That's shocking. I really thought you had come around to her." Enzo poked.

"Enzo." I reprimanded and gave him a pleading look. Whenever Gage got in these moods, he was so hard to be around.

Enzo looked at me and shrugged, giving me the look that he would back down.

I had done the rough numbers in my head and knew that Gage, Gideon and myself were no's and that Enzo and Jace were yes's, which left Dresden and Calix.

This was going to be a long night, no matter which way this fell.

CHAPTER NINE

SNOW - BOSOM BERRIES

THE BOYS CAME DOWN from the showers and didn't speak to me except for Barrett who told me to wash up before dinner so they could talk.

I quietly obeyed and walked up the stairs.

The shower room was a large open area on the third floor. I saw all the stalls around the outside, but decided on the middle one since it seemed to be the one that had the most privacy. I slipped out of my clothes and walked into the shower, letting the water hit me in the face. The warmth trickled down my body and soothed my tight, achy muscles.

I grabbed the soap and rubbed it all over my body, realizing the scent reminded me of Gage when he was in the bedroom in front of me. I had never seen a man's body before and it looked absolutely glorious and caused feelings deep inside my stomach to stir.

When he turned around... my mind wondered to what it would feel like... to touch it... to feel it... down there. I continued to imagine him, while my hands roamed around on my body, migrating further and further down.

This wasn't the first time I touched myself, but it was the first time I did with an image so vivid I felt like I could reach out and touch it, and oh how I wanted to. The pad of my finger fumbled around on the outside of my opening before slipping in. It felt good... great, in fact.

I didn't want to stop.

I pulled my finger out and continued rubbing and swirling and slowly dipped it back in, imagining it was him... Gage, but I knew that would never happen, so I pictured Enzo. My free hand rubbed up my torso, gliding over my wet breasts causing my nipples to pebble.

"Scarlet!" I heard Enzo yell from downstairs, startling me out of my fantasy.

I quickly rinsed off the remaining soap and climbed out of the shower. I grabbed my towel and went to wrap it around me when I found Gage standing at the doorway, looking at me.

"I..."

His eyes looked like they were on fire. He didn't say anything, but turned to leave.

That was unexpected, I thought, then panicked. What if he saw me? He did see me, there was no way he didn't. Why did he stay to watch?

I realized in this moment, I was not horrified he saw me, but curious... and excited.

I quickly grabbed my outfit and put it on, and walked downstairs to find Calix in the kitchen.

He looked up at me and smiled. "Not bad, kid."

For a split second I thought he was talking about the shower, then I quickly realized my guilty conscious was toying with me and he was talking about dinner. "Thanks!" I perked up a little, even though the nerves about their decision was tearing up my stomach.

I glanced at Gage to see if I could get a read on what he saw, but he wouldn't look at me. Was that on purpose?

I searched around the room to find Enzo and he wasn't looking at me either, which told me all I needed to know.

They decided, and it wasn't good.

Barrett cleared his throat. "Scarlet." Everyone looked at him, including Gage. "We've been talking... the better part of the day, actually. It seems you have caused quite the stir in our house."

I went to apologize, but he continued talking.

"There are some here who have doubts about your story and are concerned it will bring trouble to our house."

I tried to stare straight ahead at the knot on the wall so tears didn't betray my anxiety. It was weird, I realized. I wasn't as sad about leaving the castle as I was this place. I had more interaction with these seven men in the short time I was with them than I had with all the people at the castle in the last several years.

"Will you bring trouble?"

I sighed, swallowing the lump in my throat. "I don't think I will, but I can't say for certain. I've seen more care from you all since I've been with you than I have from my family in all my years combined, so I don't imagine anyone will come from me. They probably already assume I'm dead, but I guess in some ways I have been dead to them for a while." I looked down, playing with the hem of my skirt.

Barrett listened thoughtfully, processing everything I had just said, and then nodded. "That was a fair and honest answer."

I pinched my lips in a hard line and nodded.

"We would like to welcome you to stay with us."

"Yes!" Enzo shouted, standing up.

Barrett looked at him. "Wait. Before you get too excited."

I looked between the two of them, with my gaze quickly flitting to Gage. I found myself wanting to know what he felt, even though I didn't know why I cared. When I didn't get any emotional response from him, I looked back at Barrett.

"We can't have drama in the house, so as long as that doesn't happen because of you, then you are welcome to stay here. You will need to continue to help around the house to earn your keep. That is the rule we all live by here. We all contribute."

I nodded emphatically. "Absolutely. Absolutely. I will do whatever you want. Anything. You name it."

"Stay out of my shower." Gage snapped.

I looked at him, but said nothing. I would have to learn to bite my tongue around him.

"You did good today. If you can clean around the house, do our laundry, help harvest the garden and you seem to have a skill with the bow. Those would all be a good start."

"Absolutely!"

"I will still cook, but every once in a while if you want to help with that too, that would be nice." Calix added.

"Absolutely!"

I was so excited right now that Gage's sour mood couldn't touch it.

"Perfect." He looked around the room. "We will eat dinner now and talk about sleeping arrangements."

"Oh." I would share a bed with someone? I immediately looked around the room to figure out who it would be.

Barrett chuckled. "Oh. You won't be sleeping in our rooms. We have space in the attic. There's a window and everything. It's just obviously on the top floor and there's junk we can go through tomorrow, but it can be your space."

"Oh." I laughed and then ran over and wrapped my arms around his neck. "Thank you so much!"

He wrapped his arms around me and I was filled with so much happiness I felt like I could burst.

"Me next!" Enzo said, walking over.

Barrett released me, and I moved over to Enzo. He wrapped his muscular arms around me, pressing me to him, and spun me in a circle, causing me to squeal.

I pulled my head back and looked at his beautiful face and got a feeling in my stomach. He looked into my eyes and then quickly sat me down.

A couple of the others walked over to give me a hug, but my gaze kept moving back to Gage, who wasn't moving.

"Let's eat some dinner!" Barrett clapped his hands to-gether.

"Please." Gage said flatly, unamused by the joy.

I let all the boys take their seat first while I brought the drinks and food to the table. I took the last seat at the end, opposite Gage and sat there looking at everyone, excited about what my new future held.

After dinner, Enzo and Barrett showed me to the attic, which was up five flights of stairs. It was larger than I ex-pected, almost four times the size of my room at the castle. There was a mattress and bed frame in the corner, with boxes piled on top. I looked out the little round window on the center of the back wall and saw a beautiful full moon shining through.

Enzo and Barrett helped me move the boxes off the bed onto the other side of the room, stacking them high.

"We will go through these tomorrow." Barrett said again.

"This is perfect. Thank you so much. Really. Thank you."

"Thank Enzo."

I looked at Enzo and felt a flush move through me. "Thank you."

He pinched his lips together. "You're welcome."

Jace walked into the room. "Here's a set of sheets and a blanket for you."

I grabbed them from him while Enzo was moving the last box.

Jace walked around to the other side of the bed and pushed it away from the wall and helped me tuck the sheets under and then lay the blanket on.

"I say we celebrate now!" Enzo said, jumping up and swinging from the rafter, his muscles flexing under this weight.

"Sure."

"That does sound like a good idea, Enzo." Barrett ap-proved.

"We have a fire pit out back we haven't used in a while." Jace offered.

"Good idea. Let's fire it up! It's getting cooler out and seems like it would be a good night!"

Enzo raced down the stairs. "Fire pit tonight!"

I heard Calix yell, "Bosom Berries!"

I looked at Barrett again, my laugh turning to a smile. "Thank you again. I know I have already said it... a lot, but I will say it more. I really can't express how grateful I am to you all."

"Just don't cause trouble and we'll be good."

"You won't even know I'm here."

"That would be impossible to do."

I caught him looking at me and felt a flurry in my stomach and a flush sweep across my face.

He must have caught himself. "Let's go downstairs and join the others." He said, tapping the doorframe.

We got downstairs and everyone was in a flurry of excitement. Calix looked at me and smiled. "You have already brought so much excitement to this house! Bosom berry time and no chore time!" He laughed.

"Have you already had some of your special ale?" Barrett wondered.

"Perhaps! Tomorrow is the first time in a long time that we don't have to get up early to do chores. I'm getting smashed!"

I followed them outside as Enzo ran up, wrapping his arm around my neck. "This is going to be so awesome!"

I smiled, looking at him. "What are Bosom Berries?"

He stopped walking and jumped to stand in front of me. "Are you kidding me?" He grabbed both my shoulders. "No. Of course you aren't kidding. You had a horrible childhood. They are the best thing you will ever put in your mouth." He tapped the end of my nose and put his arm around my neck, guiding me out.

Calix already had a fire going while Dresden was walking outside holding long wooden sticks. "I've had these for a while and now we get to try them out!"

Enzo dropped his arm and ran over to Dresden, and I immediately missed our connection. I had never had someone pay as much attention to me as he did, and it felt amazing.

"Let's see what we have here." Enzo said, grabbing a stick and sliding it through his hands. "Smooth, long. Just like my cock." He laughed.

"Enzo. There's a lady here now. No more dick jokes." Jace reprimanded.

"It's ok. The dick jokes are funny." I had only ever seen one, and that was Gage's. I toyed with the idea of making my own joke, but thought it probably wasn't the best idea.

At least not yet.

"Even the way you say dick is so cute." Enzo said swiping my nose.

"Enough. We didn't keep her around to be your toy, Enzo." Jace reminded.

We all grabbed a seat, and I followed what they were doing. Calix had brought out a bowl of berries, some sort of chopped up cake, and a tray of white fluffy stuff. He held out his stick and slid on a berry, then a piece of cake, another berry, and another piece of cake, then held it over the fire, slowing twirling the stick. After a few minutes, he took it off and slowly rolled the berries and cake into the white fluffy stuff and then carefully plucked each piece off into his mouth, moaning.

"How is it?" Enzo asked excitedly.

"Better than sex."

"I doubt that." Enzo chuckled. "Maybe you need a night with Cana."

I ignored the slight sting I felt when Enzo was talking about being with another woman. It's not like we had anything, but perhaps somewhere inside I wanted it.

I slipped the berries and cake on just like Calix had done and twirled it over the flame. After the fluff, I took a seat back in my chair and plucked the berries and cake off. I put the first bite in my mouth and moaned, garnering

the attention from everyone. "Sorry... This is really good."
I laughed.

I felt a tap on my shoulder and looked up to find Gage
standing there.

"You're in my seat." He said in a flat tone.

"I..." I looked around and then stood up. "Sorry."

I don't know why I was apologizing, but every time I saw
him, my mind went back to the shower.

There were no seats left, so I stood there awkwardly, then
decided to sit on the ground.

"That was rude, Gage."

"Shut up Enzo. I don't see you offering her your chair."

"I'm fine here. Thank you." I looked at Gage. "Do you need
a stick?"

He stared at me for a second, then shook his head and
knocked back a glass of ale.

"Can I have some?" I asked, looking at him.

He hesitated a second before filling the glass and handing
it to me.

"Is Gagey poo sharing?"

"Shut up Enzo!" I said before Gage could. "You're going
to ruin it for me." I laughed, then drank all the ale. I felt the
familiar burn through my chest.

We continued to sit by the fire for hours, eating Bosom
berries and drinking ale, while the boys regaled me with
stories of their mischief.

A few times, I caught Gage staring at me and couldn't
help but wonder why. Was he seething with anger that
I was still here? Was he replaying what he saw of me in
the shower? The thought of him watching me caused my
insides to tighten.

Ignore it.

Ignore him.

My head felt weird, like I was floating in the ocean, while
at the same time feeling an overwhelming amount of happiness.

"Well, it's early in the morning. We should all probably get to bed." Barrett said.

"Just one more." Enzo chimed, swinging his shirt around his head. He had a beautifully sculpted chest, I admired.

Everyone laughed. "You've had enough." Calix said.

"Boo."

I stood up and stumbled around a minute before I felt a hand on my arm stabilizing me.

"Tha-" I saw Gage.

"I didn't want you falling on me because you can't hold your ale." He dropped his hand and started walking inside.

"Do you need any help cleaning up out here?" I asked, trying to ignore the tingling feeling on my arm where Gage had touched me.

Calix and Dresden, with their arms full, declined my help.

"Then I thank you for a wonderful evening and I will see you all tomorrow." I took a step, but felt very woozy and wobbly.

"Here." Jace said, running up. "You had a lot to drink. It can make you a little lightheaded."

I grabbed his hand. "Thank you."

By the time we reached the house, Enzo was on my other side, holding me up with his arm slipped around my waist.

Jace shot a side glance at him, but didn't say anything.

Jace parted out when we got to his room and I couldn't help but glance at Gage's door and wonder what he was doing. Was he in bed? What would it be like to be in his bed... with him? In his arms? I shook my head. No. I shouldn't be thinking about that... about him.

Enzo helped me up the stairs, and we laughed as we both continually missed steps. His room was on the level right below mine. When we got to his door, he stopped but didn't take his hands off me. "This is me."

I looked up the stairs at my door.

My door, I smiled.

"Do you need help up?" He offered, following my gaze.

"I don't think so."

"Ok. If you need anything, let me know."

"Thanks." He dropped his hand, but neither of us moved, just staring at one another. A door slamming broke us from our trance and I started walking up the stairs. After I missed the first couple, I decided to bend over with my hands on the stairs, walking up them slowly on all fours.

I heard a chuckle behind me, so I peeked between my legs and found Enzo standing in his doorframe without a shirt on, watching me.

"I fell."

He ran up a few steps. "Here. Let me help." He grabbed me around my hips and helped guide me up the rest of the stairs and across my room. I tripped, and we both fell onto my bed. I rolled over on my back and he was lying on top of me. "Oops."

I laughed and before I knew what I was doing; I leaned up and kissed him, pressing my lips against his, and then I stopped. "I'm... I'm sorry... I don't know why I did that."

He smiled, standing up. "It's ok. I liked it."

I returned his smile. "I liked it too."

He walked out of the room and shut my door. I heard a rumble like he'd fallen down some stairs, but then he quickly said, "I'm ok!"

I didn't move from my bed. I turned my head, so I was looking out the window at the star covered sky in complete bliss.

My first kiss.

CHAPTER TEN

GAGE - OUT OF MY BED AND OUT OF MY HEAD

I GRABBED THE PICKAXE and slammed it into the wall as chips of rock flew off. I reared it back and swung it as hard as I could into the wall again. It had been over two days and I couldn't get the image of Scarlet in the shower out of my head.

Her hand rubbed slowly down her body, crossing over her breasts and parting her creamy thighs. I knew I should have turned away- should have walked away- but I couldn't. *She moved her fingers around delicately.* She was inexperienced. She hadn't done that before, or many times at the very least. I could show her what to do. She would live in ecstasy for days if I helped her. I would make her toes curl and her back arch, sending those beautiful breasts in the air. *She continued circling and then stuck a finger in, gently probing.*

Who was she thinking about? Was it me? Or was it Enzo and his perky, always smiling, face?

I slammed the pickaxe again as the memory of her touching herself continued to dance around in my head. I slammed it again. Two days!

She didn't moan. She wasn't doing it right.

I could show her. I would make her come.

I bet it would taste sweet.

I slammed the pickaxe again.

Fucking Scarlet! I could feel my cock pulsing at the thought of her.

"Everything ok over there?" Dresden asked.

"Fine." I mumbled.

"Girl troubles?" Enzo skipped over.

"Fuck off."

The last two days had been nearly unbearable. He had been giddy... more giddy than usual, and it was infuriating. He wouldn't say why, but I had a feeling it had something to do with Scarlet. Everything around the house lately seemed to have to do with her.

Everyone loved her. She was great. Blah, blah, blah.

She was getting herself off in my shower, she fucking laid in my bed, and I could smell her scent all over my bowl and spoon the night she first stayed at our house. It was like she was designed to fuck with me and make me want what I can't have. My own personal torture- payback from the Goddess, I'm sure. There was a pureness inside of her and a darkness that filled me. It would destroy her and enjoy doing it.

No, people like me didn't get happiness.

Water and soap bubbles washed over her perky little nipples, sliding down her body.

I slammed the pickaxe again. I needed to do something to get her off my mind. "You boys want to go to the Ruby Tavern tonight after work?"

Enzo's eyes grew large. "You know I love me some Ruby's tavern. I haven't seen that little fae, Cana, in a few weeks. The things she does with her mouth." He kissed his fingers.

"Barrett?"

"Not tonight. Last time I went there, I couldn't walk for a few days."

Enzo patted his back. "I'm telling you. Cana is where it's at, although Gage likes those shifters. What was her name? Eloise?"

"Yes, but I don't think I'm in the mood for her tonight. I need something more."

"More? She's a werewolf."

"Yea. I'm thinking maybe two tonight."

"Ooh, the Gemini sisters." Enzo stroked his chin.

I smiled.

"My man. Something must really have you worked up if that's what you're going for. They are intense with a capital N."

"You're an idiot."

"What? N as in I.N. Intense."

I shook my head. He had no idea the problems I was dealing with. I didn't want Scarlet at the house. I didn't want her in my bed. I didn't want her in my shower, and I certainly didn't want her in my head. She needed to get out, and the Gemini sisters would help with that.

They had to.

The workday went by a little easier once I had my plan in place. After tonight, Scarlet wouldn't be a problem for me anymore. This was going to be good.

We got home just after dark and had a quick bite to eat after we washed up. Scarlet was there as usual, always smiling and gliding around. After she found me watching her in the shower, she had been a little quieter around me, which was nice. I didn't like the version of her that talked back to me. It excited the darkness with in- the challenge.

She needed to know her place.

I saw the way she was around Enzo, and it riled me up. She watched after him like a lost pup looking for a bowl of milk to lap. Why didn't she understand he would hurt her?

We all would.

Barrett shouldn't have let her stay, but the others felt bad for her.

We were not men to settle down with and have a family.

We were miners.

We had a job, and we did it.

The women in our lives were fleeting- no other purpose than to give us what we wanted, when we wanted it and nothing more.

I watched her eat the meat on her plate while talking and laughing with the rest of the men. Infuriating. I had to fight the urge to swipe her plate out from underneath her and-

She caught me looking, so I just glared at her, which was enough to cause her to dart her eyes away.

Good. Look away.

As we were getting ready to leave, I heard her ask Calix where we were going, and he looked uncomfortable. Enzo was already outside or else he probably would have felt guilty and stayed.

I stepped up, casually laying my arm on Calix's shoulders. "Ruby's tavern. You should come. You could probably learn a thing or two."

She looked confused. Of course, she hadn't heard of it.

"Well, you boys have fun."

"We plan on it." I added with a smirk.

With that, Calix and I met Enzo outside.

"What took so long?" Enzo asked, jogging over to us.

"Your girlfriend wanted to know where we were going." I teased.

"Jace?"

"Hilarious. Scarlet."

"She's not my girlfriend. Is that what she said? We just kissed the one time, and it was by accident... kind of."

They kissed? I felt my head fit to explode, but fortunately, no one else could see since it was already dark out. "Let's go get some pussy tonight!"

Enzo, Calix, and I arrived at Ruby's Tavern and the place didn't look any different from the last time I'd been here. It had been a while, but tonight was much needed. The tavern was an old house that had been transformed into the tavern. It was three stories above ground and remodeled to have three stories below ground, but that was a no-go zone for most- but not for me when I needed a little extra.

The main foyer was decorated in a classic white and black marble decor and housed the one spiral staircase leading upstairs and down. There was a glittery beaded curtain wall that separated the foyer from the tavern part of the house and when you walked through, all you saw was red. The floors and walls were covered in crimson velvet with a few black high top tables scattered around, with black velvet plush chairs in the corner. On the opposite side of the room was a long bar top with a few chairs sitting in front, which is where I was headed.

"Ruby darling." Enzo said, walking up to her, leaning across the bar to give her a kiss on the cheek.

She smiled and sang his name in her usual melodic tone, adjusting her top to show more of her cleavage.

"So sweet sounding." He smiled. "Lured anyone to their death lately?"

"Only those that deserved it." She winked. "I told you, I have put my siren days behind me."

"You can take the girl out of the siren, but not the siren out of the girl. You are as beautiful as ever and I would follow you anywhere." Enzo said, kissing her hand.

"Such the charmer you are." She looked at Calix and me. "What can I do for you fine bunch of men tonight?"

"We need to have a good time." I said.

"Do you even know what that is?" Enzo chimed.

"Leave him alone." Calix defended.

I waited for a jab from him, but he didn't.

"Enzo, I believe is looking for Cana. Gage, here, wants the Gemini's and I'm looking for whatever you think is best."

She looked in the air and was silent a moment and then started nodding. "Yes. Cana will be ready soon and the Geminis are just finishing up and for you, dear Calix," she pressed her hand to his chest. "Your heart is beating strong tonight. You are looking for a challenge. I'd recommend Eloise or Tryx."

"Surprise me," he said.

We ordered a few drinks while we waited and took a seat at one of the available tables. I looked at Calix. "Have you ever been with Eloise or Tryx?"

He shook his head, and both Enzo and I started laughing. "What?"

"Brother, you are going to be in for it tonight. Go ahead and come up with a safe word now... chances are you'll be using it."

"I will?"

His face was somewhere between worried and excited. If he only knew, I laughed.

"Oh God. He's laughing. This is going to be bad." Calix said, his face converting to full worry now.

"No. It will be great. Mind blowing." I said, patting him on the shoulder.

"Gage?"

I heard my name and looked up to find the Gemini sisters standing at the base of the stairs wearing nothing but sheer white panties and matching bra with a little fur trim around the edges.

"Go get 'em tiger." Enzo said, holding his hands up like claws.

I walked over to the sisters and they each hooked their arm around mine, leading me away. As we started walking up the stairs, I saw Tryx coming from one of the lower level floors and chuckled while at the same time saying a silent prayer for Calix.

They directed me to the first room on the fifth floor. In the middle of the room was a swing hanging from the ceiling while on the wall to the right were all sorts of accouterment, ranging from whips, chains, handcuffs, spiked balls and more.

"What are you in the mood for tonight, Gage?" The first asked, shoving me on the bed while the other pulled off my shoes.

"I need to forget someone."

"Potion or no potion?" The second asked.

"No potion."

They both looked at each other and smiled. "We can help then."

"Perfect."

The first sister laid me back on the bed. "Any preferences?" She asked, unbuttoning my shirt.

"None."

"Excellent." The first said, pulling off my pants. "Oh my."

They both stood up and started to slowly undress one another, although there wasn't much to take off. "Do you like to watch?" The second asked, falling to her knees.

My mind wondered back to watching Scarlet in the shower, and I just moaned. Fortunately, they thought it was meant for them because the second grabbed the other from around the waist and pulled her to her mouth. The first grabbed onto her hair and pulled her in tightly as she stood there, being lapped. Her moans echoed throughout my mind.

Holy shit.

After a few minutes, the second stood up and walked over to me. "My turn." She said crawling on the bed as she propped herself over my face, her sweet juices already at the rim while the other sister took my cock in her hand and slowly sank her head down, taking me in her mouth.

The second sat her wet pussy on my face and I ate like it was the last fucking cake in the world while the other bobbed her head up and down on me, taking me in, swirling her tongue around. I could feel my tip crashing into the back of her throat and hear her gagging just a bit, while her teeth gently scraped the sides of me. I grabbed the legs of the one on my face and pulled her in closer, so I could sink my tongue in as far as possible.

The first one cupped my balls while she continued to bob and then slowly pulled off, moaning. The one of my face asked, "Do you want some help down there, sister?"

"I would love it."

She turned around on my face so she was looking at her sister and bent over to join her as they both started at the base of my cock and licked and sucked the sides to the very tip where they preceded to make out with each other for only a second, while they continued, slowly pumping each time. I felt like I could explode, but as if sensing it, they both stopped.

The one climbed off my face and they each grabbed my hand and pulled me off the bed. Sister one walked and sat on the swing adjusting the height a bit while the other one directed me in front of her. "Fuck her."

Startled for a brief second at the command, I recovered and pulled her hips to me, slamming into her. She let out a wail of pleasure and leaned back. Her sister walked over and stepped over her sister's face while she looked at me. "Fuck her harder."

I continued to pound into her sister as she stared at me while getting lapped like a savage beast. This was hotter than I could have ever imagined.

Scarlet was out of my head now.

CHAPTER ELEVEN

SNOW - A WARNING AND A QUEST

I LAID IN MY bed, staring through the window at the moon. The house was quiet since most of the boys had gone to bed some time ago. Enzo, Calix and Gage still weren't back and part of me wondered what was taking them so long.

I thought about Gage's offer to go to the tavern and part of me wanted to show up and prove a point, even though I knew it was a snide, off-handed comment. The part he added about the tavern teaching me something was a jab no doubt at the scene he saw in the shower.

I walked downstairs and grabbed a glass of water and a blanket and sat outside, enjoying the cooler weather. Winter was always my favorite time of year, something about how everything seemed quiet and at peace filled me with comfort.

I wasn't outside longer than an owl's hoot when I saw three figures walking through the woods. I tensed at first, then recognized the wide shadow of Gage, walking behind two figures, one of which seemed to be limping.

"Scarlet..." Enzo mumbled when he got to the porch, like I had caught him doing something he shouldn't have.

"Hey boys."

"What are you doing out here?"

"I couldn't sleep, so I thought I'd sit out here for a little." I looked at Calix. "Are you ok? You're walking a little funny." I chuckled.

"He got rode by a werewolf." Enzo said, patting him on the back.

I nearly choked. "A what?"

"A werewolf. Tell me you have heard of those." Enzo bent over, pleading.

I laughed. "Yes. I have. It was just unexpected."

I noticed Gage's gaze on me before he spoke, almost like he was trying to figure something out. "What did you think the Red Tavern was?" Gage asked, leveling his eyes at mine. I could tell he was trying to rile me up.

"I don't know."

"Seems like there's a lot you don't know."

"On that note, I'm going to bed." Calix said, hobbling up the stairs.

"Let me help you." Enzo offered, eager to get out of this conversation.

Gage didn't move and neither did I. Part of me wanted to show him he didn't intimidate me while the other part just wanted to be in his presence. My body felt alive when I was around him and I couldn't figure out why. Was it because I had never experienced someone like him before?

"Did you get ridden by a werewolf?" I asked him jokingly.

He laughed. "Why does it matter to you?"

"It doesn't. You're still out here, so I can only take that to mean you want to tell me about your sexual exploits. Perhaps try to rile me up or get under my skin."

"Do you want to know?"

"I don't care."

"I was with the Gemini sisters."

I nodded. "Two?" I felt a pang of jealousy, but I wasn't going to let him see.

"Yes, and it was magical."

"Sounds fantastic. Hopefully, you won't be such a dick now." I said flatly.

He chuckled. "I doubt that. You still seem to bring out that side of me."

"I do?" I moved forward and saw him tense and noticed his breathing changed. The pleasure I felt from knowing how I affected him was a rush, so I took another step forward so we were nearly chest to chest. I looked in his eyes and with the moonlight casting down on him, it was as if they almost glowed in the dark.

"What else do I bring out in you?"

He stared at me but didn't speak.

"Hmm?"

His expression turned stony, like he'd caught himself being weak. He leaned in so our faces were inches apart. "Are you going to kiss me like you kissed Enzo?"

"Do you want me to? Did that make you jealous?" I asked, not moving, letting his warm breath curl around me.

I felt like we were in a hunters' game, both of us trying to get the other to break, and it was intoxicating.

His eyebrows lowered. "You wouldn't be able to handle me."

"Is that a warning or a challenge? Because I never back down from a challenge." I closed the gap so our lips were only inches apart.

"No. I've just seen how inexperienced you are." I saw the devilish grin slide across his face as his gaze settled on my lips.

He had seen me, I thought he had, but wasn't certain. Heat flashed through me, causing my blood to boil and my cheeks to flush. My core tightened as a mixture of embarrassment and lust created a confusing mix.

He wanted to embarrass me and so I'd slither away like some hurt animal, but that's not who I was. I wasn't going to pretend I was experienced. I knew it and he knew it. It wasn't because I didn't want to, rather, I didn't have the opportunity. I have the opportunity now and whether he wanted to admit it or not, I knew I had an effect on him.

"Then show me." I leaned forward and gently placed my lips just beside his mouth and pulled back, looking up at him through my lashes.

His eyes flashed as he sucked in a breath, and I could tell that was not the reaction he expected.

"You couldn't fucking handle me." He repeated, his voice shaking slightly.

"I think I could." I whispered, cautiously letting my hands rest on his chest. My body was buzzing right now, and I was throbbing between my legs as moisture began to puddle. How was it possible the mere sight of him caused my body to react like this?

"So you want to fuck me? Is that it?"

He licked his lips and I wanted nothing more than to press mine against his and taste them, taste all of him. I let my hand slide down so it was resting on the outside of his pants, pressed against his hard cock. "What if I said yes? Then what?"

He stared at me for a moment without speaking, as his eyes darted back and forth between mine.

I raised my eyebrows. Was this it? Was this what he wanted? Was this actually happening?

"No." He said simply, answering my internal dialogue.

"No?" I was confused. I could tell by the bulge in his pants he wanted to.

He straightened up, pulling away from me. "No. I don't want to sleep with you."

He pushed past me and walked inside.

That was it.

That was the end of our conversation.

I stared at the door, flabbergasted, and then sat in the chair. No. No, he didn't want to sleep with me?

That was a lie. I could see it in his face he wanted to.

I tried to steady my breathing because I was more alive than I had ever felt.

It was Gage. He did that to me.

After I calmed down, I walked inside to a dark and empty room. All the lights were off and it was deathly quiet.

I walked upstairs to my bedroom after pausing at Gage's door, wondering what would happen if I walked in. Would he push me out or would he give into the temptation and take me?

I fell into bed, staring out the window, trying to figure out what had just happened until I fell asleep.

"Darling?"

"Mama, is that you?"

The room slowly came into focus. It was the same room as last time, with a little more detail.

The walls were a wet stone that was quickly being replaced with wall paper as I looked around the room. There was a beautiful deep, dark blue on the bottom half and dark green on the top with a golden ribbon criss-crossed throughout.

Sitting in her chair in the corner was mama.

"You need to be careful with those miners. There's darkness in some of them."

"But they have been so kind, taking me in." I shook my head. "How do you know about them?"

"I know a lot of things."

"You said last time I had to go home and help papa."

"Yes. He needs you, but not before you're ready."

"Ready? Ready for what?"

"For your battle with the dark Queen."

"I don't think I can fight her."

"You can. You are stronger than you know."

"You said she practices the dark arts. She will have magic."

"You have power too." She stood up and crossed the room.

"I'm not a witch."

"Her being a witch doesn't make her powerful."

"It sure helps. I can't compete with that..."

"You don't have to be a witch to wield power, Snow."

"She seems to use it to wield her power. I mean, look at what she has done to Papa. Do you know how he is?"

"He is fine. He is safe... for now."

"What do you mean?"

"There are things you need to know that I can't tell you."

"You said that last time."

"And it's still true today."

"Who can tell me?"

"Find a white witch by the name of Persephone."

"Persephone?"

"Yes. She can tell you what you need to hear. But you must hurry and find her."

"Where? Where is she?"

"Find a purple mangor. Bring it berries from the bosom bush and tell it what you seek. It will help guide the way."

"A purple mangor. I've never seen a purple mangor before."

"Ask the wind and nature will provide."

She started slipping away again, fading into a fine mist.

I yelled out for her to stay, but it was too late.

"Scarlet! Scarlet! Wake up."

I opened my eyes and saw Enzo standing over my bed. "What?"

"You were screaming. Crying out."

"I was? I'm so sorry."

He climbed into bed and wrapped his arms around me. "Do you want to tell me about it?"

I heard a creak at the door and saw someone walking away. I couldn't tell who it was, and it felt weird to call out for them now.

"I don't really remember much." I lied, because even though I felt like I could trust Enzo and all the miner seven, she warned me to be careful.

"You seemed terrified."

"I did?" I rested my head on his chest.

"You're safe here."

After a few moments, I asked. "Have you ever heard of a purple mangor?

"The bird?"

"Yea."

"Not a purple one. Red and blue, but never purple."

"I didn't think so either."

"Why? Is that what your dream was about?"

I mumbled a noise, not really sure what to say. How do you tell someone, you're dreaming of your dead mother who you've never met and she's telling you that you need to talk to the wind to find a bird that doesn't exist so it can lead you to a white witch that will tell you something that you need to know about yourself so you can defeat the dark Queen who also happens to be your stepmother and a witch? I took a gasp, running out of breath in my head just thinking through all of that.

"Do you want me to stay with you?"

I looked up at him. "Would you?"

"Sure."

I rested my head back on his chest and closed my eyes.

Chapter Twelve

Huntsman - An Encounter with a Siren

I HAD WANDERED THE mountainsides for days now without a trace of Snow. While she was good with a bow, she was too young and naïve to last this long in the woods without help, and a beautiful woman like her would be no match for beggars and thieves.

I had to find her, but why?

The dark Queen tasked me with killing Snow and bringing her Snow's liver and heart as proof.

Was I really going to kill Snow?

I honestly couldn't say right now. If I didn't, I know the Queen would kill me. Was Snow's life worth more than mine?

I stopped in a house that had a small sign posted out front.

Ruby's Tavern.

Hopefully, they'd have something good to eat, since it was the first building I'd seen in hours. I walked into the elegantly decorated black and white foyer and had a feeling this was not the tavern I had been expecting.

"Welcome." A woman said from behind the bar in the other room. Her voice was light and melodic.

"Hello." I replied, taking off my hat.

"What can I do for you this evening?"

I looked around and saw a few men waiting at some tables, and then looked back at the bartender. "You wouldn't have anything to eat here, would you?"

The woman laughed. "We have lots of things to eat. What exactly are you in the mood for?"

Catching her mischievous grin, I settled for the less obvious answer. "Food?"

She smiled knowingly. "You aren't from around here, are you?"

"Is it that apparent?"

She shrugged her shoulders. "Maybe just a little."

"So... food? This was the only place I have seen around for a while."

"You just have to know where to look in these areas." She studied me for a moment. "We rarely serve food, but you're in luck. I just made a stew last night and brought it in for the girls. I could probably get a little for you."

"Thank you. I would be so grateful."

"I'll be right back."

She returned a few minutes later with a bowl full of stew that was steaming hot. "Thank you. How much can I pay you?"

She batted her hand. "It's on the house, darling."

"I can't take it for nothing."

She lifted her chin and studied me for a second. "Two Yergamots."

"Done." I pulled the coins out of my pocket and handed them to her. "Not many people deal in Yergamots around here." I said taking in several large spoonful's of stew.

"I know. It's mostly only used around the castle." Her tone changed. "Tell me. What is it you're doing out here again?"

Shit. She was sly. A test and I didn't even see it coming. "I didn't say." I shifted more upright in my seat as a tingle crept down my spine.

She looked at me, waiting. "I could make you tell me."

"I'd hate if you did that. We were getting along so well." The air was rapidly shifting around me, but I wasn't picking up anyone else close to me, just her.

"Who are you working for?" She stood upright, clearly sensing my uneasiness.

"I can't say."

Her eyes narrowed at me. "See, the thing is, I have a business to protect and, therefore, customers to look after. If you're doing the bidding of the dark Queen out in these areas... well... I don't think that's going to bode too well for my people. She's not been the nicest to our kind and I feel like if you're here... one of them may be in trouble."

"I have no need for any of your people. I'm merely passing through." I dropped my hand from the bar and placed in on the handle of my knife, but leaving it tucked in its sheath.

"I see."

"I probably should go now." I said pushing away from the bar, careful not to move too fast. I was in an unfamiliar place, in an unfamiliar town with an unknown threat. I had quickly looked around the bar when I entered and didn't surmise a threat, but I was getting the impression I may have underestimated the barkeep.

"Wait." She put her hand on my shoulder and then slowly started to whistle, letting her head sway side to side like a boat rocking on the ocean. I felt myself getting lulled into a relaxing state. "Who are you searching for?"

I shook my head, but her whistling felt like it was carrying me away to the clouds.

"Who?" she moaned softly.

"Snow White."

"The princess? I thought she died years ago. No one has seen her."

"Locked away."

"By the dark Queen?"

I nodded, feeling like a complete dope. Part of me wanted to stop talking, the other part was glad to share everything with her so I could listen to her beautiful song.

"What does she want with her?"

"Her heart... and her liver."

"Black magic."

I shrugged.

"What would the Queen want with the Princesses heart and liver?"

I shrugged, still feeling like I was floating through the clouds, without a care in the world.

"Are you going to kill her?"

"I don't know yet."

"You can't."

The whistling stopped and I looked around like I had knocked back about ten ales too many. The room was spinning and I felt woozy. I took in a deep breath and looked at the bartender. "I really wish you hadn't done that."

"Me too." She said, troubled. Was she nervous because she knew my true intentions or because she knew something about the Queen?

"Why are you so worried?"

"You can't give her the heart and liver of Snow White. If it's what I think..."

"What?"

"Rumor is the old Queen couldn't get pregnant. Her and the King tried for years and then one winter day she pricks her finger after being startled by a bird... a black bird. After that visit, she's pregnant with Snow and soon after childbirth, she dies."

"Yes." She was saying a lot of words and I was still coming out of my drunken stupor, but everything she said seemed accurate.

"What if?" The bartender was pacing. "Oh... no... no... no. This can't be good."

"What? What is it?"

She stopped pacing and looked me dead in the eyes, slamming her hands on the counter. "You cannot find Snow and kill her. The dark Queen cannot have her liver and heart."

"Why not?" What did she know I didn't? "Tell me."

She shook her head. "Not yet. I need to make sure."

"Make sure of what?"

"You need to leave."

"But."

"Now. Leave. You can't be here. I can't be seen with you. The Queen can't know you've been here."

"The Queen knows you?"

"Leave! Out!" I heard the whistling and in a second I felt my turning and walking towards the exit.

Once I got outside, it was like the trance had been lifted, but I instinctively grabbed my head to make sure it was still attached to my body. Satisfied, I patted my leg, calling the dog over, and made my way to the woods. I need to get back home.

"What are we going to do, dog?"

She looked up at me with the eyes of a wise person before she barked and ran off.

"Don't leave me!" I shouted after her.

A moment later, I heard her barking wildly like she was trying to tell me something. I found her on the edge of the woods, standing over a wild boar.

She had managed to catch a boar twice her size.

As if sensing my needs, she gave me an answer to the question.

I was going to kill the boar and take its heart and liver back to the Queen.

Chapter Thirteen

GAGE - HUNT FOR THE PURPLE MANGOR

FUCK!

I pounded my fist into the bed.

An hour! I lasted a bloody hour.

The Geminis were great! Fantastic! But I got home, and she was sitting outside. At first I thought she was waiting for us, then realized she wasn't and I didn't know what bothered me more.

And the way she pushed back! The way she always pushes back.

I hit the pillow, this time sending feathers flying in my room.

She kissed me. No fear. Just kissed me. I could still feel the softness of her lips just to the side of mine. She knew what she was doing.

And then now! Her screams woke me from my restless sleep and like a dummy I went to check on her, only to find fucking Enzo in her bed.

It should have been me.

No!

It shouldn't be any of us.

Why didn't she see that?

I punched the bed one more time for good measure, then laid down. I'd have to figure something out.

The next morning, I watched her walk down the stairs yawning, followed by Enzo.

"Sleep good?"

She cut her eyes at me, daring me to say something else.

"There was this howling that kept me up last night."

She continued to glare.

Enzo chimed in, defending her. "She had a bad dream."

I pouted my lips. "Oh no. A bad dream?" I mocked.

"Fuck off." She said, pulling up a seat at the table.

Calix choked, and Enzo smiled from ear to ear.

"Lighten up." I recoiled. I felt a little guilty for being mean, but the other part, the more logical part, knew it's what needed to be done. She had to see us for what we were and if I was the one that had to show her, then so be it.

The next several days passed much like the others. I had noticed Scarlet was a little quieter, like something was weighing on her, but she wouldn't share it with us, not even Enzo, who she seemed to have grown rather attached to.

"I'm going out today." She said, grabbing her bow and quiver off the wall.

"Where are you going?" I asked before I could help myself.

She turned and looked around the room, then landed on me. "I'm sorry. Were you talking to me?"

I put my paper down. Everyone else was doing other things around the house, so it was just her and I... alone... in the living room. "Don't flatter yourself. I don't care. I was just trying to be polite."

"You are never polite."

I shrugged my shoulders.

"Ok then. See you later." She turned and started walking outside.

Damn it! I stood up and ran after her, grabbing her wrist, spinning her around. I felt a spark tingle beneath my touch and dropped her wrist like it was a live wire.

"What do you think you're doing?"

I rolled my eyes. "I have no fucking idea."

It was the truth. My head was telling me to run away, but the other part was jumping up and running after her before I could stop myself.

"I'm going now."

"I'm going with you." Shit! It was like there were two people inside of me fighting for control of my mouth.

She laughed, then stopped. "Oh. You're serious."

"Yes. You shouldn't be going out on your own. You don't know this area well and you could get into trouble."

"Careful, you may sound like you care."

"I don't."

"So you keep saying, yet you're standing out her convincing me on why you should go with me." She studied me for a second before she turned and walked down the stairs.

I huffed and then followed her. "The only reason I'm coming is because I was the last person to see you. If I let you go off and something happened, I would be the one they blame and I don't need that shit."

"Got it." She continued walking without even looking at me.

"So, where are we going?"

"I don't know."

"You don't know?"

"No. I need to send a note in the wind and find a purple mangor."

"Are you mad? Purple mangors don't exist."

"They do. They have to." Her voice held a note of tension in it.

I grabbed her wrist again, this time more gently. I couldn't help but notice her soft skin under my rough and calloused hands. "What's going on?"

She looked at me. "I can't really say."

"Does this have to do with why you left home or with the nightmares you have at night?"

She pulled her wrist from my hand and continued walking.

"Scarlet!" I sighed, running after her, hating myself every second. I don't run after people, especially women.

"I think we should go this way." She pointed to the right and pushed some branches out of the way.

"Off the trail? I don't think that's a good idea."

She turned around to look at me. "It'll be-" she screamed and slipped out of view.

"Shit! Scarlet!" I ran to where she was last standing and skidded to a stop and looked down.

"I'm fine." She said, standing up and dusting herself off. "It was just a tiny hill."

"That's a nine or ten-foot drop."

"I guess you should go back home then." She continued walking, batting branches and twigs away from her.

She was completely mad. She was wandering through the woods, looking for a bird that didn't exist. The thought she was mentally unstable never crossed my mind, probably any of our minds. Perhaps that's why she left and the entire story of being locked up was a lie, or maybe she was locked up for a different reason and somehow escaped.

I skidded down the hill and walked after her.

"Tell me more about your childhood."

She looked at me and I could tell the question made her nervous.

"Why?"

"Because I want to get to know you."

"That's bullshit."

"For a lady, you have a dirty mouth."

"That's a sexist and fucked up thing to say." She looked over her shoulder and smirked, causing me to chuckle.

She stopped in a panic, looking around. "What was that?"

I looked around, my body tensing. "What? I don't see anything."

"Nooo... it... it sounded like you laughed."

"Ha. Ha. Very funny."

"There it is again, only that held the usual note of sarcasm." She playfully punched me in the shoulder and continued walking.

"So seriously... what are we doing out here?"

She looked at me, biting her lip, and I felt something tingle inside of me.

"Seriously... we are looking for a purple mangor."

"I really don't think they exist."

She sighed heavily, like she wanted to tell me something, but was scared. "I had a dream a few nights ago."

I remembered and then a flash of seeing Enzo laying in her bed with her crossed my mind and I felt my fists clench.

"It was my dead mother."

"Shit."

"Yea. She was standing in this room and she said I had to get back to the ca- to my home to help my father."

I didn't talk, because she looked like she had more to say.

"I think he's in danger... from my stepmother. She is an evil and vile woman."

"Aren't they all?" I joked, but it didn't seem to land.

She cast a glance at me that told me that wasn't the case.

"So your mother came to you and told you to find a purple mangor? Do you think it could have been a metaphor?"

She shook her head.

"Did she tell you how to find this bird?"

She pulled her lips.

"How?"

"She said to ask the wind." She spun around in a circle. "Look. I know it sounds crazy and you probably think I'm crazy, too."

She started crying, so I cautiously walked over to her and held my arms out. She surprisingly walked into them and wrapped her arms around me, pressing her face into my chest.

"It's ok. I think you're a little crazy, but I will help you."

I felt a small chuckle, but she didn't move and neither did I. She felt so small in my arms, so delicate, but I had a feeling that's not who she was. From everything I have seen, she is small, but mighty- a fighter.

The wind blew, and she stepped away from me. "Help me find the purple mangor."

I started to answer her, but stopped when I realized she wasn't talking to me. She was talking... to the wind? I watched in amazement as it whirled up around her, causing her shirt and pants to flutter, and her hair to twist straight up, and then it stopped.

Her hair fell and her clothes stopped fluttering.

"Who are you?"

She smiled. "Scarlet."

"Are you a witch?"

She laughed like I was joking, but I wasn't. "No."

"I've only seen witches communicate with nature."

She shrugged.

There was a flutter of a breeze near a bush and she started to run towards it.

"Come on!"

"Seriously?"

She didn't turn around, but continued to run. In this instance, she reminded me of a young child, running carefree through a field. She was practically emitting a light, as excitement and curiosity flowed through her.

Another ruffle of a bush or flight of birds and she would steer this way or that. It was like nature was communicating with her and she was following. Had I not seen it with my eyes, I probably wouldn't have believed it.

I don't know how long we had been following the path or where we were, but we came to the edge of a plunge pool at the base of a waterfall.

She stopped and looked up in amazement. "Isn't it beautiful!"

"Yes, yes, it is." She caught me looking at her, so I quickly diverted my attention to the waterfall. "So, what do we do now?"

"I don't know. I guess we wait."

"We wait? For how long?"

"I don't know." She looked around. "But the sun is high in the sky and mangors don't typically come until it's twilight out. So we have some time." She looked at me and I saw the look of mischief in her eyes. "I'm going to go for a swim. Care to join?"

"No. I'll stay here."

"Suit yourself." She started slipping out of her clothes.

"What are you doing?"

"I don't want to get my clothes wet. Do you know how cold I'll be tonight?"

"So maybe you shouldn't go in then..."

"But I want to."

"Do you always do what you want?"

"I never had the opportunity before, but now I do, therefore I am."

I chuckled until she took her top off and was standing in front of me, completely naked- her soft and supple skin begging to be touched.

Shit. She had no reservations.

I looked away until I heard the splash in the water.

"You should totally come in. The water feels great!" She said, bobbing up and down.

"No thanks. I'm good here."

She ducked under the water and popped up a few seconds later, before she rolled over to float on her back, as the water covered her skin like thin silk.

I watched her for an immeasurable amount of time as she simply enjoyed this moment and I couldn't help but wonder if she was telling the truth. Had she really been locked up in a small room most of her life, hidden from everyone?

She ducked under the water again, swimming towards the waterfall. Where was she going?

She popped her head up for a second, then dipped back under. I waited for her to pop back up, but she didn't. I stood on the edge of the bank looking for her in the water, but there was nothing, only the little ripples from the falling waterfall.

"Scarlet?" I called.

Silence.

"Scarlet!" I yelled a little louder.

Silence.

Shit! Did she drown? Did some animal get hold of her? She was stupid for going in there! Who knows what kind of creatures lived in that water.

I walked around the edge of the bank but didn't see her.

"Scarlet!" I shouted.

Silence.

I tore off my boots, pants and shirt and dove into the water, swimming to the last place I saw her. I took a deep breath and dipped under the water and saw her swimming towards me. Was she a fish?

She waved me towards her, so I swam over. She grabbed my hand and pulled me along.

We popped up a second later behind the falls.

"Change your mind?" She playfully splashed water on my face.

"I thought you died."

"And you came after me? I think you like me." She said, tapping the end of my nose.

"Unlikely." I said, pushing her head under water.

I second later I felt her try to climb on my back and take me under, but her weight wasn't a match for me.

"Nice try." I leaned back, and we both crashed under the water.

She quickly swam out from under me and pushed me, even though she moved more than I did. I watched her swim up to get air as her perfect little ass was on display under the water.

When I came up for air, she was waiting to splash me in the face with water.

"Careful. You don't want to start something you can't finish."

She splashed me again, laughing. I leapt forward and grabbed her, taking her under the water, our bodies pressed chest to chest. She was fighting me, trying to get loose, but I tightened my grip. Our faces were inches apart and then, as if something moved through the water, everything changed. She wasn't laughing any longer. Instead, she was staring at me and I could feel something inside me change. She wrapped her legs around me and I could feel my dick pressed against her and I immediately went hard. Her eyes grew wide with excitement and curiosity.

This was not how today was supposed to go.

Chapter Fourteen

SNOW - TRUTH REVEALED

I FELT HIS LENGTH between my legs and my stomach tightened. I knew I should move, but I didn't want to.

I wanted to feel him there.

I had fantasized about this moment and right now I wanted nothing more than to feel him inside me.

He swam us up to the surface and I took in a breath, but neither of us let go.

"Scarlet..." He hissed.

"Don't." I pleaded for him to stop talking. "Let this happen."

He shook his head slowly. "I'm not a good guy. None of us are."

"I don't need some prince to come rescue me." I slid my hips forward, rubbing along his shaft pressing my hips to his, as a warm tingle danced between my legs.

"You don't know what you need." His words were quick between his shallow breaths.

"I know what I want." I leaned in and kissed him just outside his mouth, feeling his cock slide between my legs, pressing right at my opening. "I know what I've wanted since the first time I saw you." I kissed him on the other side of his mouth, our lips barely touching at the corners.

I rocked my hips back and then forward slowly, letting my swollen clit rub along the top of his shaft as I shifted my legs, locking them around him tighter sending his cock further between my legs. I heard him suck in.

"Scarlet." He moaned my name, and it sent shivers down my spine and caused my stomach to clench and my breast to swell.

"Please." I leaned forward, rocking softly over him as I bit my bottom lip.

He shook his head. "Don't do that." He said breathlessly, his eyes intently watching my lips.

I could tell his resolve was fading. "Don't do this?" I bit my lip again, slowly scraping my teeth over it. Knowing what it was doing to him made me feel alive, causing my entire body to spark.

"Fuck." He growled, as one hand pressed on my lower back holding me close to him while the other snaked around the base of my neck pulling me towards him. He pressed his lips to mine, sucking in my bottom lip before forcing my mouth open with his. His lips were soft and warm as his tongue pulsed in, hungry, the same time his hips rocked us, causing his cock to split my folds.

I wanted to feel him inside of me, so I kept shifting my hips to feel him pressing at the opening, but he would shift again, placing me back on his cock. It was infuriating and erotic as hell all at the same time. He rocked faster and I gave up the fight and took what he was giving. I needed more. More of him, more friction. His hand slipped lower down my back and under my bottom as he dipped a finger in. I gasped as pleasure blossomed in my belly.

"Fuck me." I pleaded, hungrily.

"Scarlet." He moved his cock against my clit faster and faster then pulled his finger out, rubbing my wetness around my clit, before sliding two fingers back in. "I'm going to make you come so hard you will only think of me when you pleasure yourself in my shower."

"I only think of you now." I groaned as the pressure continued to build.

He kissed me hard, as he started to finger-fuck me. I felt my body start to take over as I rocked back and forth on his fingers. I wanted more of him in me, I needed more of him in me. I pressed down on him trying to get as much as I could. A moan escaped through our kiss, which only seemed to amplify his need. He shifted his fingers, so they continued to pulse in and out while another finger rubbed against my clit.

I felt it coming, the insatiable wave of pleasure. I arched my back giving him as much access as he needed. He greedily took my breast in his mouth and sucked in hard, the bite of pain sent a shock down my back before turning to pleasure. I wrapped my hand around his head pressing him to my chest. Take it, take all of me, I wanted to say, but didn't.

My body was spooling up. "Fuck, Gage." I continued to rock as his fingers continued to fuck me, his shaft rubbing on my clit now, fast and furious. "I want to feel you inside of me. I want you to fuck me Gage."

"I can't."

"I need you."

His lips crashed on mine, his tongue pulsing in sync with his hips as his cock pressed harder onto my clit. His fingers were no longer moving in and out, as I just rode them, feeling his hardness against me, my body begging for release.

"Come for me." He commanded, between kisses.

My body obeyed and it felt like my body exploded around him. "Oh my... fucking Goddess." I continued to ride his fingers as his length continued to rub my clit. I let out another gasp. "Shit. Fuck. Oh." My body continued to convulse around him, as my body melted onto him, pleasure taking over every part of my body.

"Fuck." He pulsed a few more times then stopped. He looked at me and I looked at him. Neither of us spoke as our breathing returned to normal.

"That was... amazing. That feeling." I released my legs and arms and floated on my back in the water in complete bliss.

"That was called an orgasm."

"I want to do that again."

He laughed. "It is a pretty glorious feeling."

"It's always like that?"

"If you do it right."

"Will you show me?"

He studied me for a minute and I was scared I had over-stepped. I knew that whatever this was between us was only temporary.

"I'm not a good person."

"I don't care. I want that again. I'm not looking for a husband right now. They had me locked up for years. I want to explore. I want to live." I swam back over to him. "So help me live, Gage. Let us take what we want from one another with no strings." I grabbed his cock in my hand. "Teach me how to please you." I ran my hand back and forth, slowly pumping it, feeling it grow harder in my hand. "Let me feel you inside me." I pressed the tip of his cock to my pussy and wanted so badly to let it take him in.

He leaned forward and then pushed away at the last second. "I can't." He moaned and then swam back towards the waterfall.

I stayed there, watching after him in complete shock. My body was still buzzing. It was clear that he was fighting some internal battles. I had been right before. He wanted to fuck me, but there was something stopping him.

After he dipped under the waterfall, I moved. It was probably getting darker out and I needed to be ready for the purple mangor, I tried to convince myself.

Goddess, I hope it existed.

By the time I got to the plunge pool, Gage was out of the water and putting his pants back on. I stayed in the water one more second, admiring his beautiful chiseled body. It was perfection.

I eventually climbed out and got dressed, sitting on the edge of the bank. Gage had found a spot in the grass behind me and had laid down with his eyes closed.

I knew he wasn't asleep, but I gave him his space... for now.

I don't know how much time had passed. I had counted seven thousand and sixty-nine ripples in the water when I heard the wind again. It was like nature was singing me a song.

"Gage." I tapped his foot.

He sat up, "Wha-"

"I think it's time."

The tree near the edge of the water started swaying gently back and forth. Bright pink and white blossoms opened, filling the entire tree in its beauty.

"Wow." I said in amazement.

It was like the tree was opening its doors to the night, welcoming it in. As if unfurling its branches, a flurry of birds flew from the depths inside the tree, taking to the air in a beautiful dance, moving with the wind.

The wind, as if it was alive and reeling with excitement, continued to blow and sway. I grabbed my hair, holding it out of my face so I could continue to watch the show.

Suddenly, the wind stop and the birds fell to the water with such precision like someone had snapped their fingers.

They quietly swam as if nothing had happened.

"What was that?" I turned to Gage.

He shook his head. "I have no idea. I've never seen anything like that before."

A moment later, a bird the size of a small elephant flew out of the tree and walked over to me.

A *purple mangor.*

I couldn't believe my eyes. Not only was it a giant bird, but it was a mangor- a purple mangor.

"Holy shit."

I looked at Gage. His eyes were enormous. "I told you."

He glanced at me, but didn't speak.

The bird stopped just in front of me and tilted its head down. I cautiously reached out and placed my tiny hand on its enormous beak. It looked so small in comparison.

"What are you doing?" Gage choked out.

"It won't hurt me."

"Until it bites your hand off!" He whispered.

The bird cocked its head like it was studying us.

"Hello." I said, and its round little eyes centered on me. "I'm seeking Persephone, the white witch."

"A witch?" Gage shuffled. "Are you mad?"

The bird began to peck the ground at my feet aggressively.

"It's trying to eat you." Gage said, standing hurriedly.

I quickly scooted back to stand up, so I was now the same height as the bird. It stepped forward and continued to peck aggressively.

Gage grabbed my arm. "We need to get out of here. This was a bad idea."

I jerked my arm from his grasp. "It's not going to hurt me."

"The fuck it won't. It's pecking at you now, like it wants to eat you."

"Eat!" How could I have forgotten! I ran to my bag and grabbed a handful of bosom berries and tossed them on the ground in front of the bird. It looked up at me and then gently picked the berry off the ground with the tip of its beak and tossed its head back, swallowing it whole. "I have to feed it bosom berries."

"What?"

I tossed a few more on the ground and slowly walked over to it. "I'm sorry I forgot the berries." I laughed.

The bird looked at me and then bent back down to retrieve the remaining berries from the ground.

I thought it was time to ask my question again. "I'm looking for Persephone, the white witch... I need to know about." I looked over my shoulder at Gage. "I need to know about me and I was told she would have the answers."

The bird took a step forward and rubbed its beak around me, up my legs, around my arms, almost like it was trying to nuzzle, but I got the feeling it was doing something else. Then it turned and walked away.

"What was that?" Gage asked.

"I don't know." I shrugged, watching it disappear back into the tree.

"Is that it?"

"I don't know Gage." My tone came off a little more irritated than I intended. "I've never done this before. I know as much as you do."

"Incorrect. You knew how to find it and that they existed."

"I was told that in a dream and was hoping it was right."

A moment later, a woman in a white flowing gown walked out from the tree. Her hair was long and red and curled around her face. She walked- almost floated- over to me.

"Snow. You have grown."

When she said my name, I felt like my body seize as the air shifted around me and could almost feel Gage's body react, but I didn't want to look to find out.

"Persephone." I started, but didn't really know how to word the rest. "My mother, she... she came to me in a dream and instructed me to find you. She said there were things I needed to know that she couldn't tell me, but you could."

"My dear Snow." She wrapped her arm around my shoulders and guided me away.

I quickly glanced over my shoulder and saw Gage standing there, torn and in shock."You have led a very troubled life. Born from magic. Harvested for youth. Now, hunted till death."

I stopped walking and looked at her. "What do you mean?"

"Oh Snow. The Queen couldn't have children."

I shook my head in confusion. "I don't understand."

She sighed. "While she may have birthed you..." she paused and grabbed my hands, "you were not hers."

"What?" My knees felt weak.

"You are Merla's daughter."

"My stepmother? But how?" I felt bile rising in my throat. I was going to be sick.

"She came to the Queen as a blackbird, causing her to poke herself with a needle. In the wound, Merla could pass on the curse for the Queen to bore you, binding your life to the Queens. She needed to die for you to live."

I shook my head, speechless, as I watched the trees sway and the birds fly.

Life was moving around me, but I felt dead on the inside.

I was dead.

This couldn't be happening.

I snapped my head in her direction. "You said harvested for youth."

She nodded.

"The curse made it so that when you were born, Merla could use your youth to keep her young."

"Which is why she wanted to kill me when I turned eighteen- I was no longer a child."

She nodded but didn't speak.

"Which is why I'm now hunted till death." I said, replaying her words back to her.

"Every day you live as an adult, she begins to age."

"Why me? I can't be the only one..."

"You aren't. Huntsmen, for centuries, have hunted her children down and killed them."

"Oh, Goddess."

"Desperate for youth and vitality, she had the Queen carry you so no one would suspect who you really were. Probably the only reason you've been able to live into adulthood."

"So she used my mother as a surrogate and then killed her. She made my father think he had a child. Who is my father?"

"You were born of magic. You have no father."

I felt my stomach drop.

"I... I..." I couldn't formulate a thought or sentence. I didn't even know what I was trying to say. I looked at her as thought after thought raced through my mind. I tried to grab on to one, but I couldn't focus.

I was filled with an ever rising rage.

I wanted to scream- to yell.

She had to be stopped. She was pure evil.

I took a deep breath.

"She won't stop coming after me." I whispered as the realization set in. I thought I had gotten away from her, but now I realized it was just a dream. She would be coming after me.

"She won't stop until you are dead."

"How do I stop her?"

"You have to kill her."

"How do I do it? How do I kill the dark Queen?"

Her eyes fell. "You must find all her children and kill them."

"Holy fuck." I ran my fingers through my hair and pulled. "Kill children. You want me to kill children? What the fuck?" I paced hurriedly in a circle.

"I didn't say that is what I wanted. You merely asked me how do you kill the dark Queen and I told you. Take away her lifelines."

"I can't do that."

"You do it now or she will when they turn eighteen."

I shook my head. "No. That's... I... Damn it. Shit. Mother-fucker." I kicked the dirt. "There has to be another way."

Persephone didn't speak.

"How many children are there? How do I find them?"

"There are thirteen."

I choked. "Thirteen? Thirteen children?"

"Soon to be fourteen."

"She's pregnant?"

She raised her brows. "This one will not be born of magic."

"My father…"

"Is not the father. It is the healer's baby."

"Healer?"

"From the night you shot her with an arrow."

"I hate I missed."

"You would not have been able to kill her without killing yourself."

"What?"

"You are tied to one another. You weren't eighteen yet."

"Wait, so you're telling me if I were to try to kill her… that her children would also die?"

"Yes. Very morbid, I know." She sat on a log. "She may be evil, but she is clever. She played on people's sympathy for children to protect herself." She held up her finger. "You would have to successfully kill her thirteen times. One time for each child."

"So you're telling me that no matter what I do, thirteen children are going to die?"

"Yes."

"Fucking hell. You're a good witch. Can you not use your power to fix this? To reverse the curse?"

Her lips pinched into a hard line. "I'm not a good witch, simply a white witch. I wish I could reverse the curse my child. Right now, you're the only one with the power. Which is why she will come after you."

"I don't have any power."

She smiled at me knowingly, but I didn't know what that meant.

"Child, you have more power than she does. I can sense it in you. You just don't know how to use it."

"Or access it." I laughed, finding this entire conversation amusing. "Wouldn't I know if I was a witch?"

"You are part of Merla. You have power. Have you never noticed how nature responds to you? Hear the songs on the wind, see how the animals are naturally drawn to you? Have things ever just happened and you couldn't explain why?"

As she was speaking, memories would pop up in my head of instances in my childhood when water troths would explode when I was angry, how I could tame a wild horse with a touch, how I listened to the wind to find the purple mangor. "I've never thought about it before."

"You have power without even trying, Snow. You are powerful beyond measure. I imagine the Queen can sense it as well, which is probably why you scare her."

"Can you teach me how to use it?"

She shook her head slowly. "I cannot."

"You can't or won't?" I barked.

"I can't."

"I don't understand."

She rested her hand on my shoulder. "That is a story for another day." She looked up at the darkening sky. "It's time for you to go."

She was speaking the words and was fading back into the tree.

I stood there, unable to move.

I don't know what I expected, but I was not prepared for what I heard.

I felt a hand snake around my waist and found Gage standing beside me.

"I think we need to talk."

CHAPTER FIFTEEN

MERLA – SECRETS AND BETRAYAL

"MY QUEEN." THE FRUMPY woman in brown cloth poked her head in the dining hall. "You have a guest."

I rolled my eyes at the interruption and let my fork drop to my bowl with a loud clatter to show my annoyance.

"I'm sorry my Queen. I can tell them you're busy."

"Yes." Why was she such an idiot? She should have thought about that before she came to interrupt me. I looked down at the guroo on my plate, its tentacles still moving. The slimy delicacy was good for revitalizing youth, which was greatly needed. Since Snow's escape, I've been feeling more tired and found two wrinkles on my forehead.

Wrinkles!

"Should I–"

I cut my eyes at her and she stopped talking. As she slowly closed the door, I heard her say a name.

I yelled out a garble of sounds, not quite sure what her name was.

She opened the door again. "I'm sorry, my Queen. Did you say something?"

"Yes. Did you say the huntsman is here?"

"Yes, my Queen. I'm asking him to leave now."

"Nonsense. Bring him in right away."

Confused by my change, she stumbled over herself, then mumbled something to the huntsman.

A moment later he walked into the room carrying with him the silver box.

My eyes grew wide and I can barely contain my excitement. "You found her!"

He nodded, but didn't speak.

I nearly tripped over myself racing to him and snatched the box out of his hands and took it back to the table to slowly opened it and then snapped the lid shut with excitement. I gently opened it again, this time letting the lid fully rock back, observing with the greatest delight a set of two beautifully preserved organs- a heart and a liver.

"Well done huntsman. I have heard great things about you and your family. You come from a long lineage of royal servants, unlike your fellow huntsman." I felt a flash of fire sweep across my eyes at the memory of all the other huntsmen I had killed for their betrayal. "But that was in the past and they have all paid the price."

He nodded, but didn't speak and showed no sign of sympathy.

Did he not understand? All my children, those huntsmen had killed over the years. A shiver went up my spine at the horrible thought. It wasn't their deaths that bothered me, so much as the years of wasted youth I could have extracted from them.

It's ok though.

They took my youth, so I took their children.

One by one, I killed them and sent the parents' pieces of their children in a silver box... every year on the anniversary of their death.

A warning to all others who would try to cross me.

For good measure, though, I began surrogating my children out. Snow was the first.

Surely the others wouldn't be as difficult as she had been.

She was always a horrible child, so many mistakes made with the first, I suppose.

I would have to go check on the others. The second one should be getting close to age.

"Chef!" I yelled.

He came scurrying out of the kitchen a second later.

I handed him the silver box. "Prepare these for me. I will have them for dinner tonight."

"Right away my Queen." He looked in the box, then his eyes shot back up to me, but he didn't speak. "Will the King be dining with you?" He asked with a slight stutter.

"Not tonight. He is still resting. He's taking his daughter's betrayal so hard."

"Of course," he nodded, and exited as quickly as he came.

I looked at the huntsman. "Good work indeed. The woman who brought you in will get the rest of your money."

"I will leave you to your dinner, then." He bowed and started backing away.

"Nonsense. You will stay and celebrate."

His lips pinched. "Very well Queen." I ignored the grimace hiding behind his eyes. He should be lucky to have dinner with someone as beautiful as I am.

He took a seat at the table, several chairs down from me.

"Tell me huntsman. What do you like to do?"

"I like to hunt, Queen."

"You know." My finger tapped on my chin. "I have ignored the fact you never call me 'My' Queen. Am I not your Queen?"

"You are... my Queen."

I nodded my head up and down.

"Very well."

The chef came out a moment later with a platter adorned in a variety of garden vegetables and in the center were two perfectly cooked pieces of meat, waiting for me to sink my teeth into. The excitement building within me was nearly untamable. I felt like I was going to explode.

I picked up my fork and knife and cut into the heart and it sliced through like melted butter. I cut a small piece off and held it to my lips.

"Good bye Snow." I placed it on my tongue and slowly began to chew.

I watched the Huntsman look at me, with no expression on his face. "Care for a piece?"

He shook his head. "No thank you, my Queen."

"Very well." I batted my hand in the air. "Chef. Get him whatever he would like. We are celebrating tonight."

The huntsman waved his hand. "I will take what you have here."

"That is just potatoes and vegetables."

"I have eaten just a bit ago."

I sighed in minor irritation. It would be hard to ruin my mood tonight. "Fine." I backhanded the air.

I cleaned the tray and felt quite full. I touched my skin and felt it was tighter than before. "Amazing."

"Thank you my Queen." The chef said over my shoulder.

I rolled my eyes and was in too good of a mood to tell him I was talking about my skin rather than his cooking. I felt it was lacking, tasty, a bit more gamey than the other hearts I've had in the past. I imagine it was his inexperience.

"Well, I must be going now, my Queen."

"So soon?" I stood up and swayed over to him.

"Yes. I must get home to feed my dog."

I laughed. "Such responsibility. Why feed them when you can eat them?"

He looked at me questioningly.

I was in such a good mood I let him in on a secret since it no longer mattered. "Snow White was my daughter."

"Impossible." His brow furrowed as he studied my face.

"The former Queen was my surrogate. After the huntsmen had killed my children, I needed to find a way to protect them." And me...

His eyes held a look I couldn't understand, like pieces of a puzzle were falling into place. "There are others?"

I gazed at him, letting my eyes settle on his soft features. "Yes... so I will have some other jobs for you in the near future."

He nodded, "Very well." He stood up from the table. "I really must go now." He wiped his hands on his pants. "Dinner was excellent. Thank you."

"Very well. I'm going to bathe and relax. It's been a very taxing day."

The frumpy woman was back with his remaining pay as we were walking out of the dining room.

"Until I need your services next time, Huntsman. Expect a call from me..." I didn't know when my next child turned eighteen. I would have to find out. "Sometime soon maybe."

"I look forward to it, my Queen." He disappeared down the hall and was gone.

I waited at the windows overlooking the field and watched the beast of a man walk through the scorched grass, his knife popping up and down on his hip while he walked. I couldn't help but fantasize how big his cock would be and how fantastic he would be in bed.

Perhaps I would call him back for other services earlier than expected.

I walked down the hall and looked around to make sure it was empty before pulling on a candle stick mounted on the wall. I heard the steady clicks and sounds of locks unlatching. A moment later, the large portrait of the late Queen had unhooked from the wall.

I had allowed it to stay up to appear more amenable to the King.

I closed the door behind me and walked down the dimly lit staircase as it descended further under the castle. The cool, wet air whipped up around me.

It had been so long since the King had used the dungeons. But not me.

I heard the clattering of chains off in the distance and knew the little mice were skittering to their corners, out of sight, but I wasn't interested in them.

Not tonight, anyway.

No, these men and women would serve me on a later day when I could figure out their purpose. If not, I would dispose of them.

I walked to the end of the hall, past all their cells, as the clicking of my heels echoed throughout. I placed my hand on the wall, temporarily removing the curse and allowing the stones to separate, revealing a hidden chamber.

The room was dark, except for a single light that shone down on a thin bed in the middle of the room. I approached, expecting to see a decaying corpse of a woman- a shell of what she used to be.

"Hel-" I stopped mid-sentence, closing the short gap between us.

She was still laying there, peacefully sleeping as she had done for the last several years, but her skin. Her skin looked as youthful as it did yesterday!

This should not be the case.

She should be a rapidly decaying corpse. Wrinkly. Gray skin.

But no!

She looked perfect.

I turned on my heel and stomped back the way I'd just come, filled with a level of rage I was having problems suppressing. I burst through the paneling in the hall and closed the portrait, heading straight for my bedroom.

I was standing in front of my magic mirror a few minutes later.

"Mirror, mirror on the wall. Show me the location of Snow White!"

The mirror swirled into its typical gray silk ribbon and then revealed. "She is on the seventh mountain."

"No!"

"My Queen. I cannot tell a lie. You made it so."

A knot lodged in my throat. "Snow White is dead. I just ate her heart and liver." She touched her face. "I feel younger right now than I felt yesterday."

"My Queen, you look as youthful as you did yesterday, but Snow White is not dead. She is living on the seventh mountain in a house with seven miners."

"Yes! Yes! I heard." I snapped, pacing around my room. I ran to my window to look for the huntsman, but he was gone.

"If you need something done right, then don't send a man to do it!"

I will go handle her myself and deal with the huntsman later.

CHAPTER SIXTEEN

GAGE - BATTLE WITHIN

"Do you know how to get us out of here?" I asked Scarlet-Snow, unwinding my arm from around her waist.

I still couldn't believe she was Snow White. I'd heard rumors she had died years ago, but there was never an official ceremony.

"No." She looked up at me, her eyes a mixture of apprehension and shock.

A red mangor walking up to us caught our attention.

"Grab onto one another." The bird said.

Snow looked from the bird to me, perplexed.

"Hustle now. I don't have all day."

Snow walked towards me, pressing her chest to mine as she wrapped her arms around my waist. She paused, looking up at me, almost questioning if it was ok, so I returned the gesture holding her in my arms. I felt her body release as she pressed her cheek to my chest.

This was not the same girl as earlier. This one was troubled, fragile, and something inside of me ached for her. It was a new sensation, one I hadn't let myself feel before... ever. I wanted to hold her and keep her safe. Let her know I was here and that I would protect her, but the words caught in my throat.

The bird walked over and placed its beak on our entwined arms, and with a pop, it transported us to another place.

Baffled, we unwound our arms and looked around. We were in the middle of a small town, standing just outside of a tavern.

"Do you know where we are?" She asked, watching a small elf with large ears push a wheelbarrow of hay by.

"I don't." I watched the townspeople hustle around as if we hadn't just popped in from thin air.

I looked up at the old wooden inn, which had a small sign tacked above the door that read Mernie's Tavern. With the daylight quickly turning to night, we needed to find somewhere to sleep.

Inside were a few wooden tables with a bar on the far left side of the room and to the right, sitting behind the desk, was an older woman wearing a gray shirt, donning a blue cap.

"Welcome to Mernie's Tavern. What can I do for you both?" She nearly cheered.

"We need two rooms, please." I said, stepping to the counter.

She pulled her face. "Best I can do is one. We have a lot of people in town searching for that missing girl."

I rolled my eyes, not caring anything about who was missing, but felt Snow tense beside me. "I guess we'll take it then." I looked at Snow and saw her watching everyone move around like it was her first time seeing this many people, and then I realized it probably was the first time.

The clerk handed me a key with a large tag reading 269 in chipped gold paint. I nodded as she pointed to the set of stairs in the middle of the room. It was kind of hard to miss the giant staircase, but whatever.

We walked into the room and found one bed with a small bathroom to its left and a little window on the opposite wall.

Snow ran over to the window and looked down. "I wonder who's missing."

"I don't care." I said simply.

"Why are you in a bad mood again?" She looked at me over her shoulder before walking to the bed and bouncing up and down on it.

"I'm not."

"You are. I thought we had moved past this."

"Because of what happened in the water?"

She looked at me but didn't speak.

Why didn't she understand? She keeps looking at me as if I am a good man and I'm not.

"We need to talk."

She sighed.

"Why didn't you tell me the truth?"

"What truth is that?"

I noticed her demeanor was fluctuating between defiant and distraught.

"You are Snow. Snow White. Princess Snow fucking White."

She stood up and walked to the window again.

"Yes. I am."

"Fucking hell." I ran my hands through my hair. "What... why..." I didn't know what I wanted to ask.

"I didn't say anything because I thought if you all knew, you wouldn't let me stay with you."

"Hell no, we wouldn't have. We don't need that kind of attention!"

"I..." I saw her eyes flash and before I could do or say anything, she was crying.

Shit.

"I'm sorry. I... I... She wanted to kill me."

"The Queen?"

"She..."

She continued sobbing into her hands. I had to fight the urge to console her because I needed to draw that line between us. I couldn't get attached because it wouldn't work out for us, especially now that I knew the truth, and I couldn't hurt her.

"What?"

She took a deep breath and looked up at me. "I don't know what to do. The witch... she told me..."

She started crying again. "I'm sorry... I don't usually cry. I'm stronger than this... it's just..."

"What is worse than her wanting to kill you?"

She shook her head.

"Can you tell me?"

"If I say it... then..."

"It's already true, but I can't fix it if I don't know." I bit my tongue the second the words were out of my mouth.

No!

Distance!

Keep my distance.

"You can't fix this."

"I don't understand."

"Merla... she's my mother."

I was going to speak, but it was like a word vomit. She just continued to talk.

"She basically implanted me in the Queen, who I thought was my mother, through dark magic. She visited my mother, well, the Queen, as a blackbird and cursed her. She bound the Queen's life to mine, so when I was born, I killed her to live. I have no father because I was born of magic. I'm a witch with strong powers that I don't know how to use. Merla wants me dead because she harvested me for my youth until I turned eighteen, which is why she wanted to kill me because now every day I live it is causing her to age. What else?"

She took a deep breath and continued.

"She has thirteen others like me scattered around. Apparently, I was the first. It's because the huntsmen were hunting her children down and killing them when they learned what she was doing. So she had the idea to conceal her children in other women, so the huntsmen wouldn't know."

It felt like a rock had settled in my stomach.

"What else is there? I feel like I'm missing something."

She puckered out her lips, her tone more direct and angry than the fragile girl she was a minute ago.

"Oh right. I can't kill her, because that would kill the children she has linked herself too. Oh! And she's pregnant right now with another one. If I wanted to make her weak enough to kill, I'd have to kill the children. So basically, no matter how you look at it, the children have to die, which is so fucking unfair."

"So you would die?"

She laughed. "No. I'm no longer a child. Once I turned eighteen, she could no longer harvest me. Harvest me!"

She stood and started pacing around.

"As if I am some fucking grain in the field. I always wondered how she never aged and always looked so young."

I nodded. "She's over three hundred years old."

"What? How?"

I shook my head.

"I don't know what to do, Gage." She walked over to me and stood in front of me.

I so badly wanted to reach out and hold her, but now more than ever, I couldn't. It was like no matter how hard I tried to get away from my past, it kept finding me.

She sighed and walked to the bathroom. "I'm taking a shower."

I heard the water click on and walked over to the window. I smashed my hand against the sill in frustration and felt the beast within wanting to come out.

No. It had to stay away.

I was not the beast.

It did not control me.

I found some blankets in the drawer and laid them out on the floor and grabbed a pillow off the bed.

Snow was walking out a little while later, wrapped in one towel, while using another to dry her hair.

"Do you know if they have any spare clothes downstairs?"

"I'll go check." I tried not to stumble over my words as my cock grew hard, seeing her barely wrapped in only a towel. I needed to get hold of myself.

She was off limits before and she sure as shit is now.

I shut the door, making sure it latched. I didn't need someone getting nosy and helping themselves to my- to Snow.

I saw several villagers and huntsmen downstairs at the bar drinking and chatting about going after some beast in the woods. Perhaps I could join them to help get my mind off all the things I wanted to do to Snow in the room upstairs.

Fuck!

I shook my head and walked over to the woman behind the desk.

"Do you have any spare clothes?"

She looked me up and down. "You, darling, are a little bigger than most of my customers."

"Not for me. For the girl I was with."

"Beautiful girl. She looks familiar. What's her name?"

My gaze narrowed. "Scarlet."

She thought about it for a moment. "Name doesn't ring a bell."

"She must have one of those faces. She gets that a lot."

The woman nodded, then pointed me to a box of clothes. I filtered through them, looking for anything that looked like it would fit her, but not be too revealing. Apparently, a lot of women who forgot their clothes here were women that would fit in well at Ruby's tavern.

I grabbed the best thing I could find and nodded at the clerk and walked back upstairs.

Snow was standing in the bathroom, completely nude, brushing her hair when I walked in.

"Seriously?" I barked.

"What? The towel kept dropping."

I handed her the clothes, turning my head away.

"We're going to pretend that you haven't seen my body and I haven't seen yours? That's what we're doing?"

I jiggled the clothes in my hand without speaking.

"Ok. Noted."

She snatched the clothes out of my hand and I went to sit back on the bed, waiting for her to get out of the bathroom. I needed to go take a cold shower and think about the elf pushing hay to get my hard on to go away.

She was out a few minutes later wearing a long brown skirt and an oversized blue shirt with a look of disgust on her face. "This was all they had?"

I nodded without speaking.

She sighed and flopped onto the bed.

"I'm going to jump in the shower." Did I feel guilty for making her look like a lumpy pillowcase? No. No, I did not feel guilty at all.

"I'm going to find us some food. I'm starving." She said, walking out of the door.

I let the water hit me in the face and wash away all my dirty thoughts. The things I did with her in the water.

I felt my dick twinge with excitement.

No! No excitement.

She is a princess and I...

I'm going to hell. I mean, I already knew I was before, but I know without a doubt I am now.

I turned the water on cold and flinched as it stung my skin.

I climbed out of the shower some time later.

There was a knock on the door, causing me to throw the towel around me. "What?" I barked.

The door opened and Snow was standing there in a tight white top and the same brown skirt.

"What are you wearing?"

"The other top was too big."

"And this is too small!" Her tits were nearly spilling over the top.

"It's fine.

"It's not. You look ridiculous."

"Well, good thing I don't give a damn what you think!"

She threw the clothes she had in her hand at my face and walked away.

Damn it!

I looked down at my dick and saw it standing at attention, saluting the thing it would never have again.

Damn it!

I grabbed the clothes off the ground and tugged them on. The pants were loose with a tie top, which helped, but the shirt was a little tight, hugging my arms and upper chest. I felt like one wrong move and I would rip the seam.

I walked into the bedroom and Snow did a double take. "Fuck."

"Language."

She gulped down her food and continued to stare at me, her cheeks holding the slightest hint of pink.

I heard her mumble something as she took another bite before handing me my plate. "I got it from downstairs." She stuttered, looking away quickly.

"Thanks." I studied the chicken and vegetables- anything to help take my mind off her. Even sitting close to her was causing my body to react- to tingle.

We ate the rest of our meal in silence, neither one of us looking up.

When she was done, she walked over to me and held her hand out to take my empty plate. I handed it to her and our fingers brushed one another, causing my cock to twitch like it had touched a live wire.

Our eyes locked and my body felt like it was on fire as I held her finger gently under the plate with the tip of my pinky... yearning for that connection, dreading when she took a step away, but she didn't.

She didn't move.

She stood there, frozen like a deer.

Fuck!

She was off limits! She was off limits!

I removed my finger, severing our connection. "Well, I'm going to bed."

She nodded. "Yep. Sounds good. You too... I mean me too... me too."

She sat the plates on the floor in the hall and then shut the door and looked at me. "You don't have to sleep down there, you know?"

"Yes, I do."

"The bed is big enough for the both of us."

"No." It was the only word I could get out. Simple and effective.

"Why are you acting like this?"

"Like what?"

"This."

Because I want to take you in that bed and fuck you until the morning sun comes up. Until you can't walk anymore. Until your throat is hoarse from yelling my name out. "I don't know what you're talking about."

"I've seen the real you. The one you are when your guard isn't up."

"You haven't seen the real me." I said flatly, and it was true. She hadn't and she never could. The real me was a dark and troubled man who would get pleasure out of hurting her.

No, the real me needed to stay locked away and hidden from her, but I could feel him there, wanting to get out.

"Right. Because you're a bad guy. What if I want a bad guy?"

"No."

"So you don't care about me... is that it?"

"No."

"No? No reason... just no?"

I could tell she was getting flustered, but I didn't say anything, and she sighed in disbelief.

She glared her eyes at me, then took off her shirt and slid out of her skirt so she was standing naked again.

"What the hell are you doing?" I barked.

"I'm going downstairs to get some dessert." She said, walking to the door.

She was trying to get a reaction out of me, so I cocked my head to the side and watched her, calling her bluff.

She paused with her hand on the handle and when I didn't speak, she opened the door and I felt my pulse quicken.

"Be back in a little." She walked down the hall, letting the door close behind her.

Shit! I raced to the door and threw it open. I ran down the hall and threw her over my shoulder and walked back to the bedroom and threw her on the bed. Her perfect body was sprawled out, begging for me to touch her.

"So you do care?" She smirked.

"No."

She rolled to get off the bed.

"Damn it Snow! Just calm the fuck down!"

"Why won't you admit you like me?"

"Because I don't." I snapped back.

"Are you sure?" Her gazed settled around my waist.

She sat up on the edge of the bed and I should have moved, but I didn't. I liked to tempt fate even though nearly every damn part of me knew I should move- knew I should stop her, but I didn't.

"I've had a really shitty day and I want to forget it."Her hands fumbled with the tie around my waist.

She looked up at me through her lashes and I just shook my head.

"Will you help me forget?" She asked with those beautiful fuck me eyes.

"Why don't you listen to me?" I could feel my body shaking with anticipation.

"Why don't you listen to me?" She retorted. "I'm not looking for a relationship. I've been locked in a room the size of that bathroom for most of my life. I was never allowed to talk to anyone and I'm being hunted by the dark Queen. My time here has been shitty at best and who knows how much time I have left? I just want to live and experience everything." She dropped the hem of my pants, letting them fall to the ground.

"Snow." My voice faltered.

CHAPTER SEVENTEEN

SNOW - A WEREWOLF IN THE WOODS

STANDING BEFORE ME WAS a God of a man, so beautiful, yet so broken. I could almost see the two versions of Gage battling for control. The one he wanted everyone to see and the one he wanted to keep hidden. The protector versus the bringer of destruction, but whose destruction? I didn't want to think about that too much because I knew the answer deep down inside.

It would be my destruction.

There was nothing Gage could do to hurt me. I knew my days were numbered. I'd been given a death sentence from the second I was born- I just didn't know it until now. It wasn't so much a question of if the dark Queen would come for me, but when.

So I would take as much as I could until that day came.

My eyes met Gage's and I felt the mood in the room shifting. Lifting. Buzzing.

His eyes searched between mine, stopped briefly on my lips before trailing down to my breasts rising and falling with the pants of my breath. I felt a tingle between my legs and had to fight the urge to cross them. I didn't want to cross them. I didn't want to hide that part of me. I wanted him to take me, to know I yearned for his touch and the feel of his cock.

He closed the distance between us and I could almost sense he was still fighting with himself, but losing. I wanted nothing more than for him to press me down onto this bed and do what he wouldn't do at the waterfall.

I slowly grabbed his large cock in my hand, taking time to wrap each finger around his girth giving him plenty of opportunity to stop me, but he didn't. I ran my thumb over the tip before fully enclosing my hand and running it down his shaft and heard a low groan escape from deep inside him.

"Snow..." He hissed.

I did it again and felt him get harder in my hand and then again, relishing in the excitement that was building within me. I leaned in closer to it, my lips less than an inch away. I wanted to taste it. I wanted it to fill my mouth.

I looked up at him between my lashes and saw his eyes on me, waiting. So I closed the gap and pressed my tongue on the tip, before taking him fully in my mouth. I sucked him in until I felt him hit the back of my throat as his eyes rolled into the back of his head.

I slowly pulled him out and did it again, each time getting faster and faster as the animal inside of me was eager to take more. I grabbed around the base and began to pump my hand as I pulled him out and then plunged him into my mouth again. I wanted him to fuck my face, to feel this insatiable hunger that I felt. It was like I couldn't get enough of him, I wanted more and more.

His hands slipped into grip my hair which sent a shiver down my spine and caused me to puddle on the bed. Fuck this was hot! His body began to move, pressing into me, taking control.

"Fuck Snow. You need to stop." His words didn't match his actions. He continued to press on, his hips rocking into me.

I felt tears stinging my eyes, but it wasn't enough. I needed more of him and took it eagerly. I bobbed on it, hungry for more as he growled with pleasure.

"Snow you're going to make me come." He panted out.

I stopped and looked up at him. "Then come." I put my mouth back on him and sucked him in deep. I bobbed on him, high on the fact I knew he wanted this as much as I did. The power I had right now was amazing.

His grip tightened as he pounded into me.

"Shit." I heard him say just before a warm saltiness shot into my mouth and down my throat.

I continued sucking and swallowing over and over again.

"Stop." He moaned, but I didn't listen to him until he pulled himself out of my mouth, his eyes wild. "Well I'm already fucked." He sighed, as if he was talking to someone else.

"What?"

He scooped me up with one arm and tossed me back onto the bed. He threw his shirt off and crawled on top of me, his eyes penetrating into mine. I felt the tip of his cock pushing right at the outside of my entrance and I shifted to press into him harder.

He looked at me with a smirk spread across his face. "No."

I don't know why I found that word so hot.

He leaned down and kissed me on my jawline line, leaving soft trails down my throat to my chest. He cupped one breast while taking the other in his mouth and I felt my stomach clench.

His warm tongue swirled around my nipple and then he sucked and bit just hard enough to send a feeling between my legs, causing me to gasp.

"This is going to be so much fun." His lips trailed the dip between my breasts as he moved to the other one, taking it in his mouth.

As he continued to suck, his hand slid down my stomach and pressed against my opening and I gasped again, causing him to smile.

"So wet." I felt his smile on my skin. He slid a finger in and my back arched off the bed. My body felt electrified.

"Fuck me Gage."

"Settle down." He said taking my breast in his mouth, the warm wetness over my nipple caused my stomach to flutter.

He moved up, taking my lips. I melted into his touch as his tongue made his way in. I wrapped my arms around his neck, moving my hips in rhythm with his finger pulsing.

"Give me more." I pleaded.

He broke our kiss and started going back down again. He went past my breasts, kissing down my stomach and landed just above my sweet spot.

"Don't scream." He warned, blowing his warm breath between my legs.

I nodded, so excited with anticipation I couldn't say anything.

He slowly pulled his finger out and sucked my juices off them. Holy fuck that was erotic as hell! He pushed my legs wider, fully exposing me to him before he slowly pressed his mouth to my opening. He blew another warm breath before running his tongue up my slick folds from the bottom to top.

"So fucking sweet."

"Goddess help me." I pleaded, arching my back giving him more access. He sucked on my clit before lapping up my seeping juices.

"There's no helping you now. You're mine." He said before diving in, pressing his tongue into me.

My desire surged, nearly spilling over. My fingers raked through his hair grabbing on for dear life as my body moved on its own, rocking my hips up into his mouth. He continued to eat hungrily, pressing and sucking and swirling. I felt his tongue flicker about as a tingle moved through my body.

He leaned back a little and then readjusted, centering his face and pressing in again.

I let out an uncontrollable moan, causing him to stop for a second. I looked down at him and his face perched right between my legs.

"Don't scream."

"No promises."

I felt him smile as he pressed his tongue in again, his arms hooking around my legs, holding me to him. I bucked my hips up like a wild bronco, needing to feel more of him in me. He released an arm and pressed two of his fingers in as his mouth continued to suck and lick. I moved faster and faster, fucking anything that was in the way, my body taking control.

I bucked one last time and cried out in ecstasy, shattering into a thousand pieces. I felt wave after wave crash around me. He didn't stop, pushing my orgasm to the very edge. I came long and hard as my entire body began to shake with delight, so charged that I feared if I touched anything, it would surely shock me.

"Stop. Stop." I pleaded, the pleasure almost too much to handle.

He looked up at me from between my legs, his eyes hungry.

He grabbed my hips and slid me down in one swift motion, pressing his lips to mine. I could taste my sweetness on them and feel his erect cock pressed at my base.

He stopped kissing me and pulled up to look at me, "Are you sure you want to do this?"

"Fuck me now." I panted.

"It's going to hurt."

"I don't care. Fill me with your cock." I felt like it was teasing me, gently pressing against my opening, like someone waiting to come in the door after being invited.

I raised my swollen lips up to meet his, wrapping my arms around his neck and pulling him into me.

"Fuck me Gage." I said on his lips.

"Snow."

"Fuck me." I reached down and grabbed his cock centering it on me, desperate to have it inside of me.

His kiss was deep and possessive as he drove into me in one swift motion. I felt the sting from within, but each time he pressed into me, it turned from pain to pleasure as he filled every inch of me.

"Oh, my." I said, feeling him inside me as my body stretched around him. "Oh, my..." My voice lowered in ecstasy.

I pressed my feet into the bed, bucking my body up to meet his, driving him deeper into me. "Shit, Snow."

I needed more of him.

I wrapped my legs around his waist as he continued to pound into me, ignoring the headboard hammering into the wall in the perfect rhythm of his thrusts. I didn't care if anyone else could hear it. All I cared about was him and me right now. In this moment.

I squeezed my legs tighter around him.

He stopped and my legs fell just as he flipped me over onto my stomach. He centered himself on me again and pressed into me, filling me even more than before.

"Oh..." I felt the wave building inside again. "Oh..." It was the only word I could get out.

He grabbed me by the hips and slammed into me over and over again.

"Gage." I cried out.

"Not yet."

I bit down, but felt the wave building.

"Not yet."

He pulled out and I felt empty.

"Turn around." He commanded.

I saw him lying on his back.

"Sit on my cock."

I crawled over to him, straddling him and centering myself on him. I slowly sank down and felt this feeling pulse through me as I stretched further around him. His eyes rolled into the back of his head before he opened them again and watched me. I slowly popped off and then sank down slowly again, wanting to feel every second of this in case it never happened again.

I pressed my palms onto his rippled chest as I slowly moved up and down on his shaft. His hands moved to my breast holding them, playing with him.

"Fuck me Snow." He commanded and it was like something lit a fire inside of me.

I began moving faster as his cock drove up into me, my breast bouncing freely in his hands. He grabbed the sides of my hips and lifted me before crashing me back down. A delicious pain seared through me, scorching a path deep to my core. He did it again and again filling me deeper and deeper. My head dropped back as I bounced uncontrollably on top of him. "Gage." I whimpered out, causing him to thrust his hips up each time I came back down on him. "Fuck."

I began working my clit, my body once again taking control of itself, hungry for all Gage had to offer. I felt the wave building again as I worked it faster and faster.

Gage sat up, pressing both his hands to my back as if he wanted to press himself all the way into me. I wrapped my arms around his neck, crashing my lips to his, grinding and moving.

He was hungry and I was here to feed him what he needed. What he'd been fighting.

I continued to rock back and forth until I got to the peak again.

"Come with me." He demanded and I fell apart as wave after intense wave crashed. My body was shaking in ecstasy as he continued to pump through his release before stilling. I stayed on him feeling our combined release spill around his base. Our chests were heaving in unison trying to catch our breaths.

He brushed the hair out of my face and just looked at me for a moment before kissing me on the nose.

I rocked my hips closer to him, wanting to stay like this for just a minute longer, breathing in his scent and our sex. I ran my fingers along the back of his neck. "Thank you." I climbed off him and walked into the bathroom to clean up.

When I walked back in the room, he was pulling his pants on.

"Will you stay in bed with me?"

"Snow." His voice lowered an octave.

"I know. I'm not asking you to be my boyfriend. Just lay with me. It doesn't make sense for you to sleep on the floor after all of that." I shrugged.

He hesitated a minute before climbing into bed and opening his arm. I climbed in beside him and tucking my head into his neck. I would take whatever moment I could get with him. My body was still buzzing with pleasure as I laid there, swirling my finger around on his chest.

The next morning I reached across the bed to feel for Gage, but he wasn't there. I opened my eyes and looked around the room to find it was also empty. I had no pre-conceived ideas of what I expected, but I didn't expect him to leave.

I sat up in bed, rubbing my face, when I heard someone at the door.

I wrapped the sheet around me and waited.

Gage walked in with two plates of breakfast and coffee.

"You're up." He said, looking at me.

"I am." I smiled immediately. He had brought me breakfast. He said he was a dangerous man, and while he could be a dick sometimes, I felt that was more of a show he put on rather than who he really was. I needed to figure out why he thought of himself the way he did, because maybe if he could see he wasn't a horrible person, he would let me in.

"I didn't know what you would like, so I got you a little of everything."

"It's perfect. Thank you." I reached for the food, causing the sheet to fall.

He looked from my chest to my eyes and stumbled over his words before saying gruffly, "We need to head out soon. We're about a full day from home, somewhere between mountain two and three."

I ignored the growing bulge in his pants. "Oh. We're close to the castle."

"Yea. A little too close for me."

I nodded, unable to speak since I had stuffed a muffin in my mouth.

"I think we should stay off the main roads as much as possible until we get closer to home. The woods will provide more protection from prying eyes."

"Ok, makes sense."

We finished eating breakfast, and I put on my clothes from the previous day. I didn't feel like the shirt and skirt would do well in the woods.

Gage paid our bill at the front desk and we set out, walking to the end of the road where it met the woods.

When we were far enough in the cover of the woods, I turned to Gage. "Why do you think you're a dangerous man?"

He cut his eyes at me.

"What? I'm just trying to understand you better."

"You don't need to understand me." He was back to his usual gruff self, the Gage from last night was gone.

"I need to understand everyone."

"Not me."

"I will, eventually."

He batted a branch out of the way with such force it snapped and dangled on the tree.

"How long have you been with Barrett?"

"Why do you want to know?"

"Just trying to make conversation so the day goes by a little quicker."

He was quiet for a moment, then answered, "Just over ten years."

"That's a long time."

"Not long enough."

"Why?"

He sighed with frustration. "Because, it's not."

"What would you like to talk about?"

"Nothing. I want silence. I need to be able to listen."

"What are you listening for? I don't really think the dark Queen will be roaming through the woods."

"It's not the Queen I'm concerned about."

"Then wh-"

Gage clasped his hand over my mouth and froze. His nose was in the air and he was looking around intently, like he smelled something. I turned my head to look at him and pulled his hand away. My pulse was pounding through my ears with a steady thump, thump, thump.

I wanted to ask him what he was looking for, but he was still searching the woods.

He grabbed my arm. "Let's go." He said, nearly jerking me to the left.

I stumbled on a log and tripped, but he yanked me back up and glared at me.

I whispered, "Well, if you hadn't yanked me."

We were walking slowly, although I got the feeling Gage was hunting. His knees stayed bent, his head was on a swivel and his breathing was steady, in and out, in and out. He let go of my arm briefly to hold his fist up, indicating we were stopping.

He sensed something, but still hadn't told me what it was. I looked around but couldn't see or hear anything.

We took another step and then another. He found a large tree that had fallen and tucked me under it. Grabbing me by the shoulders, he stared into my eyes. "Stay here and do not make a sound."

I nodded as I pulled an arrow out of my quiver and laced it in my bow, laying it on my lap.

What was going on? What did he sense that I couldn't?

He leapt over the log in one swift motion, an easy six foot vertical, and walked in the direction behind me. He told me to stay put, so I fought the urge to get out and look, which in itself was irritating. I was not some damsel in distress he had to baby.

I was a capable woman who could hunt.

I started to move when I heard a twig breaking on the ground, followed by a slight ruffle of leaves. I could tell by the sound it was not Gage, but someone else... something else... and it was getting closer.

Another twig breaking. Another leaf crunching.

I grabbed the bow off my lap, slowly pulling the arrow back. If I had to jump out and shoot, I needed to be ready.

I heard another set of twigs breaking, but these were a little further in the distance.

Two?

While I felt capable, I still wish Gage was with me. Two on one would definitely be harder.

I heard another twig breaking, and this one was right over me. I held my breath, not wanting to make a sound.

"Hey!" I heard Gage yell off in the distance.

The leaves shuffled above me.

"Shit." Gage said, his voice faltering, but there was something else in it. Something I couldn't place. Recognition?

I heard a low growl from above me.

It was an animal of some sort, large, by the sound of it.

I heard it walking away from me, towards Gage's voice, the growl growing louder.

"What do you want with her?"

Was he talking to the animal? About me?

"You can't have her." Gage snarled, which set the animal off.

I heard its pace picking up, like it was charging towards Gage.

I poked my head up, ready to shoot my arrow if given the chance. Gage had to be protected.

I popped my head above the log and was not prepared for what I saw.

A giant wolf was running full sprint at Gage with his teeth pulled back over its white hot gums and standing arms open, ready to fight, was Gage.

I panicked. He couldn't take on a wolf that large by himself. Its stomach was nearly four feet off the ground. Panic tore through me. Was this the beast in the woods the people in the town were talking about?

I wanted to yell at Gage, but all that would do was distract him.

I watched the wolf close in, faster and faster.

It leapt in the air at the last possible second, lunging after Gage, who ducked and rolled under it. "I'm not going to fight you."

Why was he talking to the wolf?

The wolf skidded to a stop, facing me with Gage in the middle of us.

The wolf looked from Gage to me.

Gage looked over his shoulder.

"Damn it Snow."

The wolf started charging, but not at Gage. At me.

I went to raise my bow, but my fingers slipped on the arrow, causing it to tumble on the ground. I quickly bent over to pick it up as fast as I could, but I was so nervous I couldn't concentrate. When I peeked up, I saw it was closing in fast, with Gage running behind it.

"Snow. Get down!"

I grabbed my bow and was standing back up just as the wolf was several feet out, and that's when I heard it. The shredding of clothes, followed by one of the loudest and most ferocious growls I'd ever heard.

Skidding to a stop was a large black wolf.

Gage was a werewolf.

CHAPTER EIGHTEEN

GAGE - REHASHING THE PAST

SHIT!

I looked over my shoulder and saw Snow standing there, and he saw her too.

If you won't fight me on your honor, maybe you'll fight me to protect her.

Unlikely.

Let's test out the theory, shall we?

Garrison! I warned.

Fight me.

No!

Then I will maul her to death and you can have Snow's death on your conscious too!

I glanced at Snow and saw the panic in her eyes. She was starting to raise her bow to shoot him, and I had mixed feelings.

Did I want her to kill him?

Part of me did.

The arrow slipped.

Garrison, stop!

Are you going to protect her brother?

"Snow get down!"

I'm getting closer, Garrison taunted.

You touch her, and I will kill you!

There it is! He shouted in excitement.

What?

You care for her. You allow yourself to be too weak, brother, you always have.

You call yourself strong, but you went after innocent children.

She's not a child, and they were not innocent. They were food for the evil witch. The huntsmen and us did them a favor.

He wasn't slowing down.

He was less than six feet from her.

Fine. You have me.

I ran after him and jumped into the air, shifting. I heard my clothes shredding as my bones broke and reassembled.

I landed hard, skidding to a stop just in front of him.

Garrison turned to face me and I could see the smug satisfaction in his eyes and Snow... Snow was staring at me in complete shock. Or was it horror?

Did she finally believe now... what I've been telling her?

I'm not a good man.

I am a beast.

I told you never to let me find you again. Garrison said with a growl.

It's been fifteen years. You need to learn how to get over it.

Get over it! Get over it? Because of you, the dark Queen captured and murdered father.

You're lucky it wasn't the both of you.

He charged at me, leaping into the air, teeth bared.

I reared up on my hind legs and pushed him back.

You've gotten stronger.

Again. It's been fifteen years.

He landed behind me and stood watching as I growled at him, squaring off to fight.

He wasn't moving.

Why wasn't he moving?

What are you doing?

What do you mean, brother?

Stop calling me that. I'm not your brother. You made that clear when you and father disowned me.

An unfortunate event. The sarcasm was clear in his voice.

I was eight years old! You both wanted me to kill that child. Weak.

Not a monster.

You are a monster. We all are. Look at how Snow is terrified of you.

Keep her name out of your mouth. I reared up and landed hard on the ground.

Snow? We're friends. He said matter-of-factly.

The fuck you are.

Do you want to find out? Although, do you think she'll look at you the same now?

You did this on purpose, didn't you? Realization was slowly setting in. He set me up.

Brother. The tone in his voice told me everything I needed to know.

Damn it. It was all some ploy to get me to shift in front of her- show her the person I really am and I fell for it.

You've gotten smarter, at least.

Why are you such an asshole?

You left me. His words held a bit of pain in them.

You banished me. You gave me no choice. I barked back.

You could have stayed and fought.

Fought? Fought against who? There was no way father was going to let me stay- not after I disappointed him.

You could have tried.

Tried? I would not kill children. Why do you care?

He pawed at the ground. *I don't care.* The asshole was back. The brief glimpse of his humanity was gone.

I glanced over my shoulder and saw Snow was still standing there watching.

Why are you even here?

Looking for Snow.

I told you. There's no way you're getting her. I will kill you if you try.

Brother, brother. Calm down. If I wanted her dead, I would have killed her in the town you two just came from. You said yourself; she is no longer a child and by the sounds of last night, I would say no longer a virgin.

I lunged after him.

He laughed, jumping out of the way. Although, he started circling around. *The Queen paid me a lot of money to find and kill her.*

The Queen? You're working for her now? If father only knew. I said in disgust.

Calm down. See. I'm in a bit of a pickle. I was hired to bring back her heart and liver.

I readjusted, so I was perfectly in between Garrison and Snow. I knew he was right. He could have gone after us before now, so this was all a game. He wanted me to show my true self to Snow, but why?

You seem to have a strong affection for her. Careful not to let the Queen find out.

I couldn't care less about her.

He laughed because he knew I was lying. *No need to pretend with me. She is a beautiful woman. Say... does she know?*

Know what?

That the Queen is her mother. He huffed. *Imagine my surprise when she let me in on that little secret. I could never figure out how she stopped having kids but stayed so young.*

Snow just found out and is devastated.

Then help me.

Help you?

Hunt down the other children. Snow is the first, which means the Queen is still using the others. We obviously need to go after the youngest ones first.

And kill them?

Yes.

No. *That's not who I am.*

He laughed. *Who you are? The Queen is going to keep coming after Snow. Every day she stays alive is a day the Queen grows weaker. If we can find and kill the others, then we can finally be rid of her once and for all. Think of all the people's she's killed.*

I'm not doing it.

She killed our father!

Our father killed himself when he hunted down her children. What did you all think was going to happen? You don't go against the dark Queen without risking your life. If you both thought she wouldn't come after you, then you were living in a fairytale.

I must have touched a nerve because Garrison lunged forward at me.

What did I say? I sneered, jumping out of the way.

You never gave a damn about father.

I was eight years old, and he wanted me to kill another child. It was bad enough he used me to lure them away, but to actually kill them! Do you know how hard it is for an eight-year-old werewolf to be abandoned? How hard it is to survive? The things I had to do. I shuddered at the thought.

Tell me, brother, what was so hard? Did you have to kill to stay alive?

When I didn't speak, he continued.

You did have to kill. He giggled in delight. *How many? Five? Ten?*

He waited.

More than that, brother? Oh, you have been a naughty boy. Does Snow know?

He looked over his shoulder at her.

No, I guess she probably doesn't.

I'm not telling you. I'm not going to relive that time because I've moved on. I found B-

Who? Who did you find?

It doesn't matter.

It does to me.

The fuck it does. You didn't give a shit about me back then and you sure as shit don't care about me now.

You're right. I care about Snow.

Do you even know the meaning of the word?

I know enough. Look. I will not hurt her. I need her alive. The longer she is alive, the weaker the Queen becomes and then as I find her children...

She would never forgive you.

Unlike you, brother, I can separate my feelings. You care for her, whether or not you want to admit it, and that makes you weak. You can't do what needs to be done.

And you can?

I'm a hunter. I would kill Snow if I had to protect the others from the dark Queen. I don't think you could. So help me. Help me find and kill the others like you were born to do. Help save Snow's life.

I've already told you, I'm not going to help you.

We'll see if your mind changes when the Queen comes after her. I just hope you don't have her death on your conscious too.

With that, he turned and ran off into the woods.

I watched to see if he was coming back, but I could smell him getting further and further away.

A few seconds later, I felt a hand on my shoulder and turned to find Snow standing there.

Her eyes looked soft and understanding.

Why didn't she understand?

I am a beast.

I snarled at her, and she recoiled in fear.

Good.

Back away.

I'm dangerous.

I snarled again, slowly stalking towards her.

"Gage! Stop!"

I didn't.

"You won't hurt me."

I reared up on my hind legs.

She stumbled backwards over a stick but regained her balance briefly before she fell.

"I don't believe you. I know you're in there." Her voice trembled unsure.

I hunched down and bared my teeth.

She raised her arrow at me.

Good.

Fear me.

There were tears in her eyes. I could see it was breaking her.

Before she could fully take aim, I darted off into the woods, leaving her on her own.

I watched from a distance and saw her standing there, lowering her bow, looking around.

"Gage!" she shouted. "I know you're still out there and can hear me!"

Silence.

"You aren't a monster, no matter how bad you want me to believe it."

She looked up at the sky. "Help me find my way home."

It only took a second, but Mother Nature responded like it had before. The wind kicked up around her, sending her scent to swirl all around me, suffocating me like a noose.

I watched as it guided her home.

Chapter Nineteen

MERLA - HATCHING A PLAN

I WAS LOSING MY touch.

In a fit of rage, I swiped my arm across the dresser in my room, sending everything smashing to the ground. The sound of glass shattering echoed throughout the room.

Historically, people feared me and now a measly huntsman thought he could take my money and try to trick me?

He would pay with his life. That was certain.

But how?

All the ways I had killed people filtered through my head, but none of them seemed dark enough. Brutal enough.

No. This needed to be special.

He tried to embarrass me... to use me.

An example needed to be made so no one would ever dare cross me again.

It needed to be a long, drawn out torture.

As ideas flowed through my mind, excitement slowly replaced the anger I felt.

Perhaps this was a gift. The huntsman had given me a gift.

I haven't executed someone in so long and I missed the smell of blood in the air and the look of fear in people's eyes.

No. I dismissed it. Too quick and not painful enough.

How could I make it public, but also make it gruesome? I sighed, irritated by the laws that had been put into place over the last several years, making executions more humane.

Humane?

No. That is not how you controlled your kingdom. Without fear, people would do what they felt like when they felt like it.

Perhaps they needed to be reminded of who they were dealing with.

"My Queen," the frumpy woman bustled in. "Is everything ok? I heard glass breaking."

I jerked around to stare at her. How dare she enter my chambers without my permission.

"It's fine! Get out!" I snapped, waving my hand in the air.

Again, I thought in furthered frustration. No respect. No fear.

I would make them fear me.

"Wait." I softened my tone.

She paused and walked back in.

"When was the rule changed for executions?"

She smiled, happily. "Oh, maybe seventeen or eighteen years ago. It was the first order the king passed after the birth of his daughter."

"Fucking Snow White." I mumbled.

"I'm sorry. What did you say?"

I dismissed her question, waving my hand in the air. "Nothing." I walked closer to her and relished in the fact she tensed up. She feared me, as she should be. "How would we overturn the rule?"

"You want to allow executions?" She asked, perplexed.

"Yes. I believe that is what I asked. Are you daft?"

She hurriedly shook her head, "No, my Queen. I wanted to make sure I understood the question, that is all."

I raised my chin, looking down my nose at her. "So?"

"The King would have to overturn it."

"The King? In his fragile mental state, I'm not sure..." I let a single tear roll down my cheek and walked to stand by the window.

"Perhaps the courts would accept a paper signed by the King?" She offered slowly.

I turned to face her. "A paper you say?"

She nodded nervously. "A doctor," she paused, then continued, "could sign a document about his current state," she quickly added, "but ensuring he is of sound mind to make the change." She clasped her hands in front of her again. "And then a second document could be written and signed by the King... reversing the ruling. A certified carrier could then deliver it to the courts, reversing it..."

I narrowed my focus on her. "I see.

She stood up straight. "Should I line up a doctor for the King? He was looking rather ill earlier when I checked on him."

I nodded slowly. "Yes please. I had feared the betrayal of his daughter would weigh too heavily on him. She was the last thing he had to hold on to from his late wife and now... she has tainted her image." I shook my head, grabbing my side. "I'm still dealing with the trauma myself."

"You are beyond amazing, my Queen."

I rolled my eyes, turning away. "Very well. Be on your way and let me know once it is all arranged. I will handle the document the King needs to sign and get that to you soon."

"Absolutely my Queen." She nodded and backed out of the room.

I walked over to the mirror on the wall once I was alone. "Mirror, mirror on the wall... where is that bitch Snow White?" I spat through gritted teeth.

The very thought of her name, the way it felt on my tongue, caused me to seethe with anger.

"My Queen, she is in Falkum's Forest currently, on her way back to the seventh mountain where she lives with the seven miners."

"Show me!"

"Very well, my Queen."

The mirror swirled like it was made of silver satin ribbon and showed Snow trekking through the forest with her bow on her back.

A devilish smile spread across my face.

She was alone.

Foolish girl!

She was going to make this too easy.

I paced around the room. What to do? What to do?

I gazed out the square pane window at the grounds people doing their mundane jobs. They were fortunate because they didn't have actual problems to deal with. Their largest concern was trying to figure out which pile to shovel the shit into.

Peasants.

So simple, blending into the background.

A thought crossed my mind.

I could shift into an old peasant woman and no one would suspect me.

Brilliant!

There was one in the dungeons I could use. Only problem to solve was her life.

Once she was dead, I could shift into her skin and viola!

This would be perfect!

I will leave in the night.

CHAPTER TWENTY

SNOW - TRUTH TOLD

I CAN'T BELIEVE THAT bastard left me in the middle of the woods on my own!

I looked up and saw the house in the distance, snaking up the tree with smoke coming out of the chimney.

Would he be there? If he was, what would I say to him? What would he say to me? Part of me was pissed that he left me, the other part was not sure how things would be between us after this trip. The soreness between my legs was a gentle reminder of what we shared.

I opened the door and found Enzo swinging from the exposed beams, while Calix chuckled from behind the bar top in the kitchen.

Enzo saw me walk in and dropped just in front of me. "Scarlet!" He grabbed my hands. "Where did you go?" He spun me in a circle.

I looked from Enzo to Calix.

Calix nodded. "He's been in the ale most of the afternoon."

"I can tell." I giggled.

Enzo looked over my shoulder. "Is Gage with you?"

He hadn't come back yet. My mind wondered where he could have gone. "No."

"That's odd. You both disappeared yesterday morning."

Was it only yesterday morning that we left? So much had happened in such a short amount of time that it was hard for me to wrap my head around. "He came with me-"

"Did you off the miserable bastard?"

"I-"

Enzo leaned in, his scent swirling around me. "No one would blame you if you did."

I couldn't help but wonder if they knew about him... the real him.

They had to know, right?

I smiled. "I didn't. We separated on the way back."

"You did? Where did you go?"

"Let her rest. She just got back from traveling." Barrett said, walking in.

I looked at him and nodded and there was something in his eyes... an expression I couldn't quite place.

"Scarlet. You can head to your room and rest for a bit. We will call you when dinner is ready." His words were clipped.

Was he dismissing me?

Had Gage made it back here before me and told him the truth about who I am?

I stared at him for a second, debating on calling him out for dismissing me or just letting it go. I decided on the latter and headed towards the stairs while Calix and Enzo watched, equally shocked.

When I got to my bedroom, I fell back onto my bed, sprawling out. I had a brief flashback of Gage on top of me, which caused my legs to quiver and my insides to tighten.

Before I could do anything to take the edge away, there was a soft knock on my door.

I bolted upright, wiped my face and patted my hair back as if that could hide the dirty thoughts in my mind.

"Come in."

Barrett.

He closed the door behind him and moved to sit on the edge of the bed.

I don't know if it was because I was horny as hell right now or if it was because I never paid attention to Barrett before, but the way he walked into my room- the authority in his saunter- turned me on. He was equally hot as the others, with his muscles, defined jawline and brown hair, but there was something else that seemed to light a fire in my pants right now.

I readjusted, so I was facing him. "Did you come to tell me why you dismissed me earlier?" My tone and words came out a little harsher than I intended, but I didn't apologize.

A smile parted his lips and then he sighed. "Gage talked with me."

Shit. How did he get back here so quickly? "Oh. Where is he?"

His lips pinched in a hardline. "He's... taking some time on his own for a little."

"What did he say... when you spoke?"

It was hard to believe so much had happened in such a short amount of time. There were a couple of big bomb-shells he could drop on me.

He studied me for a moment before he spoke. "He told me about your trip."

"He did?"

He nodded. "Look, I'm not going to lie. The fact you're a princess on the run from the dark Queen... it makes me a little nervous."

Ok. So he told him the truth about who I am. Check.

He continued. "With that said, I also can't just turn you out."

I exhaled in relief.

"But."

I hated buts... well, not men's butts. Round. Hard and squishy at the same time. I fussed at myself. Focus Snow, this was serious.

"You have to tell the others tonight. They will get a vote."

I nodded.

"It could bring attention to our house that we don't want and everyone should get a say."

"I understand."

"If it's worth anything to you, I have enjoyed having you around. I've grown rather fond of you."

I smiled as worry caused a pit to form in my stomach.

He lightly touched my knee and looked at me. I felt a fire flash inside my eyes before he stood and walked out.

"Hey," I called after him.

He stopped and turned around.

"Is he ok? Gage?"

He nodded and walked over to me, like he realized he forgot to say something. "Also, let's not mention what you saw today... with Gage."

My brow furrowed.

"It's not something he wants the others to know."

"But you do?"

He nodded. "I found him."

"You found him?"

"Yes. He'd been abandoned by his family when he was eight and had to survive on his own in the woods. I found him a few years later, but those years he was alone were rough on him. The things he had to do." He shook his head. "He knew he could trust me, but getting him to open up at all was, and is, nearly impossible."

I nodded.

"He sees himself as a monster and has tried to hide who he is for so long. He doesn't want the others to see him that way." He laughed, "An asshole he is ok with, a monster..."

"I won't say anything to the others. But..." I hesitated. "He's not a monster."

"He's not now. But he's also not the same person he was when I found him. He was, for all intents and purposes... feral."

"Feral?"

"Wild. Untamed. Before he met me, I don't think he had true, positive human interaction in years."

"How did you know?"

He smiled. "That's a story for another day."

He opened the door and paused. "We have some time before dinner if you want to wash up."

"Is that your subtle way of saying I stink?"

He smiled and walked downstairs.

I stared after him for a while before I moved, with Gage consuming all my thoughts. It made more sense why he thought he was a bad person. I could see the anger in his eyes before he shifted like he was being forced to shift and then after, when he looked at me... the sadness and the pain.

Who was the other wolf and what did it want?

It seemed as if they knew each other, perhaps a friend from his past life? Although, based on the conversation I just had with Barrett, I wouldn't think Gage had friends during that time.

My heart broke for him.

I couldn't help but wonder where he went and for how long he'd be gone.

I wanted to see him and wrap my arms around him and let him know I didn't see him any differently. He wasn't a monster.

But no matter how many times I said it, he wouldn't believe me... that much was clear.

I grabbed a change of clothes and headed to the showers. I toyed with using Gage's since I figured he wouldn't be back for a while, but decided against it... and used Enzo's instead.

I walked downstairs a little while later and Enzo called out, "The Queen has arrived! We may start our feast!"

I panicked, scanning the room for Barrett, and he shook his head.

I breathed a sigh of relief and kept walking down the stairs.

"Barrett, did Scarlet tell you what she did with Gage?" Enzo asked.

"I-" I started, but Enzo cut me off.

Barrett laughed. "She did nothing. I needed him to run an errand for me."

Enzo flopped in the seat. "I thought badass Scarlet offed him for being such a dick all the time."

"I tried." I laughed. "But there's always next time."

Barrett looked at me and nodded, smiling.

I walked into the kitchen and stood next to Calix. "What can I help with?"

He gently rested his head on mine. "I've missed you. You're the only one who wants to help around here." He said the last part loud enough for everyone to hear.

"We just know how much you enjoy it." Enzo shouted, rocking back in his chair.

Gideon reached his foot under the table and pushed Enzo's chair, causing him to lose balance and fall backwards.

"Not cool man." Enzo said, huffing as he stood up.

"I was just testing the laws of physics."

"Whatever." Enzo slammed the chair down on all fours and sat down.

I laughed as I helped bring the food over to the table.

We all enjoyed a delicious pot roast and vegetables, but it was obvious the dynamic was off with Gage not here... or maybe it was just me. I couldn't help but glance at his empty chair and feel a pang of guilt.

Had that wolf not been there, he wouldn't have had to show himself. Was he embarrassed to be around me? Ashamed?

I had to get him to believe I didn't see him any differently, but that was kind of hard to do when he wasn't around for me to talk to.

I realized I was squeezing my fork a little hard when Barrett cleared his throat and lightly nudged my leg under the table. He nodded towards the fork when I looked at him. I dropped my hands below the table and straightened the small bend.

"So Scarlet, tell us where you ran off too." Enzo chimed, shoving a bite of food in his mouth.

I glanced at Barrett, who smiled. "Perhaps we can have that discussion after dinner." His words were slow and quiet, but his tone was final.

Enzo puckered his lips and mumbled something under his breath.

Barrett looked at Jace. "Were you able to get those healing herbs from the witch doctor yesterday?"

Jace nodded. "We're well stocked."

"Perfect. Never know when we'll need it." I felt like he was talking to me when he spoke.

After dinner, I helped clean off the table and washed the dishes. The more time passed, the more nervous I felt.

Barrett walked through the kitchen, giving my shoulder a light squeeze.

Shit.

Was that a sign? Was it time?

I took in a deep breath, but didn't move.

"Group." Barrett announced, gathering everyone's attention. "We need to have a family talk."

"Mannn." Enzo whined. "I didn't do anything. I swear!"

Barrett chuckled for a second, surprised by Enzo's guilty conscious. "No, we need to have a conversation and vote." He nodded in my direction and everyone looked at me.

I wiped my hands on my pants, both nervously and to dry them off, then stood by the table to look at everyone.

I took in a deep breath. My stomach was full of knots and my hands were trembling.

"What's going on Scarlet?" Enzo asked, confused.

"First off... that's not my name."

"I knew it! I told you," Enzo said lightly back, gripping Calix's shoulder. "She didn't look like a Scarlet."

"It's Snow... Snow White."

Gideon's lips parted as he cut his eyes to Barrett.

Enzo's chair came crashing back down as he mumbled, "Oh shit. I didn't expect that."

I hurried. "I'm sorry I lied to you all. I was scared if you knew the truth you wouldn't let me stay and I also..." I shook my head, burying my face in my hands.

"So you're the Snow White. The princess, Snow White. The Snow White that no one has seen in years and thought was dead." As if putting all the pieces together, he slapped the table. "Well shit, that makes sense." Enzo bellowed.

"There's more..." I mumbled, taking in a deeper breath.

Gideon crossed his arms across his chest. I don't know why I kept being drawn back to him. He was never kind to me- not rude, but never kind. It was like he suspected me from the beginning, but he never said anything and now was proven right.

"I don't know where to begin with this next part." I looked up, hoping something would give me inspiration or encouragement. "Part of what I told you was the truth. The dark Queen left me locked up in a room from basically the time she moved into the castle after my mother died until I escaped. I've been having dreams about my mother, but she was warning me. She told me I needed to find Persephone to learn the truth about me... about who I am... so that's where I went."

"The white witch?" Jace asked.

"Who are you?" Enzo asked, sitting forward, excitement filled his eyes like this was some fairytale and not my real life.

I kept my eyes glued to him, his stare giving me the silent reassurance I needed to tell the next part. "She told me I was born from magic, harvested for youth and hunted till death." My lips pinched in a hard line. "I was born from magic. She told me that..." I felt a tear on the rim of my eyelid. "She told me the dark Queen is my mother."

Everyone except Barrett gasped.

"I had no idea." I tried to reassure them, feeling an uneasiness in the room. I ran them through the details of how and why I was born and why the dark Queen wants me dead.

Once I finished talking, everyone stared at me for a moment without speaking.

Barrett stepped forward. "Scar- Snow. If you want to wait in your room, we will vote and let you know the outcome."

I nodded, looking at everyone's faces one more time before I left, hoping it wouldn't be the last time.

I heard Enzo ask about Gage's vote while I was walking up the stairs and heard Barrett say he had already given it. As I passed his room, I got the strange urge to just climb into his bed and cuddle up with this comforter, but I ignored the feeling and continued to climb the stairs.

I waited patiently, pacing around the room, and then decided to get my pajamas on. If they were going to evict me, they wouldn't do it tonight... I hoped.

Some time later, there was a soft knock on my door. I opened it, expecting Enzo or maybe even Barrett, but instead found Gideon. I tried to get a read on his face, but he gave nothing away. Always so stoic.

I followed him silently down the stairs as my heart tried to beat a hole through my chest.

When we got downstairs, Gideon took his seat, and I walked in front of the kitchen island and put my hand on it for support.

"The vote was unanimous." Barrett started, and my heart fell. "We want you to stay."

"Wait, what?" I was shocked. Unanimous. Gage? Gideon? They voted for me to stay?

Enzo jumped up from his seat like a spring that had been forced into a box for too long. "Come here, girl! We aren't going to let that evil woman get her hands on you! You are one of us and we protect our own." He wrapped his arm around my neck, pulling me in for a hug.

I turned into him, burying my face in his neck as tears fell uncontrollably. "Thank you." I looked up at the group. "Thank you all so much."

Gideon, showing no emotion, warned, "You will need to watch the dark Queen. She will come after you."

I nodded.

"She has spies everywhere," he continued. I got the feeling it was from personal experience perhaps... is that why he is so guarded? Untrusting of others? Untrusting of me?

With Enzo's arm still around my waist, he looked at me. "So since you're a witch... what kind of powers do you have?"

"What he really wants to know is if you can make his dick bigger?" Calix chimed in.

"My dick is plenty big enough," he defended, then cut his eyes at me and whispered, "But if you could... let me know."

I laughed, then turned my gaze to the rest of the group. "I don't know what kind of powers I have. The white witch mentioned something about being about to speak to nature, having a connection with animals, but aside from that, I have no idea. I asked her to help me, but she said she couldn't." I shrugged. "I don't know why."

"Because she's a white witch, she can't interfere with dark magic." Jace interjected.

"I'm not though..."

He shrugged. "You can't say for certain. You were born from dark magic, so one would have to assume you have dark magic in you."

I had a shiver run up my spine. "I'm not dark."

"I don't think so, but that's why she couldn't help you."

Calix popped out of this chair. "Enough of this!" He clapped. "This calls for a celebration."

"We'll get the bosom berries." Enzo announced, shaking my shoulders back and forth.

I looked up at him and smiled.

"Come on, Snow." He quickly kissed my forehead and pulled me to the front door.

CHAPTER TWENTY-ONE

MERLA - GARDENING IS GOOD FOR ONE'S HEALTH

I BATTED A BRANCH out of my way in frustration and snatched my skirt, which had gotten stuck on the trunk of a small broken tree on the ground. I heard the rip of the fabric as the sharp stump tore a hole through it.

Cheap fabric.

I had taken a number of layers from the frumpy woman's closet and was starting to get hot. It had taken me a full day to get this far and the sun would be setting soon.

But it was for a good cause- Snow's death.

I envisioned her frail, lifeless body in my arms as I cut into her chest.

I crested the top of a small hill and let out a sigh of relief. In the distance, I saw a house built into the side of a tree and recognized it from my mirror.

The miners' house.

And to my delight, there was smoke coming from the chimney, which meant she was home.

I picked up my pace and saw the mangy brown horse Snow had used, parked out front of the house feasting on some vegetables in the garden. It looked at me and reared up, causing me to take a few steps back.

I pointed my finger at it and whispered, "Reducio."

With a zap, the horse shrunk and was no larger than a miniature pony.

He looked down and started to charge at me again, but when I held up my finger, he skidded to a stop, turned and ran off.

I riffled through the bag on my side and pulled out a mirror and examined my face to make sure I was still in the woman peasant's body from the dungeon. I only had so much time in her body before the decay started to set in and began to smell.

I pulled the mirror away quickly. The sight of my dirty, wrinkled, and haggard face with an oversized wart made me nauseous. I stuffed it back into the bag and quickly pulled out several chains and necklaces, and hobbled to the door.

I gave it a gentle, elderly knock, and waited.

Nothing.

I gave it another knock, this time a bit louder.

Nothing.

My patience was wearing thin.

Just before I was about to knock again, the door swung open and there she was. All bright eyed and bushy tailed.

"Oh. I'm sorry. I didn't know anyone was here." She was standing in the frame with a basket on her hip, looking very homely.

I changed my voice to what I imagined a frail woman would sound like. "Oh dear. It's quite alright." I shifted uncomfortably from side to side. "I was hoping... if you'd be interested in some of these fine necklaces here." I held them up, but let my arm shake from the weight.

"Oh, my." She looked behind me. "Have you walked all this way?"

I nodded. "My cart got stuck in some mud a ways back, but I was hoping perhaps you and your husband could help an old woman out and purchase a piece or two of fine jewelry. A house as grand as this and a neck as beautiful as yours deserves to be adorned in finery."

"Oh." She laughed gratingly. "I'm not married."

I peeked around her arm. "You have a table for so many. I thought for sure a young and beautiful woman such as yourself would have a husband with many children."

She laughed. "Maybe one day."

Not likely. "Well." I shook the necklaces in my arm.

"I don't know if I need a necklace now, plus I have no money."

"Oh." I lowered my arm. "I was hoping to sell at least three more of these this month so I could buy some food for my children."

Her face fell. Always such the soft heart. I smiled at the thought of holding it in my hands in mere minutes.

"How many children do you have?"

"Five children... full of energy." And delicious youth.

Her eyes focused on me. "Are you alright? Your eye..."

"My eye?" I reached up to touch it.

"It's twitching."

"Oh... it does that sometimes. Old age..." It shouldn't be the body decaying... I hadn't been in it long enough. Perhaps the old hag had a twitching eye already? I never noticed, granted I never paid much attention to her. I looked around. "Do you think I could come in and wait for a bit? Let my feet rest before I go back to my cart?"

She looked over her shoulder, hesitating, so I dropped my leg and let out a gasp.

"Yes, yes, of course." She backed out of the door. "The men will be home in just a little while and will be able to help you with your cart."

"Oh, goddess bless you, child."

She smiled and guided me over to the couch.

"Such a big house you keep."

"It's great. I was just about to go harvest some vegetables in the garden. Will you be ok in here on your own?"

"Yes. Let me rest for a moment and I can come out and help you."

"Nonsense. You have had a long and tiring journey."

"It's not a bother. My mother always said gardening was good for the health."

She giggled, "I, also, find it relaxing."

"I'll be right out in a little."

She closed the door, and I heard her melodic voice filtering in through the windows and felt my body cringing at the sound. I walked around the kitchen, letting my fingers glide carelessly over the counter, and stopped at the knife block. My fingers padded across the handles of each of the knives, landing on the center one. I pulled it out and the sound of the metal scraping sent a euphoric feeling through me. I put the knife in the skirt's pocket and continued moving around the house.

I wandered up the wooden staircase and stopped on the first floor. I opened the door to the left and stepped into a rather small room with an enormous bed and a dresser. I bounced on the edge of the bed, but was distracted by Snow yelling out something.

I moved to the window and peeked through the curtains to see her looking out across the field with her hands on her hips. I laughed when I realized she was looking for that stupid horse!

So long horsey!

The sun setting in the sky caught my attention. I was running out of time! I needed to kill her before those stupid miners returned home.

I bolted out of the room and down the stairs and gathered myself before opening the front door. "Is everything ok? I heard you yelling something." I said in a meek voice.

She looked over her shoulder briefly, then turned back to digging up the potatoes. "Yes. My horse. He must have run off."

"Shame. I didn't see a horse. I can keep an eye out for him, though."

"Thank you, you're so kind."

"The kindest." I mumbled under my breath.

"What was that?" She brushed the hair out of her face with her arm.

"I asked where you needed me."

"Oh. Down there would be good. Lots of potatoes." She laughed.

"Yes, of course."

I reached in my bag and grabbed a necklace out and coiled it around my hands and walked over to her. I heard her humming some song and excitement filled me, knowing that would be the last song she'd ever hum.

I reached around her neck and pressed the necklace to her throat, pulling back as hard as I could.

"Poor Snow. Always so trusting." I said through gritted teeth.

She let out a gasp and a moan as she flailed about. She reached up, trying to grab onto my arms, but the cloth prevented her from getting a firm grasp.

I pulled harder, pressing my knee into her back for leverage, but felt my strength falter for a second. "No!" I cried out.

I could tell one of my children had been killed. It was like an electric shot zapped through me. All that youth wasted, I thought in fury.

I looked down at Snow and saw her looking up at me, eyes wide with panic as realization set in.

"You. You did this!" I pulled hard and watched as her face turned a rainbow of colors before her arms fell to her side.

CHAPTER TWENTY-TWO

ENZO - WE PROTECT OUR OWN

"When is Gage going to be back?" I moaned to Barrett. "I had to do part of his section today because he wasn't around."

Barrett patted me on the back. "A little extra work is good for you."

I rolled my eyes. "So... Gage?"

"He'll come back soon."

"What's he doing?"

Barrett cut his eyes at me, which told me I needed to drop it.

"Fine."

He held his hand out. "Stop."

We all froze.

"What's wrong?" I whispered, sensing he was not playing.

There were sticks breaking in the brush up ahead.

Barrett's face contorted, confused.

A second later, a miniature horse that looked just like Snow's, only a quarter of the size, walked up to me.

Barrett looked from the pony to me and back to the pony.

"Shit! Get back to the house." He commanded.

"Snow?" I didn't wait for his answer before I took off running.

I felt the wind whipping through my hair and stinging my eyes as I raced by tree after tree. I glanced behind me and saw the others running, but falling off quickly.

Over the years, we had discovered I had extraordinary speed, but didn't know what I was or where I came from.

Barrett found me in one of the towns when I was a teenager, after I had managed to steal a stone from him. I thought it was a satchel of coin when I was lifting it and almost tossed it when I realized it wasn't, but there was a symbol on the front which I thought was interesting. I thought it to be some sort of talisman, so I held onto it for good luck.

And good luck it brought me. Barrett managed to track me down when no one else had even gotten close. I thought for sure he was going to kill me and perhaps he even tried, but I managed to dodge his several attempts at grabbing or punching me. I felt this tingle move through my body when he got close to me, like something was waking up, even though I'm not quite sure what it was. It seemed like he felt it too because a few times he would pause and adjust and after a while I felt like he was no longer trying to hurt me, but rather study me.

I don't know how much time passed, but he eventually stopped and took a step back, his face perplexed and then offered me a place to stay. I thought it was a joke at first- a ploy to catch me off guard, but we talked for several hours at a pub and I don't know if it was the ale or the look in his eyes, but that night I went home with him and never looked back.

I was approaching the house and saw Snow laying on the ground by the garden. "Shit."

I skidded to a stop near her head, throwing dirt up, and fell to my knees.

"Snow! Snow!" I yelled, shaking her gently.

Her face was as white as snow.

I saw the necklace around her throat and pulled it off, tossing it to the side. There was a red line, burned into her skin where it had been pulled across her throat.

Who would do something like this? The force someone would have to use to cause that level of a wound...

I lightly tapped her face. "Snow. Wake up!"

I heard movement behind me and quickly turned to fight, but stopped when I realized it was the others.

Jace ran beside me and dropped to his knees. "Put her head down." He commanded, and I followed.

His ear dropped to her nose and mouth. "She's not breathing." He tilted her chin up and placed his mouth on hers.

"What happened?" Barrett asked.

I shook my head. "I don't know. She was on the ground when I got here. There was a chain around her neck, so I took it off and threw it over there." I nodded.

Barrett looked around. "I'll be back." He took off running behind the house.

"Jace." I begged, hoping for any piece of good news.

He ignored me and started pressing on her chest.

"What can I do?"

"Pinch her nose and blow some breaths into her mouth."

I followed what he said as he continued to press on her chest.

Jace pushed me out of the way and laid his ear to her nose and mouth. "Damn it!" He balled up his fist and pounded it on her chest.

"Jace?" I asked, concerned. I had never seen him mad and right now there was a look of anger and frustration penetrating out of his every pore.

"Come on, Snow!" He pressed his lips against hers again and then continued pushing on her chest.

She laid there like a rag doll with her arms flopping this way and that with each compression.

"Snow." I said, holding her face in between my hands.

"Blow in her mouth." Jace commanded again.

I pressed my lips to hers and blew twice and felt something.

A twitch.

"Jace." I called his attention.

He looked at me, then down at her.

"Snow?" I whispered.

I saw her lips curl into the smallest smile.

"Snow." I grabbed her head and sat it on my lap, wiping her hair out of her face.

A few seconds later, she opened her eyes and looked right into mine.

"Snow." I leaned over and kissed her forehead.

She took in a deep breath and sat up, looking around at everyone with her hand grasped tightly in Jace's. "Where is she?" Her voice trailed off, but sounded like she had swallowed an entire bag of glass.

"Who?" I asked, looking around. "No one was here when I got to you."

"It was an old woman. She was..." she rubbed her throat. "She was selling necklaces."

"The necklace." I pointed at the necklace I had thrown and Calix ran to pick it up. "She tried to strangle you with it. I found this wrapped around your throat."

She winced. "I don't understand. She... she seemed so... nice."

"Who was she?"

Snow shook her head.

Barrett came running back and looked at all of us. "Is she ok?" He asked.

Jace nodded. "I think so. She will have some bruising around her throat and be hoarse for a few days, but I think she'll be ok."

"Did you find anything?" I asked.

He held up some thin brown fabric, a satchel, and a kitchen knife. "I found it behind the house with some footprints, but they disappeared."

"Disappeared? It was her, wasn't it?" Snow asked solemnly, rubbing her throat.

Gideon looked around. "Let's get her inside."

"Come on." I lifted her up as she leaned into my chest and wrapped her arms around my neck.

Calix and Jace walked over to the cabinet and started pulling out some herbs and dropped them in hot water. A few minutes later, Jace was cradling a mug, bringing it over to her on the couch. "Drink this. It will help your throat feel better."

He looked over at Calix, who was riffling through the kitchen drawers and cabinets. I imagine taking an inventory to make sure nothing else was missing.

"Thank you." She smiled, pulling my attention back to her.

Barrett sat on the edge of the couch and placed his hand on her knee. "What can you tell us?"

I looked from his hand to her, back to his hand and then to Jace, who had also noticed this odd gesture.

She shook her head, clasping the warm cup in her hands like it was her lifeline. I could feel her shaking beside me, but knew she was trying to be strong for all of us. I wrapped my arm around her shoulders and gently squeezed her.

She placed her hand on mine. "I was going outside to harvest the vegetable garden when she was standing at the front door. She said her cart had broken down a way back and wanted to know if we could help her. I told her no one else was home and then she offered me some necklaces she was selling. She was so old and frail looking, with wrinkles and a wart." She shook her head, trying to wrap her head around everything.

I rested my head on hers and cut my eyes at Barrett. He knew what I was thinking.

I'm sure what we were all thinking.

I wanted to go to the castle and wrap my hands around the dark Queen's throat and kill her. I could almost literally feel my blood boiling I was so angry.

Flashes of Snow laying on the ground... the necklace burned in red around her throat... Jace pounding life back into her chest.

Barrett nodded his head at me- a sign I needed to keep it together.

I had been known to make reckless decisions in my past and I'm sure right now he could sense I was on the verge of making another one.

"I invited her inside to rest because she looked tired and weary. When she learned I was going to harvest the garden, she volunteered to help and said something about it being good for the soul."

She took a sip of hot tea and cleared her throat.

"After some time, she came outside and the next thing I know, she pulled a necklace out and wrapped it around my throat." She paused and closed her eyes. "She said 'Poor Snow, always so trusting.'"

I felt my hand clench by my side and caught Barrett studying me.

She leaned her head into my chest while I gently brushed the hair back with my hand.

She popped her head up. "She said something else."

She closed her eyes, trying to remember.

"When she was pulling the necklace around my throat, I felt her press her knee into my back to help give her leverage, but she faltered. Her strength faltered for a moment and... and had I been smarter, I would have taken that time to defend myself." She rubbed her face in frustration.

I grabbed her hand. "It's not your fault."

She exhaled. "She cried out for one of her babies. At first, I didn't know what she was talking about, but then I remembered the white witch told me in order to defeat the dark Queen, her children would have to be killed. I think someone killed one of her children and it made her weaker... it was only for a second but she felt it."

She took another sip of tea and yawned.

I looked at Calix with a sneaking suspicion he had put something in the tea, but he gave nothing away, standing by the table watching her with his light brown arms crossed against his chest.

"She looked at me with a rage in her eyes like nothing I had ever seen before and I swear her eyes flashed a sort of green color and she said, 'You! You did this!' And then the light faded away."

She looked up at me, her eyes slowly glazing over.

"We... we have to... find them... the others..." Her eyes were closed.

"How much did you give her, Calix?" Jace asked, mildly concerned.

"I don't know. The same amount I give any of you."

"Calix!" Jace reprimanded. "She's like half our size!"

Calix scrunched his nose. "Is she going to be ok?"

Jace placed his fingers on her neck. "Pulse seems steady. Someone will need to stay with her tonight just to make sure."

"I can!" I announced quickly, garnering several looks from the others. "What? She trusts me." I knew it went deeper than that.

I wanted. No, I needed to protect her. We all did.

I glanced at Jace and Calix and saw the look on their face. We three had agreed not to pursue Snow. We liked to share women, but Snow was not that. She was different.

Although, after tonight, perhaps we should have included Barrett in the pact. We just didn't think anyone else in the house was interested in her like that, although it seemed like she had a piece of all of us right now, because the looks on these men's faces... They were ready to go to war, but we had to be strategic and Barrett would see to it that no one did anything stupid.

Barrett rolled his eyes. "Fine. You can stay with her."

"Do you think the dark queen will come back?" I asked, cradling Snow in my arms, preparing to walk upstairs with her.

"I don't know. I would have to assume once she knows Snow isn't dead, she will."

"We have to kill her... for Snow."

"I know." Barrett said quietly.

I carefully scaled the stairs with her in my arms and when I got to her room, I gently laid her on the bed, slipped off her shoes and covered her with a blanket. She reached out for my arm and held on, so I climbed in bed beside her, wrapping my arms around her.

"It's ok Snow. We protect our own." I kissed her on the forehead one more time and then laid my head on her pillow.

CHAPTER TWENTY-THREE

SNOW - OFF TO FIND A MAGE

I COULD FEEL THE warmth of the sun peppering my face and knew it was the morning. This was the fourth morning I had woken up in Enzo's bed.

I felt him shift under me, so I opened my eyes to find him propping his hands under his head and looking down at me.

"Good morning." He smiled.

"Morning." I laid my head back on his chest. "You know," I started.

"Huh?"

"I think you're milking this whole taking care of me thing to get out of doing work at the mine."

I felt him shaking with laughter. "Maybe I enjoy spending time with you." He rubbed the back of my head affectionately.

"It's been days."

"Yea. Barrett says I have to go back next week." He sulked a bit.

"Oh." I tried not to sound disappointed, but I knew I failed. I had gotten used to having Enzo all to myself. He was amazing to look at and he made the days go by fast. He was funny and always had the best stories from his days on the streets before Barrett found him. I had learned that he was quite the pick pocket, stealing to get by.

"But it's ok. We have the whole day ahead of us!" He said, tickling my sides before he jumped out of bed.

He stood and stretched his arms to the sky, causing the muscles in his arms and back to tighten and twist. He was tall and very muscular, not as big as Gage, but proportioned well for his size. He was only wearing a pair of boxers that hugged his ass perfectly. He turned around to look at me, but stopped when he saw me looking at his beautifully wrapped package.

I felt a flutter in my stomach and quickly looked away.

Even though sleeping in the same bed seemed to be a given right now, we hadn't tried anything. Well, he hadn't. Which made me wonder why? Was it because he didn't find me attractive? I made myself available each night, wearing less and less, to the point I was wearing only a shirt that barely covered my ass. But through it all, nothing.

I could even feel his hard dick pressed against my back at night when I would scoot back into him, but nothing.

I wondered if it had anything to do with Gage, then realized there was no way he could know about that and surely Gage wouldn't have said anything when he stopped by and talked to Barrett. I doubted if Gage would even acknowledge what we shared.

Which was fine. Again, I wasn't looking for anything serious. I just wanted to live and to experience... life.

Enzo jumped on the bed. "What do you want to do today?"

"I told Calix I would go into town and pick up some grocery items so he wouldn't have to do it tomorrow."

He rolled his eyes and fell back onto the bed.

I patted him on the chest. "You'll be ok."

He grabbed my hand and pulled me down, so I landed awkwardly on top of him.

I laughed and then paused when I looked at him. Our eyes locked, and I felt the weight of the room change.

This was it.

I felt my breathing slow as we stared at one another.

His hand slowly cupped the edge of my cheek and heat was radiating off of it in pulses. I turned my hand into his wrist at the same time he brushed the hair out of my face. "Your throat is looking a lot better."

It was like something snapped us- me- back to reality. "Yea. Jace has been putting a cream he created on it to help it heal."

"Oh, I know what Jace has been doing." He popped out of bed and threw on a pair of pants and a shirt.

"You seem jealous."

He looked glanced at me over his shoulder. "Whose bed did you wake up in? I'm not jealous." He winked and dashed out of the room, yelling as he descended the stairs.

I laughed, climbing out of bed and stretching. We had the house to ourselves and every morning he would yell and scream at the top of his lungs as he swung from raft to raft in the living room. He looked like a monkey, but it made me laugh.

When I got downstairs, he dropped to his feet in front of me.

"Do you want some breakfast?" I opened the fridge. "Looks like Calix left us some. I can heat it up."

He stood behind me, his chest on my back as he leaned over, pressing his cheek to mine. "Looks good to me."

I turned my head only slightly to look at him. I couldn't tell if he was teasing me on purpose or was just that obtuse, but the continued closeness and touching was sending my body reeling.

I popped my butt out into him, making him jump back.

If this was a game, then two could play it.

He laughed and sat at the table while I heated the food.

"So I was thinking we could eat then head to town. I need to get back so I can do the laundry."

"Sure, sounds good." He said flatly.

I sat down at the table. "Ok then."

I looked at him for a second, trying to figure out what had changed. He was usually never that agreeable. There was always a groan or complaint or a joke mixed in.

We finished our food and headed to town.

"Do you have any magic that can transport us there?" Enzo teased the moment we stepped outside.

"No. I was hoping my horse would be back and we could take him." Since the dark Queen came by, my horse hadn't been around. I never tied him up, because I wanted him to explore and be free, but I was kind of missing him.

"Oh." His voice dropped.

"Oh? What?"

Enzo's face fell. "I think the dark Queen did something to your horse."

I grabbed his arm, spinning him around. "What do you mean? Did she..." I couldn't say the words.

"No. No. No. I think she shrunk him."

"Shrunk him?" I asked, confused.

"Into a pony."

"Oh, my." I looked around, hoping to find him, but he wasn't here. "I need to find a mage too, so I can learn magic. I feel so useless and if, or rather when, the dark Queen comes back, I need to be able to defend myself."

"We can stop at Ruby's Tavern to see if she can help."

I smiled. "Yes!"

"But..." he hesitated.

"What?"

"Probably don't tell the boys I took you there."

"Why not?"

"You'll see..."

We decided to go to Ruby's before we picked up the groceries because we didn't want to have them at Ruby's while we were talking.

We walked up to the outside of the old house and, for some reason, I had pictured it differently. After walking in, I immediately figured out why he didn't want me saying anything to the boys. I watched a few girls wearing almost nothing lead men upstairs and down from the main foyer.

I admired their confidence and couldn't help but straighten my back just a bit.

We passed through the beaded curtains and walked into the main hall, where we found a woman standing behind a bar. She was wearing a black corset with her chest spilling over and a black sequin head band with a white feather in the cap.

"Ruby." Enzo said as we got closer.

"Enzo darling." She looked at her watch. "A little early in the day for you." Her gaze landed on me. "And who do we have here?"

"Sn- Scarlet."

"Scarlet?" Something in the way she said my name told me she knew that wasn't my name, but she also wasn't going to push.

"Nice to meet you."

She opened her arms wide. "Everyone that comes in gives me a hug." She leaned forward as her breast swept across the counter.

I gave her a hug and noticed she smelled sweet, like some sort of flower.

"What can I do for you two today? Are we looking for a couple's room or your own?"

Before I could correct her, Enzo jumped in. "Oh no. We aren't... we're here on a different kind of business."

She smiled, intrigued. "Go on."

"My friend here," he said, placing his hand on my shoulder and regrettably, emphasizing the word friend. "Is in need of a mage."

"A mage?"

"Yes... to teach her the arts."

She studied me for a minute.

Enzo continued. "She just learned she has powers."

"And her parents?"

"Can't help."

"Can't help?"

"It's a long story."

Ruby raised her brows.

It was obvious she was a woman who didn't trust blindly and while she liked Enzo, she didn't fully trust him.

"Ruby." I started. "Can you keep a secret?"

She laughed. "I run this place. Of course I can."

I took in a deep breath. I didn't want to do this, but could quickly read the room and knew we would not get anywhere beating around the bush. Ruby didn't strike me as that kind of lady. "I'm Snow White and on the run. The dark Queen is my mother and wants me dead. I just learned all of this, as well as the fact I have powers, and need to learn how to use them, so I can defend myself... against her."

Ruby looked from me to Enzo back to me and then, without warning, burst into laughter. "I like her Enzo." She continued laughing. "Snow White... in my tavern... classic." She rested her hands on mine. "I'll help you out Scarlet. I have a few mages I employ, but I will set up some time with Lilibet. She will probably be the best for you."

I smiled. "Thank you, thank you!"

"You're welcome dear." She leaned in, so her lips were pressed against my ear. "Go by Scarlet here. I can keep your secret, but others..."

I looked her in the eyes and nodded.

I was so happy, but that quickly disappeared when I heard a voice boom behind me.

"What the fuck are you doing here?"

I turned around and found a girl hanging on Gage's arm.

Chapter Twenty-Four

GAGE - BROTHERLY BONDING

Shit.

I glanced over and looked at Josie, getting dressed.

I used the word dress, loosely, since she was only wearing a sheer bra and matching panties.

I was hoping a quick visit to Ruby's tavern before I went home would help settle me and get my mind off Snow.

But it didn't.

The last week I had regrettably spent with my brother. It took me a day to find him and when I did, he had already found one of the Queen's children before I could convince him to find another way.

Fortunately, he seemed to have matured, and it seemed to bother him more than it used to and more than it bothered our father. Sometimes I wondered if our father ever had a caring bone in his body. Oftentimes I felt like we were a means to an end, being used much like the Queen uses her children.

Which then led me back to Snow.

Fuck!

"Let's go." I snapped.

Josie looked at me like a startled doe in the woods.

"I can't wait to see you again." She said, swiping her hand across my shoulders.

I nodded, but didn't speak. She was good, but she wasn't Snow.

The amount of regret I had giving into my desires and sleeping with her enraged me. It was part of the reason I had stayed gone for so long. I needed as much time away from her as possible. I could still feel her tight pussy on my cock and I hated it! I hated thinking of her.

Perhaps I would go one more day.

Barrett had only said I needed to be back before work, which meant I still had two more days.

Why rush?

We walked downstairs and her scent hit me before seeing her.

We walked through the beaded curtains and my eyes darted quickly around the room until they landed on her... and Enzo.

My blood boiled.

"What the fuck are you doing here?" I commanded.

She turned around and her eyes scanned me up and down- a mixture of excitement and something else. Anger?

I looked to my right and saw Josie was hanging on my arm.

"What are you doing here?" Snow retorted just as fast. Her eyes had hardened, and she *was* angry.

"You didn't answer my question."

"I don't have to." She snapped.

Josie shifted on my arm. "Is she your girlfriend?"

"NO!" Snow and I said in unison.

"Oh... ok." Josie mumbled, clearly uncomfortable.

Enzo snaked his arm around Snow's waist and I could feel anger swell like a wave.

Snow narrowed her gaze at me. "What are you doing? Have you been here the whole time?"

"I'm going to go." Josie said quietly, trying to pull her arm out of mine.

I clasped my hand on hers, holding her in place. "Not yet."

"Ok," she resolved, looking at Ruby. "I guess you have a few more minutes."

I looked at Enzo. "Are you fucking mad... bringing her here?"

Enzo widen his stance, clearly not enjoying being talked to like that. "Scarlet needed to talk to Ruby."

At least he wasn't daft enough to use her real name. "She did?" I didn't believe him. There is no way Snow needed to see Ruby.

"Yes, I did." Snow interjected back into the conversation. "So, why are you here?"

"I needed a good lay." I lashed out.

I saw her chest recoil in shock and heard her heart beat flutter, but she recovered quickly. "I hope you got what you wanted."

No. I didn't. "It was fucking fantastic." I narrowed my eyes at her.

"Ok... well, this seems fun." Ruby entered the conversation. "We aim to please." She looked at Josie. "Your next client is here." She nodded at the man waiting in a booth on the other side of the room.

She gently pulled out of my arms and gave me a light pat. "Thanks Gage." She kissed me on the cheek.

I couldn't help but notice the look on Snow's face and could tell it bothered her. I wanted to tell her this was all for show, but the other part- the more reasonable part- knew this was for the best. She didn't need to care for me because I would only hurt her.

Ruby looked at Enzo. "Let me chat with a few people and I will get back to you."

"Thanks Rubes, you're the best!"

"What are you doing?" I asked, my tone still a little clipped.

"I'm looking at getting a job here." Snow snarked.

Rage.

I saw red, and it wasn't the walls. "The fuck you are."

She continued. "That's not a problem, is it?"

I felt my eyes narrow to thin slits and took a beat after realizing she was trying to get a reaction out of me. "Not at all."

"Good." She looked at Enzo and reached around his waist after placing her other hand on his chest. "Are you ready to go?"

Enzo looked between us and nodded, unsure of what was going on.

Good.

He didn't need to know.

I watched them walk out and, almost like she knew I was watching, she moved her hand over his butt.

I wanted to punch something, but I needed to hold it together.

"Brother!" Garrison shouted, walking into the room a few moments later.

"Please stop calling me that."

"We are."

"Garrison. It's not the right time."

"How can you still be so uptight? That was the best... everything I have had, maybe ever."

"So happy for you." I said deadpan.

I looked at Ruby. "Thank you, as always."

"Take care of that girl. She's something special... I have a feeling."

I nodded. "I know..."

It was true. I haven't been able to put my finger on it, but there was something about her. I felt it the first time I saw her and I still feel it.

Fuck! This was a completely wasted trip since I'm leaving stressed out and thinking more about Snow than I did before I came here.

Garrison patted me on my back as we were leaving. "Everything ok brother? Who is she talking about?"

When we got outside, I looked at Garrison. "For fuck's sake. Stop with the brother shit. I have seen you more this last week than I have for the last fifteen years. We are not brothers. You made that clear when you abandoned me."

"That's not fair."

"How is it not fair?"

"That was father's choice."

"One that you didn't stop or change."

"Gage." His face fell. "I was only thirteen. I didn't really have much say, you know that."

"I know you didn't look like you gave two shits. Tell me. Did you ever try to find me?"

"Gage."

I held up my hand. "I don't want to hear it."

"Well, I do want you to know I'm sorry. I thought about you."

"Thinking about me didn't do shit." I whirled around on him. "Do you know what it was like for me?" I continued to walk and then circled back. "I was eight years old. Eight fucking years old and I was on my own. Do you know what assholes do to eight-year-olds who are on their own?"

He shook his head.

"No. You don't and trust me... you don't want to know. I learned real quick that no one was my friend. They all wanted to use me, just like father did. A means to an end. That's what I was." I laughed. "What's funny is that father got what he wanted. I had my first kill on my ninth birthday. So I became what he wanted... granted, it wasn't a kid, but some jackass who thought he could have his way with me."

"Shit."

"Yea." I smirked and continued walking.

"I'm sorry."

"Save it because the 'I'm sorry's don't do shit for me."

The rest of the walk to our house was quiet.

I expected to see Snow and Enzo there, but the house was empty.

I tried not to think about what they were doing or where they were doing it at. The look in her eyes... the hurt... I could tell she wanted to lash out at me and the way she and Enzo had their arms around one another...

"So, what are we going to do here?" Garrison asked, looking around.

"This is my home. I need to talk to Barrett to see if he's ok with you crashing here for a little while."

"Why wouldn't he?"

I cut my eyes at him. I didn't need to go into the details of what Barrett thought of him. Garrison had a slight point that he was only thirteen, but still... something could have been done. It didn't help that we weren't close beforehand. I was always some little errand boy for him instead of a brother.

I peeked out the window, expecting the boy's home any minute, and right on cue, I saw Barrett walking up the trail. I walked outside to meet him and noticed his face fell when he saw Garrison walk out behind me.

I heard Gideon mumble something about picking up strays, but ignored it.

I bounded down the stairs and met Barrett. "Can we talk?" I said under my breath.

He nodded, and we peeled away to stand by the large oak tree on the other side of the vegetable garden.

I knew Garrison had super hearing, so I wasn't really trying to stop him from hearing it, but I wanted privacy from the others.

"Is that your brother?" Barrett asked, nodding to Garrison who was still standing on the stairs.

"That is Garrison." I corrected.

"I see." Barrett said, clearly picking up on my distinction. "How's everything here?"

He bobbled his head from side to side. "Dark Queen was here earlier this week when we were at the mines and attacked Snow. Nearly choked her to death. We got back just in time and Jace had to use all his skills to save her."

"Shit." I had noticed the faint bruising on her neck, but thought it was just a shadow. "She ok?"

"She is tough as nails. She's been fine, though. Nights are a little tough, so I think she's been staying with Enzo in his room."

"And that's not a problem?"

"Hasn't been. Why? Will it be a problem for you?"

"No. Why do you ask?"

"I smelled you on her when she came back. I ignored it, but now I don't know if I should have."

"All is good here. We were traveling together, that's probably what you smelled."

He hesitated before nodding, clearly not buying it, but also not pushing it.

"So Garrison. Do you mind if he stays here for a little?"

"How long? We're kind of bursting at the seams."

"I know. Not long. The dark Queen hired him to kill Snow and bring back her liver and heart. He said he couldn't find Snow, but I think he knows her and has an affection for her and purposefully didn't find her. Anyway, he cut out the liver and heart of a boar and took it to the Queen and obviously she knows Snow isn't dead, so..."

"Shit."

"Yea. So he has no home."

"Hmm." I knew exactly what he was thinking, because I had already thought about it. The difference was that he wasn't eight years old right now.

"I know." I smirked.

"Well, he could help around the house and perhaps stay here with Snow while we're at the mines."

I didn't say anything.

"Sure. We can try it out for a little while, but..."

"I got it. Thanks."

"I'm not sure I'm doing you a favor."

"Me either," I chuckled as we walked back to the house.

Garrison looked at me. "All good?"

"Yea. You can stay for a while, but you have to help out."

"Understood."

We walked in and everyone was in the showers, getting washed up. I took this time to lay out the ground rules for him, so he knew the flow of things.

Calix came downstairs first and walked into the kitchen.

"Calix, this is Garrison. Garrison. Calix."

Calix nodded and then had a questioning look on his face.

"What's wrong?"

"I expected Snow to be back from town by now."

"I'm sure she's fine. Enzo's with her." I mocked.

"That's what I'm concerned about. They've been getting pretty close lately," he quickly added. "Not that I have a problem with that, I'm just saying."

"Of course you don't." I tried to sound as apathetic as I could, but I could see the look on his face. He was swooning over her, too. This mother fucking house and Snow!

"She is a beautiful girl. Almost mesmerizing at times." Garrison added.

I cut my eyes at him and he chuckled. Not him too!

The front door opened and Snow was laughing at something Enzo said as she walked in. She stopped and looked at me and then at Garrison.

"Hunter?" she asked confused.

"Who is Hunter?" I asked.

She pointed at Garrison.

"What the hell?"

She quickly added. "He never told me his name, so it was the name I gave him."

"You know each other?"

"I told you we did, brother."

"For the last time..." I warned, and he held his hands up.

"Brother?" She asked, looking at us.

"Don't say it out loud," Garrison joked.

"Fuck off."

"I don't understand." She looked at Garrison, ignoring me.

"It's a long story." I said.

"Can you tell me your name, then?"

"It's Garrison."

She smiled, "Nice to meet you Garrison. I don't think that was so hard."

Enzo leaned around Snow and held his hand out. "Nice to meet you, man. Gage has told us so much about you."

I rolled my eyes, regretting bringing him here.

Calix walked over. "Do you need help, Snow?"

"Please." She offloaded several of the bags she had on her arms to Calix.

"Thanks for swinging by the market to get these things."

"Always happy to help."

"You didn't run into any trouble, did you?" Their conversation faded as they walked into the kitchen.

I looked between Enzo and Garrison and didn't speak.

"Ok, well, I'm going to go change." I said, desperately wanting to escape this awkwardness.

"Do you know where I can change or sleep?" Garrison asked.

"You can take my room." Snow offered from the kitchen.

"No." I glared at her.

"I haven't been using it." She sniped back.

My eyes narrowed. "No."

Her eyes flared for a moment before she rolled them and turned back to Calix.

Enzo started to speak, but I held my hand up, silencing him. "I'm going."

I heard Enzo offering his room to Garrison as a place he could use to change as I was climbing the stairs to my room. I walked in and rested my back against the door, closing my eyes.

There was a soft knock, and I could smell her scent.

"I'm not going anywhere until you open this damn door," she warned.

I heaved off the door and opened it.
She pushed her way in and shut the door.

CHAPTER TWENTY-FIVE

SNOW - STUBBORN GAGE

I WATCHED GAGE WALK up the stairs, and I desperately wanted to run up behind him and smack him across the face. Who did he think he was?

No?

No?

He can't tell me who I can and cannot invite to stay in my room. I looked at Enzo, who seemed to be in a deep conversation with Garrison about something. I could keep staying in his room. He didn't seem to mind, and neither did the others.

Why is it that I felt irritated when Gage is around, but can't stop thinking about him when he isn't?

"I'll be right back." I said to Calix, heading for the stairs.

"Don't hurt him too badly." He teased.

I winked at him over my shoulder, causing him to laugh.

I stood outside Gage's door and took in a calming breath and then knocked.

He didn't answer. I could almost feel him staring at the door, daring me to walk away... or was it to walk in?

"I'm not going anywhere until you open this damn door."

I heard him heave off the door and gathered myself as it slowly swung open.

I stepped inside and closed the door.

"Who in the hell do you think you are?"

He looked at the ceiling and then backed away.

"So this is how it's going to be now." I stomped over to him and shoved him.

He spun around so fast... too fast and grabbed my wrists. "Don't."

I tried to pull my hands free, but his grip tightened. Something about this interaction caused my stomach to tighten and my legs to quiver. I sucked in a breath and he quickly let go.

"You need to get control of yourself."

"I have control."

He cut his eyes at me, knowing that we both knew I didn't.

I would happily strip him down right now and have my way with him... let him have his way with me if he just said the words.

My body craved him.

I craved him.

He walked over to his dresser and took his shirt off.

Fuck. Shit. Mother ass.

"Still under control?" He goaded.

"Fuck you."

He smiled.

I let out a sigh of frustration, balling my fists up, twirling in a circle.

He waited until I stopped and then grabbed his pants around his waist, hesitating.

Was he inviting me to look or warning me to look away?

I let my bottom lip drag across my teeth and he slowly shook his head before pulling down his pants in one swift motion.

My stomach was tightening all the way down to my center. I could feel myself dripping with moisture and I knew he could tell because his eyes flashed for a second... hungry... wanting.

"You think I'm going to just run over to you and what? Fuck you?"

"Thought crossed my mind."

"Do you want me to?"

He stared at me for a second, then pulled on another pair of pants.

My body was buzzing, being in the same room as him again.

I walked closer to him, still not sure if I could trust myself or him. "Why did you leave me?"

"I didn't take you as a girl to be so stupid."

"Stupid?"

"You know what I am and still you come into my room wanting more."

"What are you exactly?"

"You know."

"I know this version of you. I know the man who, against what he wanted to do, shifted to protect me. You see yourself as this monster and..." I shook my head. "You aren't."

He closed the gap between us in two gigantic steps, his chest pressed to mine. "You don't know me. You don't know the things I have done. You need to stay away from me."

I pressed forward, standing up on my tiptoes, my lips less than an inch from his, breathing in his intoxicating smell. "You don't scare me."

He closed the space between our lips even more, so they were barely touching. "I should." His warm breath swept across my face and I was so fucking hot for him right now, I could barely stand.

We stayed there breathing each other in, each fighting our own battles for giving in and taking what we wanted.

I would turn myself over to the dark Queen tomorrow, if he just reached out and pressed his lips against mine and took me on this bed. To feel him driving in to me over and over again. I could feel moisture running down my leg as my chest was heaving up and down.

"Take me." I whispered.

He didn't move.

I looked up into his eyes and saw a man torn.

"Take me Gage." I closed the distance between our lips and pressed mine against his. I pulled away and looked up at him and then went back in for another kiss. This one was deeper. He wanted it.

His tongue pushed its way in and I took all of it, grabbing him around his neck as his hands found themselves on my hips, digging into my flesh.

A light moan escaped my lips as I reached for his pants.

His hands grabbed mine and he pushed away.

"No."

"I'm getting really tired of that fucking word." I said, panting.

He pushed away from me. "You need to leave."

"Are you kidding me?"

"No." He caught himself. "Leave. Now."

"You are un-fucking-believable."

He shrugged.

"I don't know why you're fighting this."

"I'm not fighting anything."

"Tell that to your dick." I said, nodding at the bulge in his pants.

"It does that for anyone. Just ask Josie."

"You asshole." I glared at him.

"I tried to tell you." He shrugged, apathetically. It was like a switch had been flipped and there was no way I was going to break through that wall right now.

My gaze narrowed. "Yea... I guess you did." I left his room and walked up the several flights of stairs to mine and shut the door. I tried not to slam it because I didn't want to draw attention to any drama in the house.

I laid on my bed and stared out of the window, trying to let my body wind down.

Why was he being like that? It was absolutely infuriating!

I know he wanted me as much as I wanted him. I could feel it in his kiss and saw it in his pants. He was lashing out because he wanted to hurt me... why? To show me he is what he keeps saying.

I don't buy it.

I knew the real him, even if he didn't.

CHAPTER TWENTY-SIX

GAGE - ON THE RUN

IT SHOCKED ME TO see Snow in such a good mood at dinner. I was fairly certain I had pissed her off, which I didn't feel the slightest bit guilty about.

She needed to learn.

She needed to stay away.

I needed to stay away. I tried, but there was something about her that pulled me to her like a magnet, and it was infuriating. It was too dangerous for me to be around her and I didn't want to hurt her.

And I would. I know I would. It's what I do...

Most of dinner Garrison regaled the table with stories about Snow growing up in the castle. Part of me was jealous he got to grow up with her and the other part couldn't understand how he could be so close to the dark Queen for years and not go after her.

She was all my father, and as a result, Garrison talked about when I was growing up. How to kill her... how to make her pay. And there he was visiting the grounds weekly and didn't do a damn thing. Maybe if he'd done his job, then I wouldn't have-

"Isn't that right broth-" Garrison caught himself. "Isn't that right?"

"What?" I asked, less than amused.

"You used to be an amazing cook! Even at eight." He said jubilantly, like it was a good thing.

I rolled my eyes. "I had to, so I didn't starve since father was never around and you didn't really give a damn." I caught Barrett's expression out of the corner of my eye and plastered a fake smile on my face.

Calix, trying to maintain the good mood, teased, "Well, perhaps you can cook for us one night, Gage."

"Doubtful."

Snow chuckled. "He'd probably poison it or something."

I glared at her as the rest of the table burst into laughter and she glared right back with a hint of a smirk.

FUCK!

I wanted to wipe that little smirk off her face. Fuck her until her eyes rolled in the back of her head and she was reeling from the orgasm I just gave her. A memory of the night in the tavern flashed through my mind, causing my cock to twitch... I needed to get away.

"Ok. Well, if you're all done, I will take my leave." I stood up and took my plate over to the sink and made my way upstairs. I needed to get away from her because everytime she looked at me, it was like a burst of pheromones engulfed me. I knew I could have her in my bed again without even trying and while part of me wanted that, the other part knew what happened before was a mistake and could never happen again.

I laid in my bed, staring at the ceiling and could hear the house had moved the party to the campfire in the back. The smell of smoke and bosom berries filled the air. And her.

I could still smell her.

DAMN IT!

Hey. I mindlinked Eloise.

Gage?

Yes. I hated to be asked obvious questions. *Do you want to come over?*

Eesh. Weren't you just here? Did Josie not do a good enough job?

She was fine.

But you need more?

Sure. Eloise was fine. She was a little annoying at times, because she was always searching for a compliment.

Give me twenty.

Sounds fantastic. I said deadpan.

Twenty minutes. I could go downstairs for twenty minutes and not lose my shit. Plus, it may be good for her to see me with someone else. It will piss her off enough to stay away.

I headed outside and saw Snow dancing around the fire with a bottle of ale in her hand, and Enzo, Calix, and Jace dancing around her. Barrett and Gideon were in deep conversation and Garrison and Dresden were talking, while Dresden was whittling a stick.

"Gage!" Snow shouted, holding the bottle up in the air as she ran over to me.

"Snow." I said, staring down at her. She put her hands on my chest and looked up at me with those hungry eyes, like she was daring me to do something or say something.

I grabbed the bottle from her and took a sip.

"Hey! That was mine." She slapped my chest.

"I think you've had enough."

She reached for the bottle, but I held it above her head. She jumped up, trying to get it to no avail.

"Why are you such an ass?" She asked through gritted teeth.

"Why don't you learn your lesson?"

She glared at me and walked away.

I sat down in the chair and rested the bottle on my knee only to find that she had grabbed another bottle and held it up with a fuck you grin plastered across her face.

I rolled my eyes and watched as she went back to dance in between Enzo and Jace. I tried to ignore her moving and swaying her body and tried not to let the fact they kept their hands on her get under my skin.

"Knock, knock." I heard her singsong voice and turned around to see Eloise walking outside. She was wearing knee high leather boots with short black shorts and a tight glossy leather vest. She had cut her black hair short and the moon in the sky caused her eyes to glow a soft golden color.

"What are you doing here?" Enzo walked over to her.

I watched Snow's eyes follow him across the yard.

"We're going to hang out." I offered.

Eloise looked at me and then at Enzo. "Had I known you were having a party I would have asked Cana to join... she loves spending time with you boys." Eloise said letting her finger run down his chest.

"Hi. I'm... Scarlet." She said, inserting herself in the conversation with her hand out.

Eloise nodded. "Yea. I saw you at the Tav. Are you looking for a job?"

Snow laughed. "Not right now, but maybe soon." She glared at me. "Maybe you girls could teach me something." No doubt throwing my words back in my face.

Eloise laughed. "I like you."

I rolled my eyes. Of course she would. Snow seems to have that way with people.

"Well." I said, standing up. "We're going to take off." I slipped my arm around Eloise for added measure, causing her to look at me but not say anything.

"You two have fun!" Snow said without missing a beat.

"We will." I winked at her over my shoulder.

When we were far enough away, Eloise grabbed my hand and removed it from her waist. "Next time you need me to make a girl jealous, I will pass."

I looked at her and chuckled. "What are you talking about?"

"I'm a werewolf, Gage. Don't lie to me. I was practically gagging on the pheromones she was releasing when she was around you."

"I can't help she's in to me."

She laughed. "Don't bullshit me, Gage. I could smell yours too... you've got it bad for her, plus I've known you long enough to read you like an open book, like it or not. You were trying to make her jealous. I will say, though... she doesn't seem like your type... she seems too good for you."

"Ready to go for a run?"

"Thought you'd never ask." She shimmied out of her clothes and tossed them on the ground before shifting into a wolf. She was light brown with pads of white on her feet.

I shifted without taking my clothes off and watched as the shredded pieces fell to the ground.

Eloise was one of the few people who knew about me. She was the closest thing I had to family, which is why we never slept together, although no one else knew that. Our sessions usually involved running and just being our natural, wild selves.

I looked at the moon and let out a howl.

Chapter Twenty-Seven

SNOW - WET DREAMS

THE HOWL SENT A shiver down my spine.

Was it Gage?

Was Eloise a werewolf too? Is that why she came over?

Jealousy ripped through me. She could give him something I never could- that rush of running wild together. I glanced over at Barrett and caught him studying me. I didn't want him to see me pining for someone or something I could never have... again. I knew when it happened that it was likely a one-time thing which is why I savored every second of it. His feel. His touch. But along the way I had somehow fooled myself into believing he could change his mind. That I could show him he wasn't the monster he thought himself to be.

I huffed. Damn him!

I danced over to Enzo because I knew he would help me forget Gage. I hoped. "What did she mean about Cana?"

Enzo quickly glanced between the boys and then looked back at me, "Oh... uhh... nothing." He laughed uncomfortably.

I stared at each of them and could see a bit of panic in their eyes. "Pretty sure that's bullshit. What did she mean?"

Calix stepped forward and both the boys looked at him with stunned expressions. "We..."

I raised my eyebrows, waiting for an answer.

"We like to share."

"Share?"

"At the same time..."

"Oh." I realized what he was talking about. "Ohh." I started nodding rapidly. "Ok. Cool. Cool, cool, cool." I don't know why I was acting so weird, maybe because of the ale? "Like all of you?" I pointed at everyone outside and then immediately thought of Gage.

"Oh no! Goddess no!" Calix laughed. "Just us three, typically."

"Could you imagine Gage?" Enzo chimed.

Calix and Jace both laughed then realized what they were laughing at and who they were talking to.

"Right... uhh anyways..." Jace said scratching his head.

I smiled. "That seems like fun."

They all looked at one another.

"Who wouldn't want you three stud muffins?" I took another sip of ale and walked back to the fire.

I could tell they were still shocked by my reaction, but I didn't want to make it a big deal. I knew I was inexperienced in all- or most things sexual, but was quickly realizing how much I still had to learn. I didn't want to make it obvious because I didn't want them to handle me with kid gloves. I had never really thought about having all of them at the same time, but now I was definitely curious. That would seem like a lot, but then I wouldn't have to choose.

I stared at each of them and thought about what it would be like in bed with them. I felt like Jace would be kind and nurturing, Enzo would be fun and wild and Calix... I don't know about him. I was still having a hard time wrapping my head around having them all at the same time.

"You ok?" Garrison asked walking over.

"Yea."

He looked around and then leaned in and whispered. "Don't let Gage get to you... he's been through a lot and doesn't let people in." He laughed. "Who am I to talk? He still hasn't let me in..."

I offered him the bottle.

"Fuck Gage." I said a little too loudly, so I patted the air. "Just kidding, of course." I smiled at Barrett.

I don't know what it was about him that drove me crazy. Earlier tonight, when he was sitting by the fire... the way the light flickered across his dark and worn face with his constant shadow of a beard and something about the fuck off attitude affixed to his forehead was driving me crazy.

I yawned as a sudden onslaught of exhaustion swept over me. "I think I'm going to bed."

Garrison looked around. "I still don't have a bed..."

"You can stay in mine tonight until they figure something out." I looked over at Enzo and saw he was listening to us. "Assuming that's ok?"

"Yea, of course." Enzo smiled, and I noticed Jace and Calix both rolled their eyes.

"I'll stay in yours another night." I said, looking at both of them.

They both smiled and Enzo added, "I'll be up in a little while."

"That's fine."

I made my way inside, pausing briefly at Gage's door, and then continued up the stairs.

As soon as my head hit the pillow, I was out.

I softly knocked on the door.

Gage opened, filling the doorway with his shirt off.

I couldn't help but stare at the beautifully sculpted torso with speckles of dark hair spread throughout. I reached up to run my hands across it, feeling the ripples below the tips of my fingers.

"You shouldn't be here, Snow."

"I had to check on you... I was worried."

"You shouldn't be."

"I don't want to be, but that doesn't change the fact I am." He let me gently push him back, so I was standing in his room.

I closed the door behind me and stared up at him.

"You should leave." He warned.

"You should make me."

He shook his head as I closed the small distance between us. I ran my hands over his face, cupping it in my hands. The warmth of his skin penetrating down to my bones. "Your eyes are so blue... like crystals..."

"All the better to see you with." He said, pushing me back against the wall, pressing his chest against mine. He looked down at me, his lips only inches away, and I wanted to stand on my toes to close the distance. I wanted to feel his lips on mine.

My heart was thumping so hard and so loud in my chest, I thought for sure it was creating a hole to beat out of.

I ran both of my hands across his chest and down his arms. "Your arms... they're so big."

He smirked playfully. "All the better to lift you with." He grabbed me under the arms and slid me up the wall, so we were face to face.

I wrapped my legs around him and leaned in, letting our lips touch. I was hungry for his kiss, sinking into it, my tongue finding his and doing a dance. I felt my body moving, mimicking my tongue against him, pulsing and grinding in perfect rhythm. I felt my breasts swell with pure excitement and felt my insides tighten.

I pulled back for air, running my thumb across his bottom lip, staring into his crystal blue eyes. "Your mouth..." I had no words that could describe it.

I saw a playful wickedness flash across his face. "All the better to eat you with."

In one swift motion, too fast for my eyes to keep up with, he ripped off my pants and lifted me further up the wall so I was sitting on his shoulders.

"Oh, fuck."

I felt his smile on the inside of my leg as he wrapped his arms around my thighs and buried his face between my legs. My back arched at the mere anticipation of what was coming next. He looked up at me and my hands combed through his hair. He smiled again and leaned in.

The warm flicker of his tongue across my clit caused my insides to tighten immediately.

"You're so wet." He spread my legs just a little further and licked me from the bottom to the top and sank his tongue in.

"Ohhh."

He started to hum, and the light vibration sent shivers up my spine. He pulsed in deeper and deeper and then pulled out and sucked.

"You taste so good." He said before diving back in.

He shifted the weight on his shoulders and slid his arm up between his chest, and I felt his finger at my base as his tongue continued to swirl seductively. Without hesitation, he stuck his finger in and pulsed, and then added another. My body arched off the wall as I pressed further onto his fingers.

"Do you like that?"

I moaned in satisfaction, pressing my hands on the ceiling for balance.

"What about this?" He added a third finger, and I felt myself stretch around him as the pressure filled me and his mouth continued to suck and lick.

"Oh." I could feel my body getting closer to the edge, like a volcano waiting to explode.

"Not yet."

I looked down at him, panting heavily.

He pulled out his fingers and looked at me. "Not yet."

I felt my insides reeling down, like a spinning top that had lost its speed.

He leaned in closer and my body bucked, pressing my eager pussy closer to his mouth.

He chuckled. "No."

"No?"

and slowly began to pump. "Because I would really like it to be your cock right now."

"Fuckkk." He seethed between his teeth.

"I'm going to take that as a yes." I pushed his shoulder laying him back on the bed so I could climb on top of him. I ripped off my shirt.

"Fuck me." He said, reaching up to grab my breasts.

I knew he was talking to himself, but I answered. "I plan to," and then I slid down softly unto his shaft.

I heard his breathing stutter as I began to rock back and forth on him. My body was already primed from my dream, so I didn't have much further to go.

He sat up and took my breast in his mouth as I continued to rock faster and faster. "Enzo." I panted out.

He grabbed my lower back pressing me to him, sending him deeper in. I pushed him back on the bed so he was laying on his back. "No." I said, a memory of Gage flashing before me. I moved my hand and started rubbing my clit.

"Fuck, you're so hot." He grabbed my bouncing breasts.

"Enzo." I let out a muted scream at the same time he released. I felt my pussy pulsing around his cock as wave after wave crashed around me.

I stopped moving and just sat on him for a second.

"Well, that was a happy surprise," he said, looking at me.

I gave him a quick peck on his nose. "Happy surprise indeed."

I climbed off and I went into the bathroom to clean up.

Chapter Twenty-Eight

MERLA - A MOTHER'S LOVE

I FELT THE COLD hard stone under the talons of my little black bird as I landed on the edge of the castle's windowsill.

That little fucking miner!

He got in the way and ruined everything. Her heart was right there for the taking.

I squawked out in frustration and then quickly regained my composure.

All is well, though. She is dead and I feel younger!

I shifted back into my human form and sauntered over to my wardrobe to put on my black silk robe. Tonight I was going to soak in my bathtub and relish that little bitch's death.

"Mirror, mirror on the wall…" I called across the room, slipping my arms in.

"Yes, my Queen?

"Who is the fairest of them all?"

I walked over to stare at the silver satin ribbon spinning in the mirror.

"My Queen, you are the fairest here, but Snow White is still alive, and she is much fairer than you."

"No! That can't be. She's not alive. I saw the life drain out of her eyes myself. I saw her color fade. You must be mistaken." I rambled in a panicked state.

"My Queen. I cannot tell a lie."

I knew this was the truth.

FUCK!

How is that little soul-sucking bitch still alive?

She was dead before those miners got there. Were they magic? Did they bring her back to life?

With my silence, the mirror contorted back into a simple mirror on the wall.

I stared at myself for a moment, and there it was.

Another wrinkle.

She was still alive and sucking my life away!

I looked at my belly and felt the useless creature inside, growing, taking more of my life. They always did until they were born.

Nine months of agony for eighteen years of bliss and youth.

I paced the room, trying to think of what I could do next.

Snow had to die. It was as simple as that, but why was it proving to be so difficult? This is the second time she's evaded death, and I was growing impatient.

I couldn't trick her as an old lady again. She wouldn't be dumb enough to fall for it a second time, but perhaps as a child...

Yes. She always had a soft heart.

I walked over to my bench and pulled out a number of ingredients to concoct a poison that would kill her quickly. Usually, I would opt for the slow, torturous death, but Snow has managed to escape too many times! I needed it to be quick and without question.

I looked around the room for something I could use and then a deliciously evil thought crossed my mind. I excitedly, but quietly, headed down the hall towards the hidden doorway behind the portrait. The air was cool and damp as it blew up the stone staircase.

"Where is she?" One of the male prisoners rushed to the edge of the cell, pressing his face through the slats.

I paused a moment to look at him and was filled with disgust. His clothes were rags and threads, barely hanging onto his bony body, and he was filthy- covered head to toe in dirt with bloody scraped knuckles and hair that hung down, long and greasy.

"Get away from me. Your stench is filling what little clean air is down here."

"What did you do with her? Where is my Isabelle?"

"Who is that?"

"The woman you took."

"Oh. Yes. Her. She's dead. I had to use her body for something."

The man crumbled to a pile of bones on the floor as sobs filled the air.

"You're a monster." He mumbled through gasps of air.

"Thank you. I'm glad someone can appreciate me." I smiled, happy with myself, and continued the walk down the stone corridor. When I got to the end, I placed my hand on the wall, allowing the stones to separate, revealing the hidden chamber.

The air was just a touch warmer in here, more muggy than warm. I walked over to the body lying in the center of the room and picked up her delicate wrist and pulled the bracelet off and let it crash back down with a thud. "Oops."

Her face didn't react or move. I hadn't expected it to.

She'd been like this for the last eighteen years.

Like a porcelain doll frozen in time.

That's what she was. Frozen in time. Ever since Snow's birth... she transferred her life force to Snow and fell into the coma. Most had thought she had died, but no... she was still hanging on by a thread- a miscalculation in my magic, no doubt, and a constant reminder of my failure.

"You know..." I rubbed my hand across her forehead. "Everyone thinks you're dead. You should be, but for some reason, you won't die." Not that I hadn't tried, but every time I moved to harm her in some way, a sort of force field appeared around her, preventing me from causing her significant damage.

Was this what was helping Snow?

I shook my head. No. I was able to kill her! She was dead before those miners showed up and ruined everything. I know she was.

No. She didn't have this force protecting her. She was vulnerable and I would take advantage of that.

"Your daughter, or should I say my daughter, is proving to be quite the troublemaker. But it's ok. She won't be alive much longer." I said, holding the bracelet up in the light, examining it.

How thoughtful was I? Gifting a mother's jewelry to her beloved daughter. I made my way back through the now silent corridor and to my room, where I dipped the bracelet into the concoction, careful not to touch the goo. In bubbled slightly as the metal touched the greenish tinged liquid and when I pulled it up to let the excess drip off, the green faded to clear around the bracelet, leaving only a slight discoloration where my fingers were holding it.

"Perfect."

Still holding the one little piece that didn't touch the poison, I lowered it into a black velvet bag.

"Now what to do?" I smiled. "I know exactly what will make me feel better."

I decided to go downstairs and enjoy my dinner before heading out tomorrow morning.

She won't escape again!

CHAPTER TWENTY-NINE

CALIX - HOME FOR THE WAYWARD SOULS

I SWUNG THE PICKAXE into the side of the mountain as chips of rock flew off. How could Enzo sleep with Snow? We had a pact.

I swung again and felt a tap on my shoulder.

"Hey, can we talk?"

Enzo.

I swung one more time and then turned around. "Hey man, what's up?" I tried to hide my irritation, but knew I failed and part of me didn't care.

He pulled his face.

Good. I'm glad he felt guilty, or at the very least knew what he did wasn't cool.

I raised my eyebrows, waiting for him to speak.

"So last night..."

My eyebrows only grew higher on my face.

"Man. Stop! You know... are you going to make me say it?" He asked with an uncomfortable smile.

"Say what?" I crossed my arms in front of my chest.

"Dude. I had no control. She woke up in a frenzy and looked at me, then kissed me and then...she practically commanded me to do it."

I nodded.

"You know I wouldn't typically break our pact."

"So what happens now?"

"She made it clear that it meant nothing."

"Yea, I saw her after... in the bathroom."

"So you knew?" He sighed.

"Of course. Nothing can happen in the house without everyone finding out!"

"Well, like I said... I'm sorry."

"Look. I'm not mad-ish anymore. Just don't do it again."

"You know, it's hard for girls to resist this body, though." He said, puffing out his chest as he backed away.

Jace walked up to me when Enzo was gone. "Well?"

I looked at him and put my hand on his shoulder. "They had sex, but he made it seem like she wasn't looking for anything serious..."

"So you're saying there's still a chance?"

"Maybe for me... I don't know about you." I laughed, picking up the axe again.

If we took too much time to talk, Barrett would get upset. We were already a little behind since we didn't have Gage and Enzo last week, although Gage was here when we showed up this morning. He seemed extra broody and if I didn't know any better, I would say he was upset by Enzo and Snow hooking up, but that couldn't be the case because he couldn't stand her. Which I also couldn't figure out why. Perhaps he didn't get what he needed from Eloise last night.

Gage was the only one in the house who I've never quite figured out. He was the dark and broody type and always seemed angry.

When he first came to the house, he didn't talk to me for a long time, although the only person he did talk to was Barrett, and that was still on limited occasion. It was obvious he was going through some stuff, always jumpy and skittish. I couldn't imagine what he had gone through living on his own at such a young age.

I wasn't much older than him and even though my up-bringing wasn't a basket full of bosom berries, it was still more stable than Gage's. As a child, I lived in a castle as part of the help in the kitchen. I can remember from a young age, always helping with something... either washing dishes, stacking plates, stirring stews.

Barrett lived there, but I never knew his position, and I never got the courage to ask. I knew he wasn't the King or prince of the castle, but always felt like he held some kind of important position and he was always kind to me. A few times, he had caught me running around the castle, so we had developed an odd kind of friendship early on, where he would look out for me, helping me stay out of trouble.

One night, I was moving around the castle and heard him arguing with the prince. I couldn't really make out what he was saying, but saw him storm out of the library and slam the door. It wasn't long after when Barrett had his bags packed and was leaving. I don't know why, but I ran after him and joined him. He didn't question it and was happy for the company. We eventually found the home we live in now, and it's been growing ever since- almost a home for the wayward soul.

I tried to go back a few times to see my mother, but the castle looked dark and shut down, like everyone had moved out, which seemed odd. I thought about asking Barrett about it, but seeing the enormous blow up fight he had with the prince- one that I most definitely shouldn't have seen- I never said anything.

After lunch, Enzo grabbed Jace and me into a huddle. "You boys want to go to Ruby's tonight? I feel like I should make it up to you."

"You are trying to appease us with sex?"

"Yes." He said matter-of-factly.

"You know us so well."

"What do you think Snow will think?" Jace asked, resting his pickaxe on his foot.

"I don't think she will care. I really got the feeling last night wasn't about having sex with me, but more about getting the frustrations from her dream out. I almost felt like I wasn't even there." He wiped his finger under his eye like he was wiping away a tear. "You know... I feel so used."

"Well, she could have used me." I said.

Since the first day she came to our house, there was something about her. I don't know if it was her innocence, the rough life she had or something else... but I felt drawn to her. I still enjoyed going to Ruby's, but I left feeling unfulfilled... maybe guilty? Part of me wanted Snow and no one else, but I didn't really feel like I could say that to the boys without getting made fun of, although I was starting to get the feeling they felt the same.

"Me too." Jace agreed.

Gage walked over. "Enough. Stop talking about her. I'm tired of hearing her name."

"Did you want a piece of her too? Is that why you're more pissy than usual?"

"No." He walked away and continued hitting at the wall he'd been working at all morning.

He had knocked out a fairly sizeable chunk, more than most of us could do in a day. He must have come back with super strength, I laughed.

I continued working away on my section of the wall when I heard Gage drop his pickaxe and look at Barrett.

"We need to get home. Snow's been attacked." Barrett said, looking at everyone.

I watched Enzo take off without hesitation.

What I would give for super speed right now...

Chapter Thirty

GARRISON - PROTECTOR OF NOTHING

THE HOUSE WAS EERILY quiet when no one was here. I had been following Snow around most of the day and I could tell she was getting annoyed with me, so I decided to give her a little space, plus it gave me a chance to do some snooping.

I walked around the different levels and stuck my head into each of the bedrooms, starting with Enzo's since he was the highest level, aside from Snow's. I noticed for the most part, all the rooms were setup the same.

Small space with a gigantic bed, one dresser, one desk and one night stand.

Aside from the main floor and part of the second floor, the rooms were built into the side of a tree, which was partly in each person's room. Dresden's room, of course, had part of the tree notched out to form a shelf to hold books and a few potted plants.

Barrett and Gideon had the most organized rooms of the entire group on the third floor. They each had a lamp on the end of their desk with neatly stacked papers and perfectly aligned pens. I toyed with the idea of rifling through the papers to see if there was anything of note, but they mostly looked like random scribbles and I didn't want to leave my scent in the rooms for too long.

I got the feeling that most of them had some sort of gift, even if they weren't sharing it with the group. I knew Gage was a werewolf, but no one, aside from Snow, seemed to know that and I had heard stories of Enzo's super speed even though no one knew what he was. I'd seen a lot of mythical creatures in my time, but none with his kind of speed.

When this thing with the Queen blew over and I was out on my own, I'd have to do some research into creatures with super speed. I had a few contacts on the third mountain I could talk to about things like this.

I ended in Gages room and sat on the edge of his bed. Part of me wanted to see what it was like to be him and the other part, the more dominant part, wanted him to scent me in his room to know I was here. It wasn't really a malicious thought, as much as it was a reminder that I was here and wanting to work on our relationship.

When he left, I never thought I'd see him again and our bond wasn't strong enough at the time to mindlink him from a far distance, although, admittedly, I never tried. But we had spent more time together in the last week than we had spent in our entire lives. I wanted to make up the fact I abandoned him, or rather, let father abandon him all those years ago.

Looking at him, I felt guilty for all the hardships he had to endure. He wouldn't tell me everything, but I had an idea, and the images that flashed through my head pissed me off more than they should have.

I looked around his room and laid back on his bed and was fairly certain he was going to kick my ass later for doing this, but I didn't care. I didn't know how much time I had left here, so I wanted to enjoy every moment I could with him, even if that meant him roughing me up a bit.

I couldn't stay holed up in this house forever... in Snow's room.

Which brought me to my second thought.

I had watched her grow up over the years and was completely dumbfounded to learn she was the Queen's daughter.

Right under my nose.

Although... she may have been the first of the Queen's children, I wouldn't have killed. She had this pure innocence to her, completely opposite from the dark Queen. Perhaps the Queen somehow managed to pass what little goodness she had remaining to Snow when she implanted her in the old Queen's body.

The thought sickened me. All those families out there... destroyed by the dark Queen. Mothers killed and children born, all the while the families have no idea the Queen will be coming after them on their eighteenth birthday.

She had to pay. That much was certain. And the first priority was keeping Snow alive, because every day she was alive made the Queen weaker. I needed to get the house together so we could come up with a plan. All of those that had tried in the past were killed, but perhaps there was another way. We just had to figure it out.

It's been my mission, my father's mission and my grandfather's before him to rid this kingdom of that evil bitch because of all the countless things she's done.

I could feel myself getting worked up the more I thought about her.

I had taken out one of her evil spawn and while part of me felt guilty, the other part knew it's what needed to be done, even if Gage or Snow didn't approve.

I remember how pissed he was when he found me after the kill. I don't think I'd ever seen him so enraged. He said Snow wouldn't want that and encouraged me to wait while we found another way to kill the Queen, because that was the end goal.

Her death.

But she always seemed to find some way to get out of it, but not this time.

Not on my watch- our watch.

I sat up on the bed when I heard voices. I focused on them and recognized Snow talking.

The sun was still up, so it couldn't have been the boys.

Then panic filled me.

FUCK!

I raced out of the bedroom and leapt with ease in one bound down the stairs and was at the front door two steps later, swinging it open, pressing my hands to the handrail on the porch.

"Snow!"

She looked up at me and smiled, and I relaxed.

Standing in front of her was a child, no more than ten years old, wearing worn rags and a shawl draped over her head.

"Look at this Gage! Show him!" Snow encouraged the child. "It looks just like my mothers! I remember seeing pictures of her with this very same bracelet." She said exuberantly.

The girl turned her head to look at me and from under her shawl I could see the dark hair and the evil green eyes at the same time a smirk crossed her face.

Gage! Hel-

Before I could finish calling for help, I saw a bolt of red light aiming right towards me. It felt like a dragon kick to the chest, sending me flying backwards through the house.

Before everything went black, I heard Snow scream, followed by silence.

Snnnno...

Chapter Thirty-One

JACE - SECOND TIMES THE CHARM

It was like déjà vu.

We got to the house as quick as we could. Enzo was already standing over Snow's body, her head in his lap, and Gage had run ahead of us, even though he wasn't anywhere to be seen.

Enzo looked at me with panic in his eyes. "She's gone."

I shook my head. She couldn't be.

She was gone last time, and we brought her back.

I brought her back.

"She's not breathing and her skin is cold and her face is blue."

"No. We can fix her."

Barrett grabbed my arm. "Jace."

I shook my head. "No. We're going to fix her. We shouldn't have left her alone." I could feel the ache deep in my bones. I hadn't gotten to tell her... tell her how I feel about her... how we all feel about her. She was like a beacon of light that walked through our front door and lit our entire world on fire. She was our Snow. Not just Enzo's, or mine, or Calix's, or anyone else's, for that matter. She was our Snow.

"She wasn't alone." Barrett reminded.

"Where's Garrison?" Dresden asked.

Enzo looked up and answered. "Inside. Gage has him."

"Is he ok?" Dresden asked.

"He says it was the Queen, dressed as a young child. He saw the way she looked at him and before he could do anything, she shot a bolt of light at him, knocking him unconscious." He added. "He did say he heard Snow scream before he lost consciousness."

"Fucking hell." Calix yelled.

I pressed my ear to Snow's nose and there wasn't a single breath.

I pressed my fingers to her throat.

Nothing.

Not a single pulse.

Her skin was cold, and she had a bluish tinge.

I looked up at Barrett and shook my head.

"No." Enzo said, rocking back and forth.

I had never seen him cry before and here he was in his most vulnerable state, a state he never let anyone see... We all knew and accepted that his constant jovial state was his defense mechanism- the guards he put in place to not feel pain, or connection. But again, Snow transcended those barriers and had weaseled her way in. Enzo could say that she was just for fun and didn't mean anything to him, but it was plain to see that wasn't true. Again, it was him putting on a front.

Gage stepped through the door and looked at all of us, his face as hard as stone.

"Gage." I breathed.

"No."

His face never broke, but I felt the air shift around him. Around me.

He walked down the stairs and scooped Snow up and carried her inside and laid her on the couch.

"I'm going to kill her. I'm going to kill the dark Queen." His eyes flashed black, dark as night, a contrast to his typical icy blue, and then they snapped back.

"Gage." Enzo warned.

"Shut your fucking mouth right now." He held his finger up.

Barrett stepped in. "We're all hurting... mourning, but we need to remember we are family."

"He's not." Enzo said, pointing at Garrison. "We left him here with Snow to protect her and look what happened."

"Hey..." Garrison held up his hands. "I had nothing to do with this."

Gage looked at him. "Are you sure?"

"Are you fucking kidding me right now, brother?" Garrison asked, wobbling as he rose to his feet.

"Tell me you aren't working with the dark Queen and I'll believe you."

"I won't." Enzo snapped, but Gage shot him a look that shut him up and even caused him to retreat a little.

"I'm not working with the Queen. I told you. I wanted Snow alive just as much as you did."

Enzo huffed.

"It's true. She could have killed me. In fact, I'm surprised she didn't. I betrayed her, and she rarely lets that slide."

"That's the point. She could have easily killed you, but she didn't. Why?"

"Can you describe the light you saw?" I asked, curious.

"It was like this red flash and it felt like a dragon had kicked me in the chest."

"A red light?"

"Yea, with specks of green. I'd never seen it before, although I'm not one for fighting with powerful, evil, witches..."

Interesting. "It should have killed you."

"What?" Half of the house said.

"The curse she lobbed. It's a death curse. There are only a few and even fewer mages, or witches, that are powerful enough to pull them off. The one she did is called the Dolorum Inferens Mortem Curse... or painful death. She wasn't messing around."

"It was painful..." He said rubbing his chest.

"I just don't understand how you're still alive."

"I don't know." He looked at Snow and his face fell. "I failed you all, and I failed her. My job, my entire life, has been to rid this kingdom of that evil dark bitch of a Queen and every time she slips through my fingers. My job was to protect Snow." He buried his face in his hands in frustration.

"I will find all of her little seeds of youth she has implanted, and I will destroy them all. I will take away her life source and then I will kill her!"

"Snow didn't want that." I said.

"Snow is dead!" Garrison shouted. "Because that... that bitch of a Queen killed her!"

"Tell me more about her... what you saw." I asked, still holding out the slightest thread of hope we could bring her back again.

"I had been following Snow around all day and she was getting irritated, so I stayed inside," he held up his hand. "I know you don't need to yell at me now." He sat down at the table. "I stayed inside while she went outside. She said she was looking for her horse she hadn't seen in a while."

"We think the Queen shrunk her horse the last time she was here." I added, trying to give context.

"I heard people talking, and I panicked and when I raced to the door, I saw a young girl standing in front of her and Snow was smiling."

"What were they talking about?" Gage asked, kneeling by Snow's head.

It was interesting to see this side of Gage- a softer side. We had all assumed he couldn't stand Snow, but the way he was acting right now... he was hurting...

"I don't know, but Snow... she looked up... she looked happy." I paused and started waving my finger excitedly. "The bracelet. She said it looked just like her mother's! She said the girl found it in town... Snow... she was so excited and that's when the little girl turned to look at me. She had a scarf wrapped around her head and when she cut her eyes at me, I saw the darkness in them and knew it was a disguise. She smirked at me and that's when the bolt of light shot out and hit me and as I was flying back through the house, I heard Snow scream and then... nothing."

Gage ran his hands over Snow, through her hair, around her neck, down her arms.

"What are you looking for?" I asked.

"I don't know." He continued searching, lifting, moving. "There are no wounds."

"No wounds?" I asked in shock.

He looked at me. "None."

I joined him in his search, the slightest bit of hope coursing through me.

We picked up her legs, her arms, looked at her stomach, her back, ran our fingers through her hair.

Nothing.

"What does this mean?" Enzo asked.

"Could be a spell or poison." Gage said.

"She does like her poisons." Garrison chimed in.

"Would Snow have drank it?" Enzo asked.

I opened Snow's mouth and nothing showed she had ingested any type of poison.

"Well?" Enzo asked, looking over my shoulder.

"The most common poisons have distinct smells... almonds, oranges, and some have a metallic smell."

"Metallic smells?" Gage asked.

He shot a glance at Garrison and Barrett, like he was having some sort of conversation with them that no one else could hear.

"Is there something you want to share with the rest of us?" I pried. Part of me had always suspected that Gage and Barrett could communicate telepathically, but I never pushed it.

He looked at me, startled.

"You look like you have an idea." I tried to recant, not wanting to distract from Snow.

He nodded.

"Right... Can you smell something on her?"

He shook his head. "No, but this..." he pointed to the bracelet on her wrist. "That is new." He looked at Garrison.

"He's right. She didn't have that on this morning."

Enzo reached for it, but I held my hand out to stop him.

"What are you doing?" He barked.

"If it's laced with poison, it could kill you, too!"

He took a step back and sighed in frustration.

"Fine. But get it off her!"

Dresden came running into the living room a minute later. "Here. Here, use these." He said, thrusting a pair of pliers and tongs into the middle of the group.

I looked at Gage, who snatched both of the items and handed one to me. "You got this?" He asked.

I nodded and used the tongs to grab the bracelet while he used the pliers to pop the clasp.

"What do we do with it once it's off?"

Dresden ran out of the room again and was back a moment later. "Here. It's a stone pot I use to store my hot tools."

He opened the lid and sat it on the floor at our feet.

I eased the bracelet into the container and Gage and I dumped the tools in as well.

"I think it goes without saying, but no one touch those items. We don't know what they are or if they're poison-"

"Barrett." I called, looking down at Snow.

Her color was returning. I felt her arms and then her head and could feel a heat returning.

"I think..." I hesitated to say the words because I didn't want to get anyone's hopes up... but...

Her eyes fluttered open and her gaze landed on Gage. "Gage..."

He looked down at her and grabbed her hand. "Hey Snow."

They stared at one another for a brief second and then, remembering they weren't alone, he let go of her hand, stood up and walked away.

She looked around the rest of the room slowly. "What happened?"

"The dark Queen." The door slammed as Gage left. "She disguised herself as that little girl."

"Her bracelet looked just like my mother's that my father had talked about." She rubbed her face.

"It probably was," Enzo said, sitting by her head. "She probably found it and poisoned it, knowing you'd recognize it."

She sat up and looked around. "Thank you..."

"Careful." I warned.

"I feel... fine." She said, wiggling and moving different parts of her body.

"You do seem to heal rather quickly." I said, as my mind was rapidly trying to figure out why. This wasn't the first time I'd noticed this. Perhaps she had some other kind of magic.

"We thought you were dead." Enzo said, rubbing her head.

"I would have been, if it wasn't for you all finding that bracelet." She swung her feet to the floor. "I'm going after her. I'm going after the dark Queen." She looked at Garrison. "She won't stop coming."

He nodded in agreement.

"We can't kill her children. We need to find another way."

Garrison sighed.

"We have to find another way." She turned her gaze to Enzo. "I want to go to Ruby's."

I looked at Calix, shocked, who just shrugged.

"I need to learn how to do magic. I need to work with her witches. I have to be able to defend myself."

Enzo placed his hand on hers. "Ok. We'll go to Ruby's."

"Maybe tomorrow?" I suggested. "You did just come back to life... for the second time..."

She chuckled. "Fine. Tomorrow then."

"I'm going to find Gage." Garrison said, walking outside.

CHAPTER THIRTY-TWO

MERLA - BETTER DO SOME MAGIC

I WAS ENJOYING MY glass of brandy and finishing up my meal when the King walked in.

Why hadn't I killed him yet? I wondered impatiently.

I knew why. I needed his power.

If he was dead, it would wreak havoc for me.

"Good evening, darling." He waved.

I rolled my eyes.

He was a mindless drone I had programmed to be obedient and obtuse, which made me wonder what happened the night Snow escaped. How was he able to break out of the trance long enough to warn her?

Unless he was faking? No... there was no way he was that good of an actor.

I studied him as he bumbled over to the chair at the end of the table and called the servant to bring his dinner.

"My King." I sang out in the most cheerful tone I could manage.

He looked at me and smiled.

A test, perhaps?

I sauntered over to stand beside him, placing my hand on his shoulder. "I have some distressing news, I'm afraid."

He looked up. His eyes were misty swirls of gray. "What is it, my Queen? You can tell me anything." He gently laid his hand over mine.

"It's Snow. I believe I may have found her."

His face pulled, but he didn't say anything.

"Are we still in agreement that she must be executed?"

He studied my face. "Is that what we agreed to?" He asked, cocking his head, legitimate confusion twisting his face. He rubbed his head. "I can't remember..."

"We did." I nodded. "She attacked you and tried to kill me before running away."

He sighed. "If that is what we agreed to, then it must be done. What kind of King would I be if I allowed special privileges to my family?"

I studied his face, but he gave nothing away. "And you're ok with this?"

"I will not lie. It does trouble me some, but again. She has to be punished for her crimes against the King and Queen. If it had been anyone else, it wouldn't even be a question and therefore should not be a question with her."

I nodded, satisfied with his answer.

"So, when can we expect to see her?"

"I'm hoping to have her here very soon."

"Perfect." He took another bite of food. "Would you like to move your seat down here and join me?" The uptick in his voice sounded hopeful.

I dragged my hand out, feigning sadness. "I would, my King, but I've just finished and I have to check to see if we're closer to bringing Snow in." I hesitated one second. "Should we perform her execution in the town center as a symbol to the people?"

He nodded. "A fair and impartial Kingdom."

I rubbed my hand down his cheek. "Good..." Boy.

I walked out of the room, leaving him sitting at the table.

I would have to look into his lapse with Snow later. I didn't need anything impeding my final plans. I needed to know I could trust him to do the things I required.

I walked into my bedroom and locked the door, pressing my back against it.

These last several weeks had been exhausting, and the shifting was taking so much out of me, but it was fine now. I just needed to get her heart and liver and I would be good as new. Should be soon now...

I sauntered into the bathroom and slipped out of my dress. I ran my fingers along the edge of the bathtub to the handles. I wanted it piping hot tonight to soothe my achy muscles. I tossed in a bit of lemongrass and fresh lavender sprigs and watched them float around carelessly before dipping my toe in. It burned, but only for a second so I sank the rest of my body in so the water hit just under my chin.

I leaned back, resting my head on the edge of the tub, and closed my eyes, taking in the delicious scents when I felt a pair of rough hands on my neck, gripping my collarbone tightly.

I flinched only for a second before I recognized them.

I opened my eyes and saw the bearded beauty looking down at me.

"My Queen." He smiled.

"My Huntsman." I closed my eyes again, letting his fingers rub my shoulders.

His hands dipped down into the water, roughly taking my breast in his palm.

"Are you going to make me a happy woman?"

"I serve to make you happy, my Queen," his voice faltered.

I sat up, causing his hands to fall off my breasts, and spun to look at him. He was completely nude and a sight to behold.

He sighed.

"Out with it!" I demanded. I didn't have time for excuses.

"She is alive. Snow is still alive."

"What!" I yelled, causing the wind to stir up and the lights to flicker.

He looked down, ashamed.

"How is this possible? How does she keep surviving? What was the point of putting you in that house if you can't do what needs to be done? She is a fucking child!"

"She's no longer a child. Isn't that the-"

"I know she's not a child by age anymore, but compared to me, she is!"

He retreated.

I climbed out of the bath, no longer enjoying it, and wrapped myself in a towel. I had so many other plans for this evening and this was in none of them. How the fuck did she survive the poison? I put the damn bracelet on her myself!

I saw her body turn blue. Felt her skin grow cold!

Those fucking miners.

I screamed out again, running my forearm across the counter in the bathroom, sending all the bottles of lotions and perfumes crashing to the floor.

"I'm sorry my Queen."

I stared at him in a heaving fury.

"Are you still loyal to me?"

He looked confused. "Of course, my Queen."

"When I found you all those years ago living in the woods, I could have left you there. I could have killed you. I could have let those men continue to do horrible things to you. But I didn't."

I paced around him, letting my fingers glide across his taut back.

"No. I protected you. Defended you. I took care of you with the expectation you would return the favor one day."

"I will, my Queen."

His words felt empty.

"Until recently, I thought her name was Scarlet. I hadn't talked with you in a while and was unaware of the situation."

"But you're aware now?"

"Yes. Snow must die." His dark eyes shifted between mine.

"Yes." I felt my eye twitch with a hint of excitement. "Tell me. If you know now, then why didn't you kill her and bring me her heart and liver?"

"The others were there. I can't defeat them all... and my brother. He has sworn to protect Snow."

"I see. How did that Huntsman end up at your house? I didn't think you two were close."

"We're not. He had killed one of your children and I joined up with him to stop him from killing anymore. The only way I knew how was to befriend him."

"I see and what is the plan now?"

"We have no plan? Not yet."

"So I don't need to worry about a bunch of miners storming the castle?"

He laughed. "No. Snow has managed to use her looks to get the men to fall over themselves for her."

"But not you?"

"Her looks do nothing for me."

"She is very beautiful." I tested.

"She is not ugly, my Queen, but she has nothing on your beauty. You, by far, are the most beautiful woman."

I smiled. "My dear Gage..." I said, standing in front of him, letting my towel fall. "I've missed our... sessions. It's been a long time..." I stared into his dark silver eyes, almost black, and saw my Gage, not the piss ant with the blue eyes. This is the one I had created and he was mine to do with, what I wanted.

He stepped forward and wrapped his arm around my waist, pulling me into him. "How do you please a Queen that can have the world?"

"I'm sure you can find a way. You used to be good at that."

"We have the bathtub..." He shoved me against it, turning me around. "I want to bend you over and the edge of this tub and fuck you until you see stars."

I placed my hands on the edge with my ass sticking out and felt his skin press against my back as he leaned over to whisper in my ear. "Do you still have our safe word?"

My insides quivered at the thought of what he would do to me. "Bandowick."

"Bandowick." He seethed through his teeth and then pressed into me hard and fast without warning.

I cried in ecstasy, as the pain bit deep within and I felt myself stretching around him, taking him in. He pulled out and smacked my ass hard, causing a sting to travel up my back and I cried out, "Again!"

He smacked again before grabbing my hips and slamming me back into him.

"Gage." I breathed.

"Shut up!" He ordered and my insides clenched. "Where are our toys?"

"I moved them into another room."

"You moved them?" He was disappointed.

I hated to disappoint him, so I hurriedly explained. "I think you will like it."

"Take me there." He snapped, pulling out of me before grabbing my wrists and pinching them behind my back. It caused a burn in my shoulders and I whimpered in just the slightest. I knew he didn't like weakness and I. Was. Not. Weak!

I walked to a bookshelf in the bedroom and nodded towards a Dark Magic book. He let a wrist free so I quickly tilted the book down, waiting for the click and watched the bookcase swing out just a bit.

"A hidden room?" He sounded intrigued and my inner Goddess purred in delight.

I looked over my shoulder but didn't say anything.

The lights flickered on when we stepped in and on display before us was a playroom for the most naughty. I had only used it a few times with others, but dominating in here was so boring.

I needed Gage.

My Gage.

He was the only one that could dominate me and my, how I loved it.

The wall to the right had a variety of whips, chains and various restraints, in the center of the room was a four-poster bed with hooks at varying heights with a bench at the base, and on the back wall was a vertical standing X with hooks and more restraints.

"I see you've upgraded." He smiled approvingly.

"For you." I dropped to my knees, bowing my head, waiting for his command.

He smiled and then without warning grabbed a fistful of my hair and jerked it back so I was looking at him. "You've done well."

I didn't speak.

"There." He pointed to the X.

My stomach tightened in excitement. I'd been saving this for him.

He swiftly attached me to it, cuffing my wrists and ankles with the leather straps and pulled tight, causing me to scream out.

He shook his head in disappointment. "Quite as a mouse. You know the rules."

I nodded eagerly for more.

He walked over to the wall and touched a handful of things and was back a moment later with a leather ball gag. He smiled as he slowly fit the ball into my mouth and clasped the straps behind me. "There." He opened palm smacked my pussy, causing tears to appear in the corners of my eyes, but I was loving every second.

"Have you been a bad girl?"

I nodded emphatically.

"A very bad girl?" He walked back over to the wall of goodies and came back with a black leather flogger and swiped it up my leg, between my legs and around my breast, pebbling my nipples and causing my insides to melt.

"You have been a naughty girl and you will be punished."

He reared back on the flogger and smacked it across my abdomen, causing a cool sting. My legs buckled for a minute before I stood back up.

"Did you like that?" His eyes were dark with pleasure.

I nodded, so he ran the flogger from my forehead, around my face and down my neck, swiping it across each breast. I moaned out, arching my back as much as I could to feel the warm leather against my skin.

Gage sucked his tongue in disapproval and then smacked the top of my breast. "We don't beg."

I nodded, looking deep into his eyes and he smiled. He moved the flogger across each breast, watching for a reaction, but I fought to be compliant. I could feel the wetness seeping out of my eager pussy the longer he rubbed it over my skin.

He pulled it back and patted it lightly on my nipples and unavoidable moan escaped. I pinched my eyes shut waiting for the punishment, but it never came. He pulled the flogger back and ran it from my foot up my leg, slowly, so un-fucking-bearably slowly, that I nearly came as it passed the inside of my thigh. My core was clenching and I had tears running down my eyes.

"Do you want to come for me?" He asked tauntingly.

I nodded.

"You will not come yet."

I swallowed the disappointment, causing him to chuckle.

He ran the flogger up my pussy to my stomach. "So wet." He held the flogger to his face, smelling in my scent and without warning smacked my pussy with it.

My back arched momentarily in pleasure and I had to quickly regain control of my body, making sure not to come until he commanded me to.

He ran the leather back down my leg and paused again at my entrance and then he smiled walking away. I wanted to ask what he was thinking or where he was going, but I couldn't speak, nor would I dare if I could.

He came back a moment later with a set of anal beads, a metal rod, and a smile on his face. "I see these are also new."

I nodded.

"Do you want me to fuck you with these?"

I wanted him to fuck me with whatever he wanted to right now. I was so hot for his touch, I was dripping down my leg.

He removed the gag and unshackled me from the X, leading me to the bed where he flipped me onto my stomach and strapped my wrists and ankles to the posters of the bed.

"Remember our safe word."

I nodded.

He slowly began feeding the anal beads in, one at a time, each bead causing ripples of pleasure throughout. He gave my ass another smack once he was complete, which nearly sent me over the edge. He pushed the metal shaped dildo into me slowly, its cool temperature and the pressure on my ass causing my stomach to tighten. After pulling it out, he pressed it in again, faster and faster. I could feel my insides spooling up as my body took control and moved with his rhythm. He slapped my ass hard.

"You don't move."

I let out a sigh as he continued pumping, my mind going crazy, trying to keep my body still.

He shifted the bands around the end posters of the bed so my legs were spread further apart. "Such a pretty little pussy. Do you want to come for me?"

I nodded.

"Not yet." He said, continuing the torturous pushing of the dildo.

"Fuck Gage."

He slapped my ass again, so hard it was sure to leave a welt, but I loved it. No one other than Gage had ever been able to make me feel like this before. I thought at first he enjoyed punishing me, but the more it happened, I learned he liked it. He enjoyed the pain he inflicted and I encouraged it. My dark one. All those years he had been tortured and abused allowed me to create this beautiful creature.

He pulled out the dildo and pushed himself into me hard, filling me, causing my face to thrash into the bed.

"Come, my Queen. Come now."

That was all I needed. My insides erupted as a scream bellowed out from deep within. He continued to pulse into me as I was coming undone, while at the same time he was pulling out the anal beads, which also amplified my orgasm, but he wasn't done. He spit on my ass and slipped the dildo in while he continued to pound into me, sending my head spinning into another orgasm.

"Holy fucking shit!" I yelled, burying my face in the bed.

After a few more minutes, he stopped pumping and just stood there with my ass up in the air, balls deep in me.

I laid still, trying to catch my breath and steady my heart-beat.

"That..." I panted. "That was intense."

He pulled everything out of me and unhooked me from the bed. I rubbed the ache out of my shoulders and legs and turned around to look at him.

"I have missed you." I sighed.

He made a noise but didn't look over his shoulder as he continued putting the items back on the counter. I would have frumpy lady clean this up later.

CHAPTER THIRTY-THREE

SNOW - MAGIC LESSON'S

"WHERE'S GAGE?" I ASKED when Garrison walked back inside.

"I don't know. I lost his trail deep in the woods."

I tried to force myself not to worry about him, but there was something in his eyes when I woke up. He was relieved, but there was something else... something dark.

Calix sat beside me and put his hand on my lap. "Are you in the mood to eat?"

I smiled at him, resting my head on his shoulder. "Always for your cooking."

He used his hand to reach around and pat the top of my head. "I'm glad you're not dead."

"Me too." I popped up and grabbed both his hands. "Do you want some help?"

He cocked his head disapprovingly. "You were blue and cold just a bit ago. You sit here and continue to get your strength back."

"I think it's all back. I feel fine. Once the bracelet was removed, it was like I could feel my body rapidly healing."

"It is miraculous... to have that kind of power."

I nodded, thinking the same thing, but also not quite sure knowing what kind of power it was. I knew I was a witch of some sort, or at the very least had magical powers, but I needed more answers, and that's why I needed to see the girls at Ruby's. I had to know what it was and how I could use it, because part of me was terrified I had the Queens's dark magic flowing through me and I had to figure out if that was the case how I could change it.

After dinner, we decided, against Barrett's better judgment, to go outside and relax by the fire. I needed to take the edge off and the boys seemed like they also needed to relax, even though I felt like they were more tense- jerking with every twig breaking in the woods.

Gage still hadn't come home yet, so that had me concerned, but I tried to ignore it as best as I could.

"So what's the plan?" Calix asked, looking at me.

I shrugged. "I have to learn magic. I know that for sure. She won't stop coming after me, so I have to turn the tables and go after her." I held up my hand. "I know it's dangerous, but so is doing nothing. I'm going to be as prepared as possible."

Jace chimed in. "You're new to magic. You can't even cast a single spell and you think you're going to learn enough to protect you against her, someone who can create some of the most difficult and darkest spells on a whim?" His tone a little condescending.

"I don't know what else to do." I defended.

He grabbed my hand. "I'm sorry. I wasn't trying to be rude... I'm just worried about you. If anything happened..."

I put my hand on his. "I don't want anything to happen, but she is shifting into bodies."

"I didn't realize she was a Hsein." Barrett entered the conversation.

"A what?"

"Hsein. Body jumper." His face pulled.

"What?"

"In order... in order for her to jump bodies... the person has to be... dead."

"Dead?"

"Yes. So she can't stay in the bodies for too long because decay will start to set in."

"Oh my... that is repulsive."

Enzo shook with disgust in an overdramatic fashion.

"Wait." I realized something. "She killed those people then, didn't she? Oh Goddess. The little girl..." I grabbed my stomach and leaned over. "I think I'm going to be sick."

Calix rubbed my back.

I sat back up. "We have to stop her. She is... she is pure evil."

"Yes. No one is contesting that, but we have to figure out a way to do it so that we all don't get killed in the process."

"We?" I said. "I don't want you all involved. I can't have anything happen to you."

"Well, you can't stop me, princess." Garrison said. "She's been on my list for years and is responsible for killing my father and countless others. I'm going after with or without you and honestly, I think we stand a better chance if we're together."

I sighed, knowing I couldn't stop him.

"I'm in." Enzo and Calix said at the same time.

"Me too." Jace said.

"I can sharpen some wooden stakes." Dresden chimed in.

"She's not a vampire." Barrett said.

"We don't know what she is." Enzo retorted.

"True. Wooden stakes couldn't hurt, I guess."

"I will help with the plan. It's what I do." Gideon said.

"Well, there you have it, Snow." Barrett said. "We're all in."

"Guys. If anything happened to you..."

"If anything happened to you." Calix said. "You've grown on me."

"On us." Enzo said.

I leaned my head on the back of the chair and stared at the stars as the conversation naturally came to an end. These boys... how did I get so lucky? Was it my mother? I corrected, the old Queen. Did she know I wasn't hers? Is that what she couldn't tell me? I wish I could talk to her again and ask her all of these questions, I sighed.

How does someone I don't remember, feel so alive and so real in my dreams? How did she know things-current things? Were my dreams my subconscious manifesting into visions of her? I had so many unanswered questions, but the one thing I believed above all was that she guided me here. She somehow knew this is where I needed to be and the miner seven would take care of me... we would take care of each other.

"Ok..." I yawned. "I'm going to head to bed."

Everyone else jumped up and followed me in and I realized they were only outside because of me, which filled me with warmth.

I climbed into Enzo's bed and he laid beside me. A few minutes later, there was a soft knock and Calix peeked his head in.

Enzo looked at me. "Do you mind if he joins?"

"I heard you boys liked to share." I laughed.

"Not like that tonight..." Calix said.

I didn't miss the qualifier he put on it... tonight. Which meant on another night he would want to? Suddenly, thoughts of me with them both filled my head. What would it be like? I found them both very attractive... but it seemed weird.

Another minute later, there was another knock.

"Come on in, Jace," Enzo said without seeing who was on the other side.

Jace smiled. "If it's ok?" He asked looking at me.

"Of course." I smiled.

Calix had already taken the other side of the bed beside me, so Jace took the bottom near my feet.

"Do you boys do this a lot?"

"What?" Calix asked.

"Share?"

"Sexually, we have quite a few times... but this. No, we never lay together like this."

"But you're going to do that tonight?"

"There's something different about you. We all felt it the first time we saw you."

"You did?"

"Yes." Jace said.

Part of me wanted to think this was weird and try to reason away why this shouldn't be happening, but the other part of me knew this felt good... it felt right. I had grown so close to each of them for different reasons and knew I couldn't choose between them and couldn't be without them at the same time. With Gage, there was something drawing me to him, but with the boys... I don't know... it was just different.

I woke up the next morning with my arm slung across Calix's chest, with my legs laying on top of Jace, and Enzo's arm wrapped around me. I didn't want to move and just relish this feeling... this feeling of being loved.

I must have shifted enough because they all woke up at nearly the same time.

"Good morning." Calix said, tilting his head to look at me.

"Morning."

Jace sat up while Enzo rolled over on his back.

"Thank God for gigantic beds." Jace said.

I chuckled. "Sorry you got the bottom."

"He likes the bottom." Enzo chuckled.

"Dude. Not cool." Jace cut his eyes, punching him in the leg.

I laughed. "So I was thinking we could go to Ruby's today."

"I'll tell you, it's always been a dream of mine to wake up with a girl laying next to me in bed asking to go to a whorehouse together." Enzo said.

"Don't say whorehouse... it sounds..." I scrunched my nose.

"Ok gentleman's establishment."

"That's better." I readjusted so I was resting my chin on my knees. "So, is that a yes?"

They laughed. "Let's get some breakfast, then we can go."

I squealed excitedly.

We were downstairs eating a few minutes later. I couldn't help but notice the entire house was here, except Gage. I caught Garrison's eye and raised my brows, but he shook his head.

So Gage didn't come home last night.

Where could he have gone and what was he doing?

The way he looked... I don't know... I had a feeling he was going to do something stupid. Whatever it was, I just hoped it didn't get him killed.

"How are you feeling today?" Barrett walked over, grabbing my shoulders.

I rested the spoon and looked up at him. "I'm fine. We're about to head to Ruby's."

Barrett raised his brows and looked at Enzo.

"I'm not a man to deny the woman's wishes." Enzo laughed.

"You're welcome to join." I offered to Barrett.

He looked off, pondering it for a little. "I think I'll pass this time. Looks like you already have a full party."

"Just Calix and I. Jace has to run to the market to pick up some things." Enzo said.

Barrett looked at Jace and it was like they were communicating with their eyes.

"Ok. Well, please be careful." Barrett warned.

"Always." Enzo said, pushing away from the table, rocking on the hind legs of the chair.

Barrett looked at Calix. "Please."

Calix chuckled. "We'll be good."

Enzo, Calix and I got to Ruby's a little while later. When I walked in, I couldn't help but look around for any sign that Gage was here or had been here. Some part of me had hoped when he didn't come home last night, he came here.

"Scarlet, love!" Ruby shouted, throwing her arms out into the air.

I smiled, "Good day Ruby."

"Why do you never greet me like that?" Enzo whined.

"Because I obviously don't like you as much as I like her." She squeezed his cheeks into a fish face when we got closer.

"You love me."

There was a twinkle in her eye as her gaze rested on Enzo for a second before looking away. "What can I do for you lovelies today?"

"I'd like to see if Lilibet is available." I leaned in. "I was attacked again and am desperate to learn how to defend myself."

She patted my hand. "Lilibet is off today, so this will be perfect." She looked at the boys. "Are we thinking one on one or group play?"

The boys looked at one another and then declined the offer, catching both Ruby and me off guard.

"What have you done to these boys?" Ruby asked, leading me away.

"I don't know what you mean?"

She glanced over her shoulder and watched them as I ran my hand across the red velvet walls, letting my mind drift. What would it be like to work here? I had spent my entire life confined to a room no larger than a closet, and now I was free of that box. There was an entire world waiting for me... well, after I was able to get the dark Queen off my back. She wouldn't stop coming after me, so I needed to come up with a plan.

Killing her over and over again wasn't an option. Killing her children wasn't an option. There had to be something else.

Could I somehow bind her powers? Lock her away so she couldn't hurt me or anyone else again?

"Scarlet?"

I heard my name and turned around and found a beautiful girl with long dark hair, light brown skin and emerald green eyes. "Hi." I stuttered, taken aback by her beauty.

She smiled.

"Ruby said you needed some help?" She cocked her head to the side, studying me.

I could feel my heartbeat racing and my skin getting clammy. "Yes."

"You don't need to be nervous."

"I'm not." That was a lie, well, not entirely. I don't know why I was having this reaction to her. She was just breath-takingly beautiful.

"Do you want to go into my room and work?"

"Your room?"

She smiled. "Not my sex room, but my sleeping room."

"Right. Yea. Of course. Your sleeping room."

She laughed. "You're funny and cute." She turned and started walking away, so I followed her through the door behind the bar. "We don't let many people back here, so Ruby must really like you... or trust you."

I shrugged, but said nothing.

"So where did you say you're from? I don't recognize you."

"Oh. I live with Enzo and the boys."

She stopped walking abruptly, causing me to almost walk into her.

"How long have you been there?" Her tone held a hint of something I couldn't place. Jealously? Curiosity?

"Why?"

"I've just never seen you there before."

"Oh? Do you go over there frequently?"

"Not in a while." She started walking again."I was dating Barrett a while back."

"Oh, really?" I was shocked because I got the feeling he didn't really date... or have much fun in general.

"Yea. He's nice, just a little too..."

"Serious?"

"Yes." She laughed.

We got to the second platform and passed door after door.

"Are these all rooms?"

"Yea. Three levels."

"That's a lot of people."

She chuckled. "Ruby's is the most popular established in all the seven kingdoms." She stopped outside a blank wall. "This is me."

"A wall?"

"Scarlet." She lightly scolded. "We're witches. Nothing is ever like it seems." She pressed her hand against the wall. "Revelare." Gold flashes of light shot out from under her palm, revealing a door. She turned the handle and opened, inviting me in. "Your first lesson." She smiled.

I stood just at the other side of the entrance, looking into the pitch dark.

"Lights. Right. Illuminaire."

Lights flickered on across the entire room, revealing a gigantic space.

"This is all yours."

She laughed again. "It was a test. Again, the art of illusion." She snapped her fingers, and the room shrunk to a normal size room.

"Do you use magic for everything?"

"Most everything. It makes it super easy."

I exhaled. "What are you going to teach me today?"

She studied me for a minute. "I'm still trying to figure out where I know you from. You look familiar."

"I doubt that."

She let it go for now, but I could tell it was still bothering her. "I want to get a feel for your power. See how strong you are. That will indicate how much I can teach you and what you can handle."

"Ok. How do we do that?"

She sat on her bed and then patted the space beside her. I hesitantly walked over.

"I'm not going to bite unless you ask me to." She winked.

I let out a nervous laugh.

"Sit." She turned her body to face me and tucked her right leg under her left. "Let me see your hands."

I placed my hands in her palms and felt a buzz reverberate between our hands and she quickly snatched hers away like she'd been burned.

"Who are you?" She demanded.

CHAPTER THIRTY-FOUR

LILIBET - ART OF DECEPTION

I REPEATED MYSELF. "WHO are you?"

"What do you mean? What happened?" She asked, confused.

Or was she only pretending to be confused? She was powerful, the most powerful witch I had ever come across... well, besides my mother.

Oh Gods. Was she my mother? Had she somehow escaped and shifted into this... this young, naive girl to get close to me?

I stood up from the bed and shuffled backwards, holding my hands out to protect myself in case she launched a spell at me once she realized I discovered the truth.

Shit!

I should have played this differently. Shouldn't have let on I knew who she was.

Fuck! How did she find me? Why would Ruby betray me?

"Who are you?" I repeated.

She held up her hands as she stood from the bed, trying to back up.

I readjusted, ready to attack. My mother was dark and malicious.

"I'm Scarlet." She stuttered, looking legitimately scared.

I shook my head to clear it. Was I being too paranoid? "The fuck you are. I'll ask again, who are you and don't lie to me or I will blow that beautiful little head off your body."

She looked around like a caged animal trying to escape. I stepped forward, but kept a safe distance from her.

"Who are you?"

"You're scaring me."

Her voice was shaking, but it could be a trick.

"Who sent you? Does Ruby know?"

"What are you talking about? Enzo brought me here and Ruby said you could help me."

I let out a heavy sigh. Part of me wanted to believe her, but the other part knew how ruthless my mother was and how pissed she'd be if she got out.

"I don't believe you. I've never seen you around here or at the miner's house and your power..."

She was breathing fast and hard.

I started circling my hands together in a simple spell, creating a ball of light... a parlor trick.

Her eyes grew wide with panic.

"Stop! Stop! Please don't kill me. Fuck!" She ran her fingers through her hair. "Ruby told me not to tell anyone."

I stopped with the ball of light, but kept it between my hands. I was fairly certain she wasn't my mother now, because she would have seen through the cheap trick, but now my curiosity was peaked. "Go on."

"I'm Snow White. My stepmother slash mother tried to kill me on my eighteenth birthday, so I ran away and found the miner's house. They took me in, but the dark Queen has come after me twice now, three times if you include the night I escaped, and tried to kill me. The first time she tried to strangle me with a necklace and this last time with a poisoned bracelet."

"Oh, shit."

I dropped my hands, with the ball vanishing.

She lowered hers. "I'm sorry, but Ruby said not to tell anyone here."

"Understandable."

"You won't say anything, will you?"

"No. Of course not."

"Who did you think I was?"

I hesitated telling her. "My mother."

"Your mom? You were terrified."

"She is a terrifying woman. But I don't want to talk about her right now."

How do you explain to someone the last time you saw your mother, you bound her in her dragon form and locked her away in a dungeon?

"Ok. Should we start over?" Snow smiled, hesitantly.

"Yes." I sat back on the bed and patted it, but could tell she was still cautious. "So, I wasn't really going to blow your head off. That was a light ball. A little trick that most mage children learn. You seemed terrified by it, which told me you weren't my mother, because she'd obviously know what it was."

"A trick?" She walked over and sat beside me. "Can you show me?" Her eyes twinkled with excitement.

"Yes. But let me feel your magic again." I held my hands out, and she laid her hands on mine.

I closed my eyes, focusing on the energy flowing between us.

"Do you feel that?" I asked, just above a whisper, peeking at her.

She didn't speak, but her eyes told me all I needed to know.

She could feel it.

I had worked with a lot of mages before, but none were as powerful as her. Her power could be equal to my mother's if not stronger, and that astounded me. "So you have never..." I couldn't even say the words because I couldn't even understand it.

"Use my powers?" She shifted her weight on the bed. "Never. I didn't know until recently that I had them."

She looked like there was more she wanted to say, so I pressed. "How did you find out?"

She looked around the room before her eyes settled on me for a second. "So..." she pulled her lips. "I had a dream of my mother, well, the woman I thought was my mother. She died soon after I was born... I later learned it was because her life was tied to mine. It was all part of the dark Queen's plan. Anyway. I had a dream with her in it and she said I needed to get back to the castle to help my father. I needed to save him. She said there were things I needed to know, but she couldn't tell me. She told me to talk to the wind and ask it to guide me to the purple mangor who would lead me to the white witch, Persephone."

"Oh. Did you find her?" I had always wanted to meet the white witch, but my mother had forbade it, although she would never tell me why. She had mentioned Persephone's name, but it was always with an extreme disgust, which obviously intrigued me.

"I did."

"Where?"

Snow studied me and I realized I had been a little too eager. "I don't know, really. It was in the woods somewhere. I asked the wind and followed it. I remember making turn after turn, just following it along, but had no idea how I got to the large tree."

"A large tree?"

"Yea, by a waterfall." She looked away, getting lost in a thought or something.

"What did the white witch say?"

"She's the one who told me everything... about my actual mother. She said I was born of magic, harvested for youth and hunted till death."

"That sucks."

"Yea. I thought I could live peacefully on my own, but she has already come after me twice. She won't stop. Every second I'm alive, she grows weaker."

"So she harvests her children to keep herself young?"

"Yea."

"She sounds worse than my mom..."

"Who is, again?" Snow playfully pushed.

I cocked my head to look at her. "Not saying. We are here to help you out- to teach you the ways of the mage."

Fortunately, she didn't push it much further. My mother was not a good person. She embodied evil in its darkest form, something perhaps Snow could relate to. With the help of several witches, I was able to trap her. Perhaps we could do the same with Snow's mother. "So do you know how to defeat the dark Queen?"

"I haven't come up with anything yet. She has twelve other children that are under eighteen. She had thirteen, but one of the times she tried to kill me, someone had apparently killed a child because she felt it. She yelled out as if it hurt her. If I kill her, then a child would die and if I kill her children, it would make her weaker... but that's not me. I can't do that. I can't kill her twelve times if I wanted to and I can't be responsible for killing those children or even helping to kill them. I have to find another way."

I wanted to tell her about my mother, but talking about her was still too much for me. No one here knows who I really am, or who my mother is. I left that all behind me and hope every day that it stays behind me. The only way we could capture my mother was by her shifting. We knew she would shift to defend herself, because she thinks she is most powerful in that form, but we were prepared and used it against her. That half second between the transition is when she is at her weakest.

I shook my head to clear it. I needed to stop thinking about her. I needed to focus on Snow right now.

"Ok. So let's teach you some magic."

She smiled and popped up and down in her seat.

CHAPTER THIRTY-FIVE

GARRISON - RABBIT DUTY

I COULD SMELL HIM walking up before he got to the door.

The door swung open and Gage walked in.

I turned to him when he entered the house. "Hey man. Where did you go yesterday? I tried finding you, but I lost you in the woods."

He casually glanced over at me, but didn't speak, closing the door behind him.

I popped up from the couch and followed him upstairs to his bedroom. "What's going on?"

"I thought I made it pretty clear the first time you asked a question, and I didn't answer, that I didn't want to talk about it. Following me up to my room and harassing me when I'm trying to obviously get away from you is a good way to find your head smashed through a wall."

"Ok brother." I said, holding up my hands.

"Fucking hell!" He spun around. "Stop with the brother bullshit. We aren't brothers. Maybe by blood, but the men in this house are more my brothers than you will ever be."

"That's not fair. I thought we were moving past that."

"What the hell Garrison? Just because you want something to be true doesn't mean that it is. Just because I'm talking to you and allowed you to stay here for a short amount of time while you figure out how to get yourself out of the situation you put yourself in, don't mistake that for brotherly bonding." He walked into his room and slammed the door.

I nodded in the air and walked downstairs.

I thought we had made some progress in our relationship, but I guess not. His words stung a little, but I tried not to let them get to me. It was obvious he was working through something, so I just needed to let him vent.

"Hey." Dresden said, stirring something in a pot.

I nodded in his direction.

"He gets like this sometimes. He goes away for a night or sometimes a couple and comes back super pissy. It used to bother us, but we just learned that's what happens. He'll be fine in a couple of days."

"Thanks. Does this happen a lot?"

He shrugged. "Not a ton. It's actually been a while."

"Do you know where he goes?"

"No, and we never ask. Something about the fuck off he usually has stamped across his forehead tells us what we need to know." He chuckled.

Dresden was the quiet one of the bunch, always in the background, watching and observing. Over the last several days, I had gotten to know him pretty well because I posted myself on the couch and chatted with the men as they walked by. Even though I had gotten used to the solitary life as a huntsman, I didn't want to come across as rude and standoffish, although they seemed to accept that with my brother.

"What's for dinner tonight?"

"A little rabbit stew. My mother's recipe."

"It's been a long time since I've had that."

"It's a house favorite."

"Can I do anything to help?"

"I feel like you're probably a good shot. Do you want to round up some more rabbits to replenish our stock? Snow usually handles it, but she's out and I figured you could probably use something to do." He nodded at the stairs.

"Yea, I guess you're right. Maybe a little separation is what we need." Although the last several years didn't seem to do anything but further damage our relationship.

I grabbed my bow and quiver off the wall and hesitated on the front porch.

I'm going out for a hunt if you want to go. I mindlinked Gage.

When he didn't respond, I took off for the woods.

I grabbed an arrow out of my quiver and threaded it through the bow so I'd be ready. I moved deeper and deeper into the forest, thankful for this distraction.

It felt good to hunt again.

I was worried about the dark Queen coming after me, but reconciled I probably wasn't even on her radar right now with Snow out walking around.

Speaking of...

It was getting late out and I had expected the boys and her would have been home by now. Part of me was tempted to go check on them, but the other part didn't want to get that involved. Although, that part was lying to himself if he thought he wasn't involved.

We were involved and we would fight whomever or whatever to protect her. She seemed to have a way that made you want to do anything for her.

I couldn't help but think back to the time when she was younger and laying on her back shooting arrows straight up in the apple tree with no fear. If she missed the apple, her arrow would come back down on her, but that didn't stop her. It was then, I decided to take her under my wing and guide and teach her. I had never wanted to do that with anyone before, and didn't want to do it after. It was just something about her.

I was startled by breaking twigs behind me. I froze in my tracks, not moving and barely breathing.

The creature stopped.

I took another step forward and paused, and so did it.

Whatever it was, it wasn't very large.

I slowly glanced over my shoulder and saw a miniature horse. I turned all the way around to face it, dropping my bow. There was something familiar about it and the way it looked at me.

"Here boy." I cautiously walked over to it with my hand extended. "How about you come home with me?"

The horse neighed in response and walked alongside me.

When we were almost back at the house, I heard a set of voices up ahead and paused for a moment, before I recognized Snow's singsong voice.

"Snow?" I yelled out.

I turned the corner of the road and saw Snow and the others stopped in the middle of the road, talking to Jace.

"What are you doing out here, Garrison?" Enzo asked, alarmed.

"Hunting. Dresden is making rabbit stew for dinner and asked me to replenish the rabbits in Snow's absence."

Calix groaned. "Every time that boy gets in my kitchen, he moves everything around."

"Did you get what you needed in town, Jace?"

"I did," he patted his satchel.

"How was Ruby's?" I asked the others.

"Good!" Snow said exuberantly. "Watch this."

She started rubbing her hands around an invisible ball and, after a second, a ball of light appeared.

"It's just a ball of light, but pretty cool, huh?"

I laughed. "So you were gone all day, and you learned how to make a ball of light?"

She huffed. "No, I learned some other things, but I have to practice them. I will have to do several more sessions with Lilibet before I'm anywhere close to ready. She said I was picking up things quickly, all things considered." She looked at the horse beside me. "Is that...?"

"I think so."

She reached her hand out, and the horse walked right over, nuzzling her. "She did this, didn't she?" A tear formed in Snow's eye.

Jace stepped forward and then stopped.

"What?" Snow asked.

Jace hesitated for a second, then said, "When I was little, I lived around a lot of witches, and they would oftentimes shrink and enlarge things. I think perhaps if you were to say dilatare, that will make him bigger."

"Are you sure?"

"Yes. Reducio to make smaller and dilatare to make bigger."

"Do I just hold my hand out?"

He walked behind her and grabbed her arm, raising it in the air, and then flicked her wrist. "Move your hand like that when you say it."

She turned to look at him, their faces inches apart, her breathing slow and steady. "Ok."

Jace stepped back and squeezed her shoulders. "You got this."

"Dilatare." She said, flicking her hand, but nothing happened. "Are you sure that was right?"

He nodded. "Just flick your wrist a little more like this." He said, showing her. She mimicked him a couple of times and then tried again.

"Dilatare!" She flicked and a light shot out from her hands and landed on the horse and he started growing in size.

"Oh, my!" she exclaimed and jumped onto Jace, wrapping her legs around him. "Did you see that? I did it!"

He laughed, holding her. "I did. Very good job!"

She leaned forward and rested her head on his shoulder for another minute before climbing down. She grabbed his cheeks and planted a quick kiss on his lips. "Thank you!"

His eyes were wide with surprise.

"Are you going to learn how to fight as well?" I asked, bringing the group back to focus.

"Yes." Enzo jumped in. "I plan on working with her in the field near the house tomorrow.

"If you need any help, let me know." I offered as we started walking back towards the house. "Oh, by the way. Gage is back, and he isn't in a very good mood."

Snow snapped her head in my direction. "Is he ok?"

"Physically, he seems fine. Just super pissy."

"Oh." the boys said in unison.

Calix added. "Yea, he gets like this when he does his little overnight jaunts to wherever he goes."

"He'll be fine in a couple of days." Jace added.

We got back to the house just as Dresden was setting the table. "No rabbits?" He asked when I entered.

"No. But I found these instead." I said at the same time the others were walking in.

"Perfect timing." Dresden threw his arms in the air. "Dinner!" He shouted to the rest of the house and then looked at me. "Garrison, you're fired from rabbit duty."

"I will get some tomorrow." Snow offered.

Chapter Thirty-Six

Gage - History of the Dark One

"Fuck!" I slammed the door to my room when I got in and fell to my bed.

No, I needed a shower. I could smell her on me.

It had been a while since I lost my grip and found myself at her front door. I knew it was bound to happen once I realized who Snow was and once she found out where Snow was.

Of all the places Snow could have ended up, it had to be our fucking house.

I let my anger at the dark Queen consume me and in that moment of weakness, I let it take over.

The rage.

And that's when her little spell worked its way in. It was what I was scared of when it happened. It made me a different person- a servant to her.

I could feel my body going through the motions, see what was happening, but couldn't stop it.

That version of me was dark- he wanted to cause pain. He liked it.

That version of me was born out of the pain I endured when I was younger- the pain I don't speak about.

She knows the pain, though. She saw it.

She found me bruised and battered on the forest floor.

I remember looking up at her and thought she was the most beautiful thing I had ever seen. That was before I knew the truth about the darkness that lived within her, festering and feeding off her.

She took me to a little cottage on the outskirts of town and cleaned me up and clothed me. We didn't speak for days. She just silently moved around me, doing what needed to be done. On the fifth day, she somehow got me talking. Knowing what I know now, I would have to think it was a spell she cast or the tea she was feeding me. The more tea I drank, the more I wanted to trust her and open up to her... become compliant.

I remember telling her everything about me... about my dad and my brother and why I was kicked out. At this point, I didn't know she was the dark Queen, but she knew who I was.

I think it was at this moment, she realized what she had, and she started molding me. I could feel it. I could feel myself splitting in two. The Gage that I once was and the one she was turning me into it. The second Gage was dark-evil. Perhaps that's what turned her on, what excited her.

She grew that Gage and taught him how to fight, how to take out enemies and how to have no remorse.

The dark Queen found the boys who had attacked me weeks before and brought them kneeling before me. I felt it... bubbling inside me of... the rage. The hate. The anger.

I wanted to hurt them. I wanted to kill them.

I remember pacing back and forth in front of them with her standing in the corner, halfway in its shadow, watching. The excitement on her face... I wanted to please her.

I moved to the first boy and removed the knife I had strapped to my leg and walked behind him, pulling his head back and slicing it across his throat. The blood spattered everywhere and pooled onto his shirt. I looked at her and she nodded slowly in satisfaction.

The other three boys were screaming, panicked, trying to get away, but they were bound by magic- invisible ropes keeping them in place.

You did this to me. You came after me and you attacked me. I said to the second boy.

No! No! I'm sorry.

Your apologies mean nothing to me. You can't go around attacking young children. You almost killed me.

We won't do it again! I swear! I promise!

I know. I stabbed him in the heart and pulled the blade up with such force that I broke his collarbone. I let out a beastly scream as the blood sprayed all over me and then heard my clothes being shredded as I shifted.

I looked at her for approval and saw her looking at me through her lashes as she took a step out of the shadows with a malicious grin spread across her face.

I watched her flick her wrist and almost immediately, the boys shot upright and started running through the woods.

A chase.

I went for the youngest one first. I knew these woods better than they did. They had been my home for the last several years. I chased him, circling him, taunting him. When he tripped over a log, I pounced, standing over him. I could feel the drool slipping out of my mouth as I stood over him, growling. The look in his eyes was pure terror, but it wasn't there for long.

I clamped down on his throat and ripped.

I popped my head up and listened for the last one. He was the oldest of their little pack, the instigator. He was the one encouraging the boys to do those things to me. My body still hurt from what they did, although it was probably more the memory than the physical pain. I don't know if the memory would ever fade.

I found the last boy up in a tree, shivering, clinging onto the trunk for dear life, while the branch strained under his weight. I shifted out of my wolf form and looked up at him.

I can wait here all day for that branch you're on to break.

He nervously looked down and realized he didn't have much time left. He quickly tried to shift most of his weight to the trunk and was happy to see the branch rise under the reduced weight.

You're not strong enough to hold yourself to that trunk for the rest of the night, or even through tomorrow... because that is how long I will wait. I will wait you out and when you fall and break several bones, I will then torture and kill you.

I'm sorry. He was sobbing buckets of tears. *It was just a game... we were just having fun.*

I can assure you that what you and your friends were doing to me was not a game and it sure as hell wasn't fun. What kind of fucked up person do you have to be to do those things to someone just a few years younger than you, or to anyone in general?

You're right. You're right. We shouldn't have done those things. It was wrong. I'm sorry. I'm sorry. I'm so fucking sorry.

I know you are. I hope you've learned your lesson. I said, backing away.

Where are you going? Are you going to kill me? He shouted, confused about my one eighty.

I didn't respond, but continued backing away until he couldn't see me anymore.

But I could still see him.

I watched and waited...

The sun went down and the moon rose high in the sky, but he stayed in the tree, scared to climb down. He should be. He knew monsters lurked in the woods.

That's what I was.

That's what she made me.

No, not her. They. Everyone in my life to this point had made me what I am.

I heard the branches shaking in the tree and saw he was inching his way down, but I stayed where I was... watching.

He landed with a plop and stay hunched on the ground for a second, looking around. He wouldn't see me- I knew how to hide. He took off running through the woods in the direction opposite of me, so I shifted and followed him at a slower pace. I could smell his fear wafting through the woods, encircling me, causing my blood to vibrate with excitement.

I could feel my wolf eager for the chase, but he restrained.

The boy had no idea where he was going, which only caused him to be more afraid. After running in circles several times, I was getting bored. I stopped where I was and waited for him to loop around back to me and when he did, he froze- feet set apart and hands in the air in front of him.

I growled at him, causing him to stutter step backwards, tripping over a branch and landing on his back. I leapt the distance and landed my muzzle to his face and growled again. I could smell his urine pooling beneath him and then bit down and ripped at his throat.

I went back to the little cottage and found the dark Queen waiting there. She admired my naked body covered in the blood of those boys and smiled.

That was the start. The start of our dark relationship.

As time went on, she couldn't be around as much, disappearing for days or weeks. When she was gone, I could feel her dark magic fading. I could feel him, the dark one, shrinking inside me. Never gone, but hidden. Waiting.

I went out on my own, wanting to get away from her, out from under her spell, and that's when I found Barrett. It took me a while to open up to him because I thought he was sent by the Queen, a trick to test my loyalty, but over time I learned the truth and was happy to leave... to be free of her. I could feel deep inside, what she was having me do was wrong. I had traded one killer for another, but it was like I couldn't control it... the dark part of me.

It wasn't until years later when I realized it was some sort of mind control, or curse, she had placed on me. It was like a switch that would flip, causing me to feel like a mindless drone. I couldn't fight it, no matter how hard I tried.

That's what happened last night... I was so angry... filled with rage at the Queen because of what she had done to Snow... but like every other time, when the rage is there, so is he... waiting. I felt him take over and go back home... to the dark Queen.

The things we did. I shook my head.

I felt sick thinking about it.

When I left, she gave me an order...

An order that part of me didn't want to follow... that part of me wanted to reject, but the other part... he wanted to please her. He lived in the darkness.

I had to deliver Snow.

CHAPTER THIRTY-SEVEN

SNOW - SPELL MAKING

"YOU READY?" ENZO ASKED, jumping up and down, slapping his knees. It was impressive how high he could jump.

I laughed. "Yes."

He charged and grabbed me around the neck, knocking me off balance, causing us to fall to the ground. His face was inches from mine as his hands tightened around my throat. I tried to keep all the kinky fuckery thoughts out of my head and focus at the task at hand, but he was hot and I was horny. I closed my eyes to refocus and began thrashing back and forth trying to get free, but couldn't get him off. I refused to tap out, so we continued and a second later, Barrett dropped to the ground on his stomach with his face by mine and started spouting off instructions.

"Go for his eyes. You aren't strong enough to break his grip."

I released Enzo's wrists and reached for his eyes, digging my thumbs into the soft parts and hooking my fingers around his ears. Enzo loosened his grip as he yelled out a stream of expletives.

"Good, good. Now hook your leg around the outside of his and thrust up. You want to throw him over you. Use your hips and legs to help."

I tried, but couldn't get my leg around his, since two of my legs was like one of his.

"You all look ridiculous." A voice boomed behind my head.

Enzo let go of my neck and rocked back on his hind legs, still straddling me, while I tilted my head backwards looking upside down.

Gage.

"Well, at least he's helping." I spat back, rolling onto my stomach so I could face him. I was glad Enzo didn't move because I knew Gage seeing him on me would make him mad." Is that what you call it?" Gage crossed his arms. "Do you really think the dark Queen is going to choke her out?"

Enzo climbed off and we both stood up.

Barrett looked at Gage. "What do you propose?"

"I don't know... maybe magic." He threw his hands in the air and continued, condescendingly. "She is the dark Queen after all and uses... magic. You're filling her head with false hope, trying to teach her how to fight. She has no chance against the dark Queen. She's powerful and is not afraid to use it against you. We'd all been better off if Snow never landed at our door."

"What crawled up your ass and died?" Enzo asked, stepping forward.

"Enzo." Barrett cautioned.

"No." Enzo batted the air. "He walks out here and is a complete ass. More than usual! We're just trying to help her, which is more than we can say for him." Enzo nodded towards Gage. "You just run away to wherever it is you go on your little overnight trips and then come back super pissy. I'm tired of it."

"You're tired of it?" Gage asked, stepping forward, his body tensing.

Sensing where this was going, I stepped in between them and pressed my hands on Gage's chest.

He stopped in his tracks and looked from my hands up to my face.

"You can leave. You've made it clear you don't care about me and they're only trying to help. All you will do is get in the way and cause problems and quite honestly, we don't have enough time for your bullshit. The dark Queen will continue to come after me no matter what, so I have no other option! I'm not going to just lay down and let her kill me. I will fight until my last breath." I started walking away and then spun around walked back to him and spoke quiet enough so only he could hear. "I know you care and when you want to help I will be waiting, because I will take whatever I will get, but until then, stay the fuck away."

He glared down at me then turned without speaking.

I watched him walk away, my chest heaving and my pulse pounding. I tried not to be turned on by his tight ass in those pants and his shirt hugging his arms because I was mad at him. I wanted his help. I probably needed his help, but he was just giving up.

I unclenched my fists and turned to face Enzo and Barrett. "He wasn't wrong, though. I need to use the spells Lilibet taught me- I need to master how to deflect and redirect. She said those were the best ones to teach me right now so I wouldn't have to learn as many spells in such a short amount of time. If I mastered those, especially the redirect, then I could cast the Queen's spells back onto her."

"That Lilibet." Enzo said, smiling. I tried not to get jealous about the twinkle in his eye when he said her name, but I had let myself develop feelings for him, all of them really, and I didn't want them to think about others that way anymore. Which I know was hypocritical. Here I was thinking about all of them, all the time.

"I sent Calix earlier to get her." Barrett stepped up.

"I don't want to wait around for the Queen to come back. I need to take the fight to her."

Barrett and Enzo both pulled their faces and looked at one another.

"Look, I know you don't like the idea, but she won't stop coming and at least I have more control if I go after her. Plus, what if she comes and you all are here next time? I couldn't handle if any of you were hurt because of me."

Barrett shook his head. "I don't like it."

"I'm not a fan of it either, but it's all I have right now. With her body jumping, I will literally be second guessing everyone I meet. I can't live like that."

"I know. I just don't like it." Barrett said, worried. "I don't want you hurt."

"Oh, you like her... like, like her, like her." Enzo teased.

He cocked his head. "She's grown on me."

I smiled and wrapped my arms around Barrett's neck and then planted a quick kiss on his cheek. "You've grown on me too."

"What's going on out here?" Dresden asked, walking up.

"Just some family bonding." I smiled, hooking my arm around Barrett's.

Dresden looked between the two of us, then said, "So I had an idea."

"Let's hear it." Barrett said.

I didn't ignore the fact he still had his arm hooked around mine.

"So I know Calix is on his way to get Lilibet and that Snow is good with her bow annndd Snow doesn't want to kill the Queen or her children... so I had the idea to have Lilibet place a curse on the arrow that Snow could shoot which would do something to the Queen."

"Do something? Do what?" Barrett asked, intrigued.

Dresden shrugged. "I don't much about curses so I'd have to leave that up to Lilibet to let us know what she can do and what she thinks is best, but I've whittled some arrows for you. It was just an idea." He shrugged, holding out four perfectly whittled arrows.

I took them in my hands, rubbing my fingers over the smooth wood. "These are beautiful, thank you Dresden. It's a great idea. We just need to talk to Lilibet to see what kind of curse she can put on it."

Dresden blushed. "I wanted to find a way to help out, too."

"No. Absolutely not." Lilibet said, after I told her about Dresden's idea.

"Why not?" I said, a little more than irritated. It was a solid plan and probably one of the safest.

"I can't be getting any more involved with this. I did this as a favor for Ruby and had I known the truth about who you are and your intentions before, I don't know if I would have helped."

"But you know now and you have still helped and you are here."

"Against my better judgment. I always sucked at doing the sensible thing." She rolled her eyes.

"So, what's different about this?"

She sighed. "I can't. Every curse has a signature which is unique to the one who cast it. Think of it like a fingerprint. If the Queen survives, which she would since that is the whole idea, I don't need her figuring out I had anything to do with this. I have too much shit going on in my life right now. I don't need this too."

"Lilibet, you're the only one that knows the truth who can help. I can't go find another mage."

"I know." She stomped the ground softly.

"So you're putting me in a bind." I spun in a circle. "She's going to come after me again and kill me, eventually. I don't know how many lives I have left. I have to go after her and put an end to all of this and the cursed arrow is the best idea in the short term."

"Snow. I'm sorry. I can't."

"FUCK!" I screamed at the top of my lungs.

Barrett jumped in. "Can you tell her the curse and let her do it? So it will be her signature on the curse and the Queen wouldn't know. I mean, if everything goes the way it's supposed to, the Queen would be immobilized and basically put into a coma until we can figure out what to do with her and the children."

"Do you even know where they are? Who they are?"

"No." I admitted solemnly.

Lilibet sighed. "This is not a good idea."

"None of it is, but it's what we're dealing with." I snapped. "I'm sorry. I'm just... scared."

She sighed. "I get it. I did something like this with my mother. When she shifted into her animal, she was more vulnerable. I was able to cast a spell and lock her away."

"So you think we can do the same here?" I asked hopefully, but not ignoring the fact she was sharing something about her mother.

"I don't know. It's a little different."

"Why is that?"

"I don't really want to get into it right now."

I couldn't understand why she wouldn't open up to me about her mother, especially when she knew everything about me. There's no way her mother could be any worse than mine. I took in a deep breath. "Lilibet... please. I don't know what to offer you."

"Lily... please." Barrett stepped forward, reaching out to her.

Lily?

I looked at Lilibet and watched her nearly melt when she looked at Barrett. Wow. She must have, or still has it bad for him. She looked at me and then back to Barrett, who was mouthing please.

"Fine!" she yelled, exasperated. "But I swear, if this shit gets me in trouble. I really can't handle any other bullshit right now." She let out a groan. "Fuck! This is not a good idea."

I ran over to her and gave her a hug before she could talk herself out of it. "Thank you, thank you. I will repay you. I swear. I will find a way and I will repay you."

"I'll hold you to it. Who knows when I'll need a mage princess?" She pushed me away but held on to my shoulders. "Have you figured out what your animal is yet?"

"My animal?"

"Most powerful mages have shifter abilities and the power I felt within you... you definitely have to have one."

I shook my head. "I don't know. I've never felt it or had anything happen. How would I figure it out? What are you?"

"It sort of just happens. You'll get a tingling feeling and then you will feel something changing in your body and then you just sort of shift."

"So I could just be walking around one day and boom!?"

She laughed. "Not really. There will be signs or feelings days leading up to it so you can be prepared. You may hear her talking, or feel her within you."

I tried to imagine what it would be like to have something, an animal, inside of my body talking to me. Would I feel like I was going crazy? Do you talk back to it? Would my voice go an octave or two higher like it does when talking to other animals? I had so many questions right now and absolutely none of them were important. I shook my head to try to refocus on Lilibet. "How do I shift back? Are all shifters, mages?" I had images of Gage shifting into a wolf in the woods, running through my head.

Barrett looked at me and must have sensed what I was thinking, because he jumped in. "Let's worry less about this right now and more about how to keep you alive." He patted my shoulder in a very brotherly way.

"Yes!" Enzo chimed in.

Lilibet nodded and then fired a spell at me without warning, hitting me in the shoulder. I screamed out in pain as the sting ran down my arm. "What the hell?"

She smiled and jumped to the left. "Ignis Ferrum! But remember, deflect or redirect!" She laughed.

"Ignis ferrum!" I flicked my wrist and a small bolt of light shot out, but only covered half the distance between us.

"Put more force in the flick. Imagine it reaching out to me!" She bounced from side to side on her feet.

"Ignis ferrum!" I yelled again and flicked more forcefully. I was so excited that it reached her I didn't see she redirected it back to me. It hit me in my lower leg, causing me to fall to the ground in agony. "Shit Lily!"

"Lilibet!" she fired again. "Only friends call me Lily, and we aren't friends right now."

I rolled out of the way and could smell the scorched patch of earth behind me.

I heard the pop of another spell and rolled over quickly and deflected it.

"Good, good!" She said excitedly before launching another and then another.

"Damn it! Slow down." I deflected one and jumped out of the way of the second.

"Make me!" She rolled on the ground, dodging my cast, and fired another one.

I redirected it back to her, but she jumped out of the way, so I launched another, clipping her on the arm.

"Oh, that was close." She looked at the black ash mark on her arm.

She cast three more back to back. I deflected two and redirected the last.

I heard Enzo scream, and we both looked at him. Apparently, one of the deflect spells hit him in the arm.

"What the hell?" He grabbed his arm.

Barrett patted him on the shoulder. "You'll be ok, it's just a flesh wound."

"Flesh wound my ass!"

"Go inside and see Jace. He'll have something to help."

He huffed and then went inside.

I heard the crackle of another spell as I was watching him.

"Lilibet! I wasn't even paying attention."

"Looks like you were." She smiled.

"I feel like you're enjoying this too much."

"Maybe a little."

Chapter Thirty-Eight

LILIBET - THE MINER SEVEN

"Are you sure I can stay for dinner?" I asked Snow as we were walking back in from the field. What had once been luscious green grass now had several burn spots throughout it, looking like a dragon's yard.

She smiled. "Of course." She looped her arm through mine. "Thanks for helping me today. I really appreciate it."

I grabbed her hand with my other. "I kind of like you and hope you don't die."

Snow chuckled, and it reminded me of wind chimes dancing in the air. "Me too."

We walked into the house. It had been a while since I stepped foot in here but nothing much had changed.

That's not true.

Snow had changed it.

There was something that seemed different about the place, even though everything seemed the same. The air was different. There was a unity, and that's not to say there wasn't before, because the miner seven were always a tight-knit group, but something was definitely different. The way they looked at her, it was like she was theirs... all of theirs. Even Barrett's, I saw regrettably.

He was different on the field, even though he was trying to hide it, but it was a feeling.

I watched Snow talk to Calix, and she radiated light- it was hard to turn away from.

She looked at me and smiled, giving me a thumbs up before walking back over.

"Dinner's all good. Want to run up to the showers with me so we can clean all this dirt and ash off of us?"

"Need any help?" Enzo shouted from the couch. I hadn't even seen him there.

"Maybe next time." Snow called over her shoulder, walking up the stairs.

"Promises, promises."

"I have some extra clothes if you want to borrow them?"

"Sure." I said, stripping off my clothes.

Snow looked at me and blushed before quickly turning away.

"Sorry. I'm used to getting undressed in front of people." I chuckled.

"Right." She laughed, getting stripped down before climbing into one of the showers on the left side of the room.

"You have a cute body. You could totally work at Ruby's."

She turned around to look at me, rinsing the soap out of her hair. "You think?"

"Yea. Although, who knows what's going to happen after the dark Queen is gone. Would you go back to the castle?"

"Oh." She hesitated. "I hadn't really thought about that."

"You're going to stay here?"

She was quiet. "I don't know. Is that weird?" Her voice held a note of sadness in it. "This place has always felt like home, more than the castle ever did, but I guess that's because my entire life was confined to a room no bigger than the shower stall you're standing in."

"Shit. That sucks."

"Yea."

"I'm sure coming here was a lot different."

"Yea. I almost feel like I was fated to show up here... is that weird? Everyone has been so welcoming."

"Everyone? Even Gage?"

She chuckled. "Even him. He has his moments, but he isn't all that bad when you get to know him."

"I have, and he just seems like an ass all the time."

"Well..." she hesitated. "Well, yeah, he kind of is, but sometimes he can be nice."

I laughed. "I don't think I've ever seen that side."

"He tries to keep it hidden."

"You seem like you have a crush on him."

She laughed. "I don't know if I would call it that."

I wasn't going to push it, but I could hear it in her voice. She definitely had feelings for him, and why wouldn't she? He was fucking gorgeous in a bad boy kind of way. Dark hair, short beard, and crystal blue eyes that sparkled. Made me want to touch myself right here. Only a few girls had gotten the pleasure of having him and the stories they told... my mind wandered, causing my skin to flush.

Snow cut the water off and climbed out, wrapping the towel around her, bringing me back to reality.

After we got dressed, we went downstairs and helped Calix set the table.

"You know it's a good thing I love to cook so much food." He cackled.

"You are the best cook." Snow said, slipping her arms around his neck from behind.

He tilted his head onto her arm. "You know all the right things to say."

"Well, it's true."

"What about my rabbit stew?" Dresden chimed in.

"It was also delicious."

Calix leaned over to both Snow and I. "I'm still putting my kitchen back together. How hard is it to put shit back in the same place you found it? Do you think he would like if I went into his shop and moved everything around?"

"I can hear you."

Calix popped his head up and looked at him. "Well, it's true."

"Apologies brother."

Dresden sat at the table and was fiddling with a piece of wood in his hand. He was the one of the miner seven I knew the least about. He never really came to Ruby's... maybe once if I tried to think back hard enough, and even when I had come over the short time Barrett and I were seeing each other, he was quiet.

"Dinner!" Calix shouted.

The kitchen filled up with excitement and I saw someone walk in I didn't recognize. "Who are you?" I asked.

He was tall, dark, and handsome, with green eyes and a familiar resemblance.

"Garrison." He smiled.

"Gage's brother." Snow added.

"Don't let him hear you say that."

"Too late." Gage walked downstairs. "What are we now? A fucking feeding line?"

"Gage. I know it's hard, but try not to be an ass for the rest of the night." Snow said, pulling out a seat and directing me to sit in it.

He glared at her, but didn't say anything.

Holy shit. No one ever talked back to Gage, but she did. I glanced at Enzo beside me. "It's their thing. He's an ass. She puts him in his place and he takes it."

"Shut the fuck up Enzo." Gage retorted.

"He's still an ass to the rest of us, but we're used to it." Enzo continued, ignoring Gage.

"So, what is your name?" Garrison asked.

"I'm Lilibet."

"A beautiful name for a beautiful woman."

"For fuck's sake. Not at the dinner table." Gage snapped.

"Seriously, what is your problem? If your brother chooses not to be a dickhead and make polite conversation with a guest, what's it to you?" Snow pushed.

He just stared at her and shoveled food in his mouth.

That's how the rest of dinner went, them glaring at one another in silence as the rest of the table carried on in conversation.

After dinner, Calix suggested we go outside by the fire pit, and I was thankful Gage had decided to stay inside. I was used to his general broodiness, but something seemed to bother him a little more than usual and I felt it had to do with Snow, even though I couldn't put my finger on it. I tried to block him and Snow out so I could focus on getting to know Garrison better while Snow made a plan of attack for the dark Queen. She told everyone about the spell she'd cast, with my help, on the arrows Dresden had made for her.

It was a simple spell in theory, one that would just stun and immobilize the dark Queen so they could bind her with a pair of magic shackles that muted her spell casting. Once those were on her, they would be able to safely store her somewhere until they could figure out what to do about her and her children.

It was Jace's idea to use the shackles, which he happened to have a pair of in his room. No one in the house seemed to question it, but I found it odd. He had told some story about how he received them when he was a young boy after being picked on by the witches he lived near.

I looked at Snow and watched her, part of me feeling guilty for wanting to stay out of this. I had enough shit going on, but there was something about her that sort of pulled you in- made you want to do whatever you could to protect her, to fight with her, to love her.

They had a plan, and they were going after her tomorrow.

CHAPTER THIRTY-NINE

SNOW - JOURNEY TO THE CASTLE

"OH, SNOW." MY MOTHER'S *face looked worn and tired, but the room was still the same.*

"What's wrong?"

"Time is running out."

"What do you mean? Is it papa?"

"No... not yet. The Queen. She's getting angry. I can feel it."

"She's getting mad because she can't kill me?"

"Yes. She's getting help."

"What do you mean?"

"Don't trust–"

I felt a light tap on my shoulder and opened my eyes to an enormous figure standing beside the bed. I jumped before I realized it was Gage. I blinked hard to get the sleep out of my eyes, but he was still there... this was not my imagination.

He waved me towards him, and I looked around. I was laying in between Enzo and Jace. Calix had decided to sleep in his own bed tonight since he had to get up early in the morning. He had planned to prepare a feast for us all before our trek to the castle to deal with the dark Queen.

I gently stood up, and he reached over and grabbed me under the armpits and lifted me with ease over Jace and off the bed. I slid down his chest as he lowered me to the floor. I looked up at him.

His eyes seemed different than usual, darker, almost gray looking.

"What-"

He pressed his finger over my lips and gently guided me out of the room.

When the door shut, he removed his finger and whispered. "Let's go."

"Go where?"

"After the Queen."

I shook my head. "That's not the plan. We're all going to leave later."

"I don't think that's a good idea."

"You don't even know the plan." I retorted, irritated by his simple dismissal.

He replayed it back to me, word for word. "Werewolves have super hearing." He rolled his eyes like I should have known that. "The others are going to get hurt, possibly killed. You don't want that, do you?"

"No, of course not."

"Plus, if we leave now, she won't be expecting anything."

I narrowed my eyes at him for a second.

"You said you wanted my help. Well, here I am. I'll protect you." He whispered, brushing my hair behind my ear. "You trust me, don't you?"

"I do." I grabbed his hand and stared at him. He was normally not this affectionate, but I would take it.

"I need to go to my room and change."

"I have your clothes in my room," he blurted.

"You've already thought of everything, haven't you?" I smiled, patting his chest.

"I know how important this is."

We walked down the steps to his room and I saw my clothes laying on the bed and quickly changed. "Are you sure this is a good idea?"

"I thought you said you trusted me?"

"I do." I defended, even though it still felt wrong leaving the others.

He nodded. "Ok then." He peeked out of his door. "Let's go."

I followed him downstairs and grabbed my quiver and bow off the wall.

The moon was still high in the sky, and the air was cool. I glanced at Gage curiously. Something seemed a little off about the way he was acting, but I knew he wouldn't do anything to hurt me, even though he didn't seem to believe it.

"So..." I started, not really knowing what to say, but also not feeling comfortable with the silence between us.

He looked at me, but we continued walking in silence.

"I don't get you sometimes. You had nothing to do with helping on the field or the conversation last night. Honestly, I didn't even think you cared, but here you are now..."

He didn't speak for a few minutes. "I wasn't going to waste my time while you all discussed irrational thoughts and ideas that were bound to get you all killed."

"But this way's not?"

"No, and the others will be safe."

"And us?"

He glanced at me, then ducked down, pulling me with him.

"Wha-"

He pushed his finger over my mouth as he stuck his nose in the air.

He was smelling the air, I realized. Super hearing and super smelling? What else did he have?

He stood up a minute later, and we continued walking.

"Everything good now?"

He nodded as we continued stomping over branches.

"Why are we going this way?This isn't the normal path to the castle." I asked, batting a branch out of my way.

"It's quicker."

"To get to the castle?"

"Yes."

I laughed. "Go to the castle so much you know short cuts do you?"

He rolled his eye at me, but ignored my question.

"I seriously hope it's quicker, because it sucks." I jumped off a log and landed on another broken branch, stumbling into Gage.

He sighed, but continued walking. "We'll be there by late afternoon."

I ran up beside him. "Why are we really leaving before everyone else?"

"What do you mean?"

"I don't think I was unclear in my question." I grabbed his arm, stopping in the middle of the woods.

"I didn't think you all came up with a good plan."

"What's yours?" I stared him in the eyes and was caught off-guard by the darkness of them. I thought I had noticed it this morning, but attributed the color to the lack of light, but now, granted it was still dark outside, I could tell they were definitely dark, like a deep gray. Was that part of his werewolf thing, too? I shook my head irritated there was so much about everything I didn't know.

"We will show up. I will distract her and you will shoot your arrow."

"Just like that? Easy peasy?"

"Easy peasy?" He started walking again, mildly annoyed.

"What happens if I miss?"

"Don't miss."

"What happens if it doesn't work?"

"You didn't account for that in your plan last night." He said simply.

That was true, but last night there was hope. There was ideas. Now it was reality. We were literally on the way to the castle and I started to second guess the whole plan. What if I didn't cast the spell correctly? Lilibet had to help me enunciate several words over and over again. What if it's not powerful enough? So many thoughts were racing through my mind now that hadn't been. Maybe Gage was right, maybe we were unprepared.

"I don't think we should do this."

He chuckled and stopped walking. "Yesterday you were all, 'let's take down the Queen, fight to my last dying breath' and now you're being a coward."

"A coward?"

"What would you call it?"

I stared at him in disbelief for a moment. "There are a lot of what ifs that still haven't been answered and we don't even have the cuffs."

He patted the satchel on his hip.

Ok, so he seems to have thought of everything. "What are we going to do with her body?"

He looked at me, clearly irritated by all my questions. "We will figure it out. But I can promise if you don't stop talking right now, you won't make it to the castle." His words were cold and hard with no hint of playfulness in them- a threat. Gage had always been an ass, but there was always a gentle edge I could see. I was not getting that same feeling right now and couldn't help but let my mind wander back to my dream this morning.

Is he the one that I couldn't trust?

Was his name going to be the one that fell from my mother's lips?

I watched him walk in front of me and couldn't imagine him betraying me, not when he had so many opportunities before, but there was something still nagging me about him.

Around mid-day, we stopped by a stream to grab a quick bite to eat. Fortunately, in Gage's satchel was also a couple of sandwiches, carrots, and an apple.

"Gage." I asked, tentatively. "Are you ok?" I placed my hand on his.

I saw his eyes flicker for a minute, from gray to blue, back to gray. "I'm fine," he pulled his hand out from under mine. "Eat your food, so we can continue." He snapped.

"What if I want to wait for the others? I don't feel right about leaving them behind." I said, finishing my sandwich.

"No. They will catch up."

I grabbed the apple off my lap and held it up to the sun. I didn't think the apple tree had any apples for us to pick, but this one was a beautiful bright red. "They'll be a whole day behind us, especially if they don't know this shortcut." I took a bite and savored the delicious taste.

"It will all be fine." He huffed.

I took another bite. "I know you say that... but I don't know. I just want to wait for them."

He threw his sandwich down in anger and stood up. "Let's go!" He commanded.

"I'm not done yet."

"Well, you didn't seem too concerned about that when you were asking all your damn questions." He snatched the apple out of my hand and threw it as well. "Let's go."

This was not the Gage I was used to. This was a different person- a more angry and triggered person. Was this the version Gage had always warned me about? Did he know... could he feel this one living inside of him waiting to come out?

The rest of the way to the castle, I thought through every possibility I could, with the one I didn't want to waste any time on, but for some reason kept going back to.

Gage was a traitor and was going to turn me over to the dark Queen.

I couldn't wrap my head around it, but all the signs were there and in my dream, my mother started to tell me not to trust someone. Was it Gage? But how would she know? Wasn't she just a figment of my imagination? Did part of me not trust him?

I saw the castle up ahead and felt a pit form in my stomach.

This was it.

The moment of truth.

I grabbed a special arrow out of my quiver and laced it into the bow. Right now, I didn't know if this arrow was meant for Gage or the Queen. I hoped for the latter, but was still unsure. I took a few more steps and my stomach started to feel queasy.

Gage turned to look at me. It was the fifth time in a matter of minutes. Like he was checking on me, but it was more like he was waiting.

Shit.

I felt it slowly creep in, starting first at my fingers and my toes and then like a dark cloud, it spread across my skin. "What did you do?" I asked him, leaning against a tree for support. My legs felt weak like they were going to give out, but I wouldn't let them. I had to fight. My vision spun as the world moved around me and a heat flashed across my skin. I felt my head drooping and tried to keep it upright, but could tell like it was bouncing around carelessly.

He stopped walking and came to my side, scooping me up.

"Sorry princess." He said without mirth.

"Are you?" I pressed my hand to his face and watched his eyes flicker again before the darkness crept in.

CHAPTER FORTY

MERLA - REVENGE AT LAST

SNOW HAD BEEN LAYING in that bed for several hours. I paced around the room in frustration, fighting the urge to shake her awake. "How much did you give her? I said only a little." I barked out, before looking out the window again.

I knew Gage had said he left early in the morning and had taken the cut through across the mountains, but I was still nervous Snow's merry band of miner's would show up causing havoc.

"A little is a relative amount." He said matter-of-factly.

"A little... a fucking little! A pinch!" I held my fingers up in the air, waving them around in a fury.

"Pinch would have been more helpful." He shrugged.

I stomped over to him and smacked him across the face. He grabbed his cheek, but seemed unfazed.

I reached for him, but he backed away. "I'm sorry. I'm just so excited." I walked back to the edge of the bed and looked down at the porcelain doll. "This little menace has evaded me for far too long and now I have her here." I scraped my pointed nail down her arm, leaving a deep red line. "I'm surprised you were able to get her here without the others having an issue with it."

"I've already told you," he sighed heavily. "We left in the middle of the night. I imagine they're aware we're gone now."

"They won't be an issue, will they?" I straightened my back, looking at him. It wasn't that I was worried about them, I just didn't need them prolonging the inevitable.

"No. They won't be an issue." He sat in the dark green chair in the corner of the room, looking out the window. Goddess, he was a beautiful creature- strong with broad shoulders, dark hair, light grey eyes and dark facial hair. Him sitting there with his legs spread apart and his elbow resting on the arm of the chair looked like it should be painted and hung up in castles. He looked like a King on his throne.

The dark King. I smiled at the thought.

Perhaps when all of this is over and that soul sucking bitch is dead, I can get what I need from her father and then kill him off too. I loved when a plan came together.

I slowly sauntered over to him and pressed my hand to the inside of his thigh. He cut his eyes to look at me, but made no indication he wanted more, but I knew he did. I could see the hunger in his eyes.

I heard the rattling of chains behind me.

Damn her!

I jerked around to see Snow coming too. She was still groggy as she pulled her arm up as much as she could before realizing she was chained to the bed. Any other circumstance and with anyone else, this would have been excellent foreplay. Perhaps Gage and I could reenact this at some point. I felt a tingle between my legs at the thought of Gage chaining me to the bed again.

Her arm fell and her eyes closed as she swallowed a big gulp of air. Her head wobbled from side to side before she opened her eyes, blinking hard. "Where am I?" She looked around the room then her gaze landed on me, before moving to Gage. "What have you done?" She strained to sit up. "You asshole! I trusted you." The chains clanked as she moved her arms and legs to try to get off the bed.

"That's your fault, princess. I told you not to. But you couldn't keep your needy little cunt away from us." He stood up and walked beside me.

Her face contorted in confusion. "Why? Why would you do this?" She was shaking from side to side, trying to get her hands free.

"It's no use. These chains are forged from dragon's fire so I can assure you that your measly strength won't be enough to break through them." I taunted.

She huffed and laid back down, staring up at the ceiling. No doubt, her mind reeling.

"Is that it?" I nearly chuckled. "I expected more fight from you."

She turned her head to look at me, but didn't say anything.

"Nothing?" I poked her a few times like children poke dead animals to see if they're still alive, unsure if they're going to come to and lunge at them.

"What's the purpose? You have me chained to a bed in dragon chains. Gage there, is a traitorous bastard and yo u..." She looked back at the ceiling.

"Me what?"

She looked back at me casually. "It really is shocking to me. Everyone is so scared of you, the big bad dark evil Queen, but you are a coward."

"Excuse me?"

"You use magic so you don't have to get your hands dirty. You used this version of Gage to do your bidding and then you chain me, while unconscious, to a bed with dragon chains. Tell me. For someone who seems so powerful, you have seemed scared of me from the moment you stepped foot into this castle. You locked me, a little girl, in that closet for a room and now you've locked me to a bed with dragon chains." She laughed, shaking her arms. "Dragon chains. You are a coward."

"I'm no coward!" I seethed.

"Ok." She said shifting her eyes back to the ceiling.

I walked over to the nightstand and grabbed the blade out of the silver decorative box and walked over to her, dragging the blade from her forehead, across her cheek and down to her chest. I pulled it up, holding it above her, clasping the handle in both hands.

She looked at me lackadaisically, then back at the ceiling.

I screamed and thrust the knife down, watching for a flinch, but got nothing. I stopped with the tip of the knife touching her chest, a drop of blood pearling on her satin white skin.

I lifted the knife and screamed in frustration. This was not as much fun as I hoped it would be.

I wanted the fight.

I wanted the fear.

But there was nothing.

"What did you do to her?" I snapped, turning to face him.

"Do to her? Nothing. I brought her here like you wanted."

"She's... she's... broken!" I said flapping my hands wildly at her.

"Then just kill her already." Gage moaned.

I turned on my spot. "Do not tell me what to do! You are not the Queen. Do not forget your place!" I was raging mad. Nothing had gone to plan, nothing at all! I had pictured this moment for months now and I was left with a lifeless sack of shit on the bed. No, I needed something more. I needed to make her feel. I needed to make her fight.

He raised his eyebrows and held his hands up. "Fine. Don't then. I don't care."

"Fuck!" I pulled the key out of my pocket and unlocked the chains.

She sat up, rubbing her wrist, but didn't make an effort to escape, which only further irritated me.

"Come." I said, waving at her as I walked out of the room.

"Where are we going?" she asked.

"Stop asking questions," I heard Gage say. I turned around and saw him yanking her off the bed and push her across the room.

She looked up at him, her eyes lost and confused. She was probably wondering how could Gage do this to me? I trusted him. We were friends. Blah, blah, blah. I laughed at how pathetic she was. Only I knew the real Gage, the one he tried to keep hidden. No, I knew this Gage and relished in his power, in his darkness. She didn't know him at all.

"Let's have a little family dinner." I said, walking down the hall to the dining room.

I snapped my fingers at the frumpy woman, who was standing by the door in shock, her gaze fixed on Snow. "Get the King prepared for dinner."

"Yes, my Queen. Right away."

"Excellent." I turned to look at Snow, with her quizzical brow, "This shall be a fantastic last feast for you."

"I can't wait." She said dully.

We walked into the dining room and I sat her on the side closest to the door and instructed Gage to sit beside her, while I sat across from him and the King in front of her. I wanted her to look at her father the entire meal and know that he didn't care about her in the slightest.

She looked at Gage, her eyes almost pleading with him to help her, but he sat there, uncaring.

The hinges on the door squeaked as the King walked in. "My King." I moved across the room to greet him. "We have a special guest." I fanned out my arm to show Snow at the table.

"Dad!" she yelled out, standing from her seat before Gage yanked her back down.

I smiled with great satisfaction, her apathetic demeanor breaking in an instant.

"What is she doing here?" His tone was of confusion and irritation.

Perfect!

I looked at her and saw her face fall.

"Dad. It's me. Snow."

He looked at her, but didn't speak.

"What have you done to him?" She yelled, standing up again. Gage moved to grab her arm, but she yanked it out of his grip. He quickly reached for it again, much harder this time, and forced her down.

I smiled. This was the reaction I wanted. I wanted to see her fight and her horror when she realized she was alone. I wanted to break her down piece by piece.

"You bitch!" She yelled in my direction.

"Such-"

The King interrupted me. "You will not speak to your Queen that way."

"Dad?" Her brows furrowed and tears sat on the rim of her eyes.

"You will apologize." He demanded.

"I won't."

"You will." He stepped forward menacingly.

"What has she done to you? To both of you?" She looked at Gage and reached up to touch his face. He shook his head quickly and grabbed her hand and slammed it back on the table. "Don't touch me."

She looked shocked, standing there unmoving.

I sat down, crossing my hands on my lap, "Now, if we could have our final dinner with Snow."

"That sounds delightful." The King moved to kiss me, so I stuck my cheek out.

"Dad?" Snow asked again, this time much quieter, almost pleading.

"Please stop calling me that. I am the King and you will address me as such. You are not my daughter. You lost that title when you attacked me and tried to kill the Queen before running away."

"Wait. What? I didn't attack you."

"She's so troubled, darling. Let's not bring things up, she will argue about. I was trying to be nice and offer her one last meal... but she is just so ungrateful."

"You are going to kill me!" she snapped. "Da- King. Are you ok with that?"

"After what you have done, it is the only solution. We cannot let the kingdom think it is ok to attack the King and Queen without punishment."

"Ah." I clapped. "Here comes the food."

Plated on a silver tray was a roasted pig with an apple stuffed in its mouth.

"I'm not hungry." Snow chimed, staring at the pig.

"Such a shame. I thought it was your favorite."

"How would you even know? You kept me locked up in a closet for the last fifteen years."

"Come now, Snow. We don't need the dramatics." The King said, taking a bite of his food. "You should be grateful you had a bed to sleep in and food in your stomach. Many in the kingdom don't have that and you threw it away like it was nothing."

"Many in the kingdom don't have that because of this evil bit- Queen. How can you not see she's brought death and destruction to this kingdom ever since you let her step foot into this house?"

I watched the King, slipping my hand onto his lap.

Snow continued. "Have you not seen the trees, the bushes, nothing outside. The fields outside were blanketed in beautiful, vibrant flowers. The scents in the air sought after my kingdoms far and wide. Tell me when was the last time you have completed a trade with another that was favorable for this kingdom?"

The King just looked at her without speaking.

"I imagine it's been so long you can't remember. She has brought death into these walls. Did you know she killed your beautiful late Queen?"

I saw his eye twitch and jumped in. "That's enough." I said. "You've ruined this dinner long enough with your continued assault on me." I hoped Snow hadn't noticed. His one weakness that stupid bitch living in the dungeon.

"Gage." I motioned for him to remove Snow.

"What? Scared if I talk about the late, beautiful Queen your spell on my father will be broken?"

Fuck, she had noticed.

"The old Queen was beautiful and kind." She started and I saw the King's eyes flicker again.

Shit! "Gage!" I commanded and this time he stood up.

"Her long dark beautiful hair, glimmered in the sunlight."

"Get her out of here now!"

Gaged pinched her arms behind her back until she screamed out in pain.

As soon as she was gone, I turned to do damage control. I rubbed my hand along the King's cheek. "I'm so sorry darling for that. I had hoped she would have had better manners with the favor I was- we were- allowing her. I fear she is too far gone into the darkness to see that what she's done is wrong."

He nodded without speaking for a moment, his eyes focused on the doors Snow had just exited. "Yes." He spoke slowly as if trying to believe the words he was speaking. "Yes. It does appear she is too far gone." He patted his mouth before standing up. "Please let me know when her execution is. I would like to be present to ensure it all goes according to plan." He turned and walked out of the room.

I was left sitting there alone. The table was a wreck, food and napkins were strewn about and I couldn't tell if Snow had broken through to the King. I hadn't seen his eyes before he left. Even though his words sounded like my King, there was something about the tone.

I pushed back from the table, throwing my napkin down. Damn that little bitch! She was going to die now!

CHAPTER FORTY-ONE

SNOW - LAST CRY

My shoulders were burning as I wiggled against Gage's grip. "Let me go! You're hurting me!"

"Stop wiggling Princess." He answered coolly.

He continued shoving me down the hall, the clacking of my shoes echoed on the stone floor. "I know you're in there Gage. The real you, not this asshole."

He laughed. "You're annoying."

"Fuck off!"

Run Snow... run. A woman's voice echoed through the halls.

I looked around trying to figure out where it had come from and why Gage wasn't reacting, and nearly tripped over the edge of the plush carpet that lined the final stretch to the Queen's room.

"Pay attention to where you're going." Gage barked.

"I heard something..."

"Your hopes and dreams fading away?"

I glanced around quickly, really needing to come up with some sort of action plan. My window for escape was narrowing and I needed to put a plan into action.

I stiffened my legs causing Gage to lose his balance a little. I took the opportunity to weave my hand between us to his opposite hip as I used my other leg to step behind him, bending down at the same time. His grip on my wrist popped off and I was free. I quickly pushed off him, but he spun around too quickly for me. I ran back the way we had just come, passing by portraits of past Queen's and King's. I stutter stepped when I saw a picture of the old Queen, my mama.

I felt Gage's hand on my shoulder so I spun around kicking at the same time I thrust my palm up into this face, crashing into his nose.

"Bitch!" He shouted, grabbing his nose.

"I don't like to be touched by assholes."

I had no idea where I was going. It had been forever since I'd been allowed in this part of the castle. I ran from door to door, but they were all locked. Where in the hell was the main staircase!

"There's nowhere for you to go princess." Gage said, walking slowly down the hall.

"No shit," I muttered under my breath. What was I doing? I slowed to a stop and turned to face him. My only hope was bringing my Gage back because I couldn't fight both him and the Queen.

I walked towards him, catching him off guard and spoke softly. "Gage."

"Princess." He said eyeing me, curiously.

"Please come back to me."

"I'm right here princess." He threw his arms out to his side.

"I'm not talking about you asshole. I'm talking about my Gage."

He let out a low growl that reverberated throughout my chest. He was a menacing sight to behold.

"Do you remember when we were in that room?"

His brows rose, but he didn't speak.

"Do you remember the things I did to you? The things you did to me?" I felt my stomach flutter at the memory.

"Ehh, I've had better." He shrugged.

"Is that so?" I tried not to let the words sting because I knew he was trying to hurt me.

He nodded, eyeing me as I slowly walked around him, my heart beating with a mixture of fear and excitement. I gently put my palm on his chest, letting it rub up his shoulder and across his back as I circled him. It was a risky move, but I knew he was going to catch me and this way gave me a chance to break through to Gage.

"Are you a shark circling your prey little princess?"

"Do you feel like you're my prey?"

He laughed. "Not at all."

It was true. I could tell he didn't think I was a threat, which was fine with me. It gave me more time to reach Gage.

I reached up to touch his face and he snatched my wrist, holding it tightly. "Not my face." He threw my hand back at me.

I cocked my head to the side, but obeyed. I let my fingers trickle down his arm as he slowly turned his palm face up. "Gage. Come back to me." I pleaded softly.

He chuckled. "It's no use princess."

"I'll get him back." I said, pressing my chest to his looking him square in the eye.

I felt a pull inside of me and wanted to feel his lips on mine. How crazy was I?

He leaned in closer as I let his chest push us towards the wall, feeling my heart start to pound through my chest. Our lips were a whisper of a breath close, but he stopped with his hands pressed on the wall above my head, caging me in. "Do you want me to kiss you princess?" His eyes hardened.

Feeling like the air had been sucked out of me, I ducked under his arm and moved behind him. This was not working.

He had an evil smile plastered across his face.

"What's going on out here?" The Queen echoed.

"Nothing." Gage said, casting a side glance at me.

"Let's go! We don't have all night!" She commanded.

Gage grabbed my arm, his grip noticeably lighter. I glanced at him but he didn't look back, keeping his eyes straight on the door ahead.

I should have been able to get through to him. I swear I saw his eyes flicker a few times at dinner, even if I hadn't seen them here in the hall.

We got back to the room and I looked around for anything I could use. Damn it! I needed more time! Where were the others? I had hoped they would be here by now, but I knew it would take time. Too much time.

"On the table." Gage commanded.

I looked at the cold stone slab- gray, much like Gage's eyes, and then at the dark Queen. "You're ok with this?"

She laughed. "Don't try to play me. I got what I needed. The look on your face at dinner will last me life times and that is how long I will live. Life times longer than you."

"It's starting to show." I pointed around my eyes, "Wrinkles." I snarled.

I saw the rage fill her eyes in a matter of seconds. "Get her on the table now so I can cut out this bitches heart and liver!" She yelled at the top of her lungs.

"Temper, temper." I mocked. I had nothing to lose now. My only satisfaction was pissing her off as much as possible. Perhaps if she was mad enough she'd torture me, which would buy me some time. I shivered. When would anyone wish for torture?

Fight. The woman's voice echoed in my head again.

Gage grabbed the chains and tugged on them to ensure they were affixed to the hooks at the corners of the table.

"Gage." I quickly cupped his cheek in my palm. "Please. You don't want to do this. This isn't you." I saw his eyes flicker from gray to blue repeatedly.

He was fighting. He was fighting the mind control or whatever the dark Queen had done to him.

"Gage. Please." I grabbed his hand.

"Hurry up!" The Queen snapped.

Those two words made the decision. Gage looked at me, his head tilting to the side.

I got the gray eyed Gage.

He fastened the chains around my wrist, the weight of them making it hard to lift my arm. I reached for his hand one last time and caught his pinky and felt him squeeze, but he didn't look at me, so I couldn't determine the meaning behind the squeeze.

"Well, I wish I could say some nice parting words or that I'd miss you, but the truth is... well, you served your purpose and, like the others before you, you need to die."

"I'm a witch, just like you, and I curse you!" I yelled in anger.

She grabbed her chest like she'd been struck with a sharp object, catching me off guard.

She froze, her eyes shut, and after a few seconds, she opened one eye and looked at me. "Oh. I guess I'm not. Idiot child."

She raised her hand with the knife in it and looked at me, smiling. I turned my head to look at Gage, but he was stone cold, unwavering.

I closed my eyes, took in a deep breath and turned to look at the Queen. I was beating myself up for not learning some sort of useful curse.

"Care to say goodbye?"

"Go to hell, you spineless bitch."

"Very well then." She smiled and moved to stab me.

I screamed out at the same time the knife was hurtling toward my chest. I felt a pulse leave my body, like a warm gust of wind had blown out in every direction. I opened my eyes and saw the Queen stumbling backwards several feet from me and turned to find Gage, bent over grabbing his knees. He looked at me with his crystal blue eyes.

"Gage." I breathed.

He looked up at the Queen, who was regaining her footing and moved forward faster than I have ever seen a person move. He broke the chains from my wrists, snapping them like twigs, and scooped me up in his arms.

"No!!! What are you doing?" The Queen was clutching her chest with one hand and reaching towards us with the other. "Gage. I command you! Bring her back."

Gage was turning and running out of the room. I looked behind him at the dark Queen, who raised her arm and I quickly wriggled mine free. I heard her mumble the words and quickly threw my wrist out with as much force as I could, redirecting the curse back to her.

I saw the light shooting out of her hand and then shoot back towards her, striking her in the chest. She fell into a heap of cloth on the ground.

As I continued to bounce up in down in Gage's arms, I waited for her to move but she didn't.

Did I kill her?

Did she kill herself?

Gage pushed through the main doors with such force he nearly knocked them off the hinges.

"Hold on tight." He commanded.

"What?" I asked, confused, still trying to wrap my head around everything that had just happened.

Before he could answer, he slung me on his back and was shifting into his wolf under me. "Oh." I didn't know what to grab onto, so I just grabbed fistfuls of hair and squeezed with my thighs as we raced across the field.

This was the second time I had run away from the castle, although, now, I felt like a weight had been lifted off me. I was no longer running away from something, but running towards something.

I was going home.

I looked back at the castle, waiting for the Queen to step out, but instead found another woman with long brown hair in a silver gown. She was rubbing her head, looking confused.

She looked up at me, catching my eye, and I nearly fell off Gage. It felt like someone had punched me in the stomach.

It was her.

The woman from my dreams.

I recognized her from the pictures I had seen growing up.

"Mama?" I could barely get the words out.

She's been alive all this time?

THANK YOU AND WHAT'S NEXT!

THANK YOU SO MUCH for reading SNOW HUNTED. I'm so sorry for the cliff!! Ahh!! I hate it, I really do! BUT! This is a Kindle Vella, so you won't have to wait long for the story to continue. I will be posting new chapters for the second book HUNTRESS SNOW soon! I have so many ideas for spin-offs after HUNTRESS SNOW, I am thinking about doing a book about the Huntsman, Gage and Garrison, perhaps diving into Ruby's story a bit as a Siren... I wonder who her parents could be :) Then there is the obvious Lilibet! I have to explore her character, her mother and how she ties to Persephone. And last but not least, the others in the miner seven. I want to learn more about their back story and who they are. I hope you enjoyed this one!

HUNTRESS SNOW... where the hunted become the huntress! I also plan to combine the chapters into a book in the beginning of 2023!

I would love if you could leave a rating and/or review for the book. It helps with the algorithm making my book more visible and please share!

Coming soon: ***Partreon and Etsy shop***. I am working on getting character art created and other trinkets! :) Big things are going to happen and I can't wait!

I'm also looking for a **<u>street team</u>** to help spread the word! If you're interested then please send me an email at authorsnmoor@gmail.com and I can share the deets.

Check me out on **Tiktok – @authorsnmoor**

Instagram – **@sn_moor**

Facebook Page – **SN Moor Author**

Made in the USA
Coppell, TX
30 November 2022

87486759R00184